TRICIA LEVENSELLER is from a small town in Oregon and now lives next to the Rocky Mountains in Utah with her bossy dog, Rosy. When she's not writing or reading, Tricia enjoys putting together jigsaw puzzles, playing Overwatch, and watching her favorite TV shows while eating extra-buttered popcorn. Her books include *Daughter of the Pirate King*, its sequel *Daughter of the Siren Queen*, *Warrior of the Wild*, *The Shadows Between Us*, *Blade of Secrets* and its sequel *Master of Iron*, all published or forthcoming from Pushkin Press.

Also by Tricia Levenseller

DAUGHTER of the PIRATE KING
DAUGHTER of the SIREN QUEEN

WARRIOR of the WILD

The SHADOWS Between US

BLADE of SECRETS
MASTER of IRON

DAUGHTER
of the
PIRATE
KING

TRICIA LEVENSELLER

Pushkin Press
65–69 Shelton Street
London WC2H 9HE

First published by Feiwel and Friends, an imprint of Macmillan Publishing Group, LLC. All rights reserved

First published by Pushkin Press in 2022

9 8 7 6 5 4 3 2

ISBN 13: 978-1-78269-368-0

Offset by Tetragon, London
Printed and bound by Clays Ltd, Elcograf S.p.A.

www.pushkinpress.com

For Alisa,

my sister, friend, and first reader

"LET US NOT, DEAR FRIENDS,
FORGET OUR DEAR FRIENDS THE CUTTLEFISH."

—CAPTAIN JACK SPARROW

Pirates of the Caribbean: At World's End

Chapter 1

I HATE HAVING TO dress like a man.

The cotton shirt is too loose, the breeches too big, the boots too uncomfortable. My hair is bound on the top of my head, secured in a bun underneath a small sailor's hat. My sword is strapped tightly to the left side of my waist, a pistol undrawn on my right.

The clothing is awkward as it hangs loose in all the wrong places. And the smell! You'd think men did nothing but roll around in dead fish guts while smearing their own excrement on their sleeves. But perhaps I shouldn't complain so.

Such precautions are necessary when one's being invaded by pirates.

We're outnumbered. Outgunned. Seven of my men lie dead on their backs. Two more jumped overboard as soon as they saw the black flag of the *Night Farer* on the horizon.

Deserters. They're the most cowardly filth. They deserve whatever fate comes to them. Whether they tire and drown or get claimed by the sea life.

Steel twangs through the air. The ship rocks from the blasts of cannons. We cannot hold out much longer.

"Two more down, Captain," Mandsy, my temporary first mate, says from where she peeks through the trapdoor.

"I should be up there, shoving steel between ribs," I say, "not hiding like some helpless whelp."

"A little patience," she reminds me. "If we're to survive this, you need to stay put."

"Survive?" I ask, offended.

"Let me rephrase. If we're to *succeed*, you really shouldn't be seen performing impressive feats with the sword."

"But maybe if I just killed a few of them . . ." I say more to myself.

"You know we can't risk that," she says. Then she adds abruptly, "More men have boarded the ship. I think they're headed this way."

Finally. "Give the order to surrender."

"Aye, Captain." She ascends the rest of the steps leading to the deck.

"And don't get yourself killed!" I hiss after her.

She nods before traveling through the trapdoor.

Don't get killed, I say again in my head. Mandsy is one of only three I trust on this ship. She's a good gal, very bright, optimistic—and a good voice of reason, which I desperately needed during our voyage. She volunteered to come, along with two other girls from my real crew. I shouldn't have allowed them to join me, but I needed their help keeping these worthless men in line. Life these last few weeks would have been so much easier if I could have had *my* crew on this venture.

"Lay down your arms!"

I can barely make out her cry through the sounds of fighting. But then things calm down. Cutlasses clatter to the wooden deck almost instantly. The men currently under my command had to be expecting the order. Praying for it, even. If I did not order the surrender, perhaps they would have given up on their own. By no means does this crew consist of the bravest bunch.

I climb the stairs, lying in wait just belowdecks, staying out of sight. I'm to play the part of the harmless cabin boy. If these men were to discover who I truly am . . .

"Check belowdecks. Make sure no one's hiding." It's one of the pirates. I can't see him from where I hide, but if he's giving orders, he's either the first mate or the captain.

I tense, even though I know exactly what comes next.

The trapdoor lifts, and a hideous face comes into view, complete with a foul, scraggly beard, yellow teeth, and a broken nose. Meaty arms grasp me roughly, hoisting me off the ladder and tossing me onto the deck.

It's a miracle that my hat stays on.

"Line them up!"

I stand as my weapons are removed by the ugly pirate. Then his foot jams into my back as he forces me to my knees, along with the rest of my men. I look down the line and relax as I see Mandsy. Sorinda and Zimah are unharmed as well. Good. My girls are safe. To hell with the rest of the crew.

I take a moment to observe the pirate barking out orders. He's a young man, perhaps not even twenty years of age. Unusual, that. Young men are not usually the ones giving orders, especially among crews such as this one. His eyes are alight with the victory of the battle. His stance is sure, his face confident. He's probably a head taller than I, were I standing, with dark brown hair the color of a seal's coat. His face is pleasant enough to look at, but that means nothing to me when I know he belongs to this crew. He notices Mandsy in the lineup. Her hat has fallen off, revealing her long brown hair and pretty face. He winks at her.

All in all, I'd say he's a cocky bastard.

My crew and I wait in silence for whatever the pirates have in store for us. Smoke billows around us from the cannon blasts. Debris is scattered around the ship. The smell of gunpowder leaches into the air, scratching at the back of my throat.

Footsteps sound as a man walks across the gangplank that connects the two ships. His head points down, revealing nothing more than a black hat with a white plume rising from the side.

"Captain," the same pirate shouting orders from before says, "all the men on the ship are before you."

"Good, Riden. But let's hope they're not *all* men."

A few pirates snicker. Some of my men glance nervously in my direction.

Fools! They're giving me away too easily.

"I've spotted three lasses so far, but none of them have red hair."

The captain nods. "Listen up!" he shouts, raising his head so we can see him for the first time.

He's not much older than his cocky first mate. I slowly take in the faces of the pirate crew. Many can't even grow hair on their chins. It's an incredibly young pirate crew. I'd heard that the *Night Farer* was no longer under the command of the pirate lord Jeskor—that he was succeeded by a young captain, but I hadn't expected the entire crew to be so young.

"You have all heard the stories of Jeskor the Headbreaker," the young pirate captain continues. "I am his son, Draxen. And you will find that my reputation will grow to be far worse."

I can't help myself. I laugh. Does he think he can make a reputation for himself by *telling* everyone how fearsome he is?

"Kearan," the captain says, nodding to the man behind me.

Kearan rams the bottom of his sword onto the top of my head. It's not hard enough to knock me out, but it is enough to hurt like hell.

That's enough of that, I think. Mandsy's words of caution are so far from my mind now. I'm done kneeling on the floor like some servant. Bracing my hands against the wooden deck, I extend my legs backward, hooking my feet behind the heels of the ugly pirate standing there. With one yank forward, Kearan topples backward. I stand quickly, turn around, and take my sword and pistol from him before he can regain his feet.

I point the pistol at Draxen's face. "Get off the ship and take your men with you."

Behind me, I hear scuffling as Kearan finds his feet. I jerk my elbow backward, connecting with his enormous gut. There's a large splat as he collapses to the ground once again.

It's quiet. Everyone can hear the click of my pistol cocking back. "Leave now."

The captain tries to peer under my hat. I could duck under his gaze, but that would mean taking my eyes off him.

All at once a shot fires, wrenching the pistol from my hand. It lands on the deck before skittering out of sight.

I look to the right to see the first mate—Riden—placing his pistol back into his holster. A resulting arrogant smile stretches across his face. Though I would like to slash the look from him with my sword, I can admit it was an impressive shot.

But that doesn't stop me from getting angry. I draw my sword and step toward the first mate. "You could have taken my hand."

"Only if I'd wanted to."

All too quickly two men grab me from behind, one holding each arm.

"I think you talk far too much for a mere cabin boy whose voice hasn't yet dropped," the captain says. "Remove the hat."

One of my captors yanks the hat from my head, and my hair falls into place, reaching halfway down my back.

"Princess Alosa," Draxen says. "There you are. You're a bit younger than I expected."

He's one to talk. I may be three years shy of twenty, but I'd bet my sword arm I could best him in any challenge of wits or skill.

"I was worried we'd have to tear apart the ship before we found you," he continues. "You will be coming with us now."

"I think you'll learn quickly, Captain, that I don't like being told what to do."

Draxen snorts, rests his hands on his belt, and turns back toward the *Night Farer*. His first mate, however, never takes his eyes off me, as though he anticipates a violent reaction.

Well, of course I'm going to react violently, but why should he expect it already?

I slam my heel into the foot of the pirate holding me on the right. He grunts and releases me to reach down. Then I jab the side of my freed hand into the other pirate's throat. He makes a choking sound before placing his hands at his neck.

Draxen turns to see what the commotion is. Meanwhile, Riden levels another pistol at me, even whilst a smile still rests upon his face. Single-shot pistols take time to reload with gunpowder and an iron ball, which is why most men carry at least two on them.

"I have terms, Captain," I say.

"Terms?" he says in disbelief.

"We will negotiate the terms of my surrender. First I will have your word that my crew will be freed and unharmed."

Draxen removes his right hand from his belt and reaches down for one of his pistols. As soon as he has it, he points it at the first of my men in line and fires. The pirate behind him jumps out of the way as the body of my crewman falls backward.

"Do not test me," Draxen commands. "You will get on my ship. Now."

He is certainly eager to prove his reputation. But if he thinks he can intimidate me, he is wrong.

Again I pick up my sword. Then I rake it across the throat of the pirate recovering from the strike to the neck I gave him.

Riden's eyes widen while the captain's narrow. Draxen pulls out another gun from his waist and fires at the second man in line. He goes down like the first.

I ram my sword into the closest pirate next to me. He cries

8

out before dropping first to his knees, then to the deck. The boots I wear are now sticky with blood. I've left a few red footprints on the wood beneath me.

"Stop!" Riden shouts. He steps closer, pointing his gun at my chest. It is of no surprise to me that his smile is now gone.

"If you wanted me dead, you would have already killed me," I say. "Since you want me alive, you *will* comply with my terms." In a matter of seconds, I disarm Kearan, the pirate who grabbed me from before. I force him to his knees. One hand yanks his head back by the hair; the other holds my sword steady against his neck. He doesn't make a sound as I hold his life in my hands. Impressive, considering he has seen me kill two of his shipmates. He knows I will feel no guilt at his death.

Draxen stands before a third member of my crew, holding a new pistol.

This one's Mandsy.

I don't let the fear show on my face. He has to think me indifferent. This *will* work.

"For one who asked for the safety of her crew, you sure are being callous when I kill them off one by one," Draxen says.

"But for every man I lose, you shall lose one as well. If you intend to kill them all after I'm on board, then it doesn't really matter if I lose a few while bargaining for the safety of the rest. You intend to take me captive, Captain. If you wish me to board your ship willingly, then you would be wise to listen to my

9

offer. Or shall we see just how many of your men I can kill as you try to force me over?"

Riden approaches his captain and whispers something to him. Draxen tightens his hold on his weapon. I feel my heart beating rapidly. *Not Mandsy. Not Mandsy. She's one of mine. I can't let her die.*

"State your terms, *princess*." He practically spits out my title. "And be quick about it."

"The crew is to be unharmed and released. I will come aboard your ship without resisting. Also, you will bring my accessories over."

"Your accessories?"

"Yes, my wardrobe and personal belongings."

He turns to Riden. "She wants her clothes," he says incredulously.

"I am a princess, and I will be treated as such."

The captain looks about ready to shoot me, but Riden speaks up. "What do we care, Captain, if she wants to get herself all fixed up for us every day? I for one won't complain."

Soft laughter resonates from his crew.

"Very well," Draxen says at last. "Will that be all, *Your Highness*?"

"Yes."

"Then get your pampered arse over to the ship. You men"—he points to a couple of brutes in the back—"get her belongings to the ship. As for the princess's crew, get the lot of you to the rowboats. I will be sinking this ship. It's a two-and-a-half-day sail to the nearest port if you row quickly. And I suggest you do before you die of thirst. Once you reach the shore, you will take my note of ransom to the pirate king and inform him that I have his daughter."

Men from both sides hurry about to carry out orders. The captain steps forward and holds out his hand for the sword. Reluctantly, I give it up. Kearan, the pirate I'd been threatening, rises to his feet and scurries as far from me as possible. I don't get a chance to smile at his reaction, because Draxen lands a blow on my left cheek.

My whole body lurches from the force of it. The inside of my mouth bleeds from where my teeth struck skin. I spit blood onto the deck.

"Let's get one thing straight, Alosa. You are my prisoner. While it appears you've learned a thing or two from growing up as the daughter of the pirate king, the fact remains that you will be the only woman on a ship full of cutthroats, thieves, and blackhearts who haven't made port in a good long while. Do you know what that means?"

I spit again, trying to get the taste of blood out of my mouth. "It means your men haven't been to a whorehouse recently."

Draxen smiles. "If you ever try to make me lose face in front of my men like that again, I may just leave your cell unlocked at night so anyone can wander in, and I will fall asleep, listening to your screams."

"You're daft if you think you will *ever* hear me scream. And you'd better pray you never fall asleep while my cell is unlocked."

He gives me an evil smile. I note that he has a gold tooth. His hat sits atop black hair that peeks under in little curls. His face is dark from the sun. And his coat is a little too big for him, as if it belonged to someone before him. Stole it off his father's corpse, perhaps?

"Riden!" Draxen shouts. "Take the girl over. Put her in the brig. Then get to work on her."

Get to work on her?

"Gladly," Riden says as he approaches. He grasps my arm tightly, almost hard enough for it to hurt. It's a sharp contrast to his light expression. It makes me wonder if the two men I killed were his friends. He tows me toward the other ship. As I walk, I watch my men and women drift away on the rowboats. They row at a steady pace so as not to tire themselves too quickly. Mandsy, Sorinda, and Zimah will make sure they swap positions regularly so each man can get a turn to rest. They're bright girls.

The men, however, are throwaways. My father handpicked each of them. Some of them owe him money. Some of them got caught stealing from the treasury. Some didn't follow orders like they were supposed to. And some have no other fault except for being an annoyance. Whatever the case, my father gathered them all together in one crew, and I brought no more than three girls from my ship to help me keep them in line.

After all, Father suspected that most of the men would be killed once Draxen took me. Lucky for them, I was able to save most of their miserable lives. I hope Father won't be too upset.

But that doesn't matter right now. The point is that I'm now aboard the *Night Farer*.

Of course, I couldn't make my capture look too easy. I had a part to play. Draxen and his crew can't suspect me.

They can't know I was sent on a mission to rob their ship.

Chapter 2

I ENVY RIDEN'S BOOTS.

They're of a fine workmanship and black as a shark's hungry eye. The buckles look to be pure silver. The leather is firm and tight. The material folds around his calves in a perfect fit. His steps thud on the deck. Sturdy. Loud. Powerful.

Meanwhile, I constantly trip as Riden drags me along. My too-big boots keep nearly falling off. Whenever I hesitate so I can readjust them, Riden yanks harder on my arm. I have to catch myself several times before I fall to the floor.

"Keep up now, lass," he says merrily, knowing full well I'm incapable of doing just that.

Finally, I stomp on his foot.

He grunts but, to his credit, does not let me go. I expect him to hit me like Draxen did, but he doesn't. He just hurries me along faster. I could, of course, break away from him easily if I wanted to. But I can't seem too adept, especially when pitted against the first mate. And I need the pirates to settle down around me after my display back on the other ship.

This ship is empty except for the two of us. All of Draxen's men are over on my ship, relieving it of anything valuable. Father gave me enough coin to make the pirates happy but not too profitable. If I had been found traveling without any money, Draxen was bound to be suspicious.

Riden turns me to the right, where we face a set of stairs leading belowdecks. It's an uncomfortable trip downward. Twice I miss a step and nearly tumble all the way down. Riden catches me each time, but his grip is always firmer than necessary. My skin will likely be bruised by tomorrow. Knowing this makes me angry.

Which is why when we are three steps from the bottom, I trip him.

He's clearly not expecting it. He falls, but I didn't take into account that tight grip of his. So, naturally, he takes me with him.

The impact is painful.

Riden gets to his feet quickly, yanking me up with him. Then he shoves me into a corner so I have nowhere to run. He rakes his deep brown eyes down and up, regarding me with curiosity.

I'm something new. A project, perhaps. An assignment from his captain. He must learn the best way to deal with me.

While he watches me, I wonder what it is he gathers from my face and stance. My role is the part of the distressed and exasperated prisoner, but even when playing a part, pieces of a person's true self can sneak through the cracks. The trick is controlling which part of me I want him to see. For now, it is my stubbornness and temper. Those I don't have to pretend.

He must come to some conclusion as he says, "You said you would be a willing prisoner. I can see your word does not mean much to you."

"Hardly," I retort. "If you had given me a chance to walk to the brig without your help instead of bruising my arm, your knees wouldn't be smarting."

He says nothing while amusement lights up his eyes. Finally, he extends his arm in the direction of the brig, as if he is a potential partner presenting me with the dance floor.

I step on without him, but from behind me he says, "Lass, you've the face of an angel but the tongue of a snake."

I'm tempted to turn around and kick him, but I manage to hold myself in check. There will be plenty of time for me to beat him soundly once I've gotten what I came for.

I stand tall and walk the rest of the way to the brig. I observe the different cells quickly, selecting the cleanest one. Really, it looks just like the others. But I try to convince myself the dark substance in the corner is dirt.

At least the cell has a chair and a table. I will have a place to put my belongings. I don't doubt for a moment that the captain will keep his word. It is mutually beneficial for all pirate captains to be honest with one another, even if we're likely to kill one another in their sleep. No deals and negotiations would be possible between rivaling lords without some semblance of trust. It's a new way of life for every pirate. My father introduced the concept of honesty into the pirate repertoire. All the pirates who wanted to survive under the new regime had to adopt it. For anyone found being dishonest in their dealings is quickly disposed of by the pirate king.

I inspect the seat of the chair. Everything is too dirty for my liking, but it will have to do. I remove the large brown leather coat from my shoulders and cover the seat and back of the chair with it. Only then do I sit.

Riden smirks, probably at my clear unease in these quarters. He locks me in the cell and pockets the key. Then he pulls out a chair for himself and sits down, just on the other side of the bars.

"What now?" I ask.

"Now we talk."

I make a show of sighing dramatically. "You already have me prisoner. Go claim your ransom and leave me to sulk in peace."

"I'm afraid your father's money is not all we want from you."

I clutch the neckline of my cotton shirt as though I'm worried the pirates intend to undress me. This is part of the act. It would take *a lot* of men to restrain me; I have no trouble handling three at a time. And no more than that would fit in this cell.

"No one is going to touch you now that you're down here. I will see to that."

"And who will see to it that *you* do not touch me?"

"Let me assure you, I have never had need to force myself upon a woman. They come willingly."

"I find that hard to believe."

"That's because I haven't worked my charms on you yet."

I laugh scornfully. "As a female pirate raised by other pirates, I've had to fend off the most despicable and persistent of men. I'm not too worried."

"And what would you do, Alosa, if you had to fend off a man who wasn't despicable and persistent?"

"I'll let you know when I meet one."

He laughs. The sound is deep and rich. "Fair enough. But now to business. You are here because I want information."

"That's nice. I want a clean cell."

He leans back in his chair, getting comfortable. Perhaps he realizes this will take a while. "Where does Kalligan make port?"

I snort. "You're a terrible questioner. You think I'm going to hand over the location to my father's hideaway? Shouldn't you ease into the big questions? And since he is your king, you would do well to address him with his proper title."

"Since I have his daughter locked up, I think I have the liberty to call him whatever I wish."

"He will kill you and everyone else on this ship. And he will not make it quick." I felt it was about time I threw out a threat or two. That's what a real prisoner would do.

Riden doesn't look worried. Not at all. He wears his confidence as if it is merely another article of clothing upon his person.

"It will be difficult for us to return you if we do not know your father's location."

"You don't need to know it. He will find me."

"We will be several days ahead of your father's men. That's more than enough time to escape to somewhere he will never find us."

I shake my head. "You simpleton. My father has men in his employ throughout all of Maneria. It only takes one of them to spot you."

"We are well aware of your father's reach. Though I don't see how he thinks that merits his self-given title as king."

Now it is my turn to recline in my chair. "You're jesting, right? My father *controls* the ocean. There is not a single man who sails without paying a toll to him. All pirates must pay a percentage of their plunder to him. Those who do not are blown sky high from the sea. So tell me, fearless Riden, first mate of the *Night Farer*, if he kills men for shorting him on money owed, what do you think he will do to the men who have taken his daughter?

"You and this crew are nothing more than a bunch of little boys playing a dangerous game. Within a fortnight, every man on the sea will be looking for me." Of course, I intend to be off this vessel before a fortnight has passed.

"Little boys?" He straightens in his chair. "You must be younger than nearly every man on this ship."

After everything I said, that's what he held on to? "Hardly. What are you, fifteen?" I'm goading him. I know he must be much older than that, but I'm curious as to his actual age.

"Eighteen," he corrects me.

"Regardless, my age has nothing to do with anything. I have a special set of skills that make me a better pirate than most men can ever hope of becoming."

Riden tilts his head to the side. "And what skills might those be?"

"Wouldn't you like to know?"

His grin widens at that. "As I'm sure you've already guessed, this is no ordinary crew. We may be younger than most men at sea, but most of us have seen the cruelest side of life there is. The men are ruthless, each one of them already killers." For a moment his face drops, and a hint of sadness washes over him. He's reflecting on some former time.

"If you're going to start crying, could you wait until you get back on deck? I can't abide tears."

Riden levels his gaze at me. Almost as if he's not looking at me but through me. "You're truly a heartless creature, Alosa. You kill without hesitating. You can best two men at a time in a fight. You watch your own men dying without blinking. I can only imagine the kind of upbringing you must have had under the most notorious pirate in all of Maneria."

"Let's not forget the fact that I'm a better shot than you."

He laughs, showing a nice set of teeth. Impressive for a pirate. "I think I shall enjoy our talks together over the next good long while. And I sincerely hope I will get a chance to see you shoot someday, so long as I'm not the target."

"No promises."

The faint sounds of shouting rise above deck. The ship shakes as it releases more cannons. That'll be Draxen sinking my ship. Well, it's not *my* ship, merely the ship my father gave me for this mission. My real ship, the *Ava-lee*, and most of my real crew are safe at the keep. While I miss both, I'm also thrilled at the challenge ahead of me.

The steps creak as someone descends them. Draxen comes into view not long after. Three men trail behind him, carrying my effects.

"About time," I say.

The faces of the three brutes carrying my bags are red, their breathing rapid. I smile. That probably means they got it all. I do not pack lightly.

Each one of them huffs as they drop the bags to the floor.

"Careful!" I snap.

The first pirate is rather tall. He almost has to duck in order to traverse belowdecks. Now that he's dumped his load, he reaches into his pocket and fumbles with something there. A string of what looks like beads peeks out. Some sort of good luck charm, perhaps?

The second stares at me as if I'm a tasty morsel of food. He makes the skin at the base of my neck crawl. Best to stay away from that one, I decide.

The man at the back of the group is Kearan. Stars, he's ugly. His nose is large, his eyes too far apart, his beard too long and unkempt. His belly hangs over his belt to complete the look.

I think that my opinion of him can't get any lower when I notice what's in his hand. He tosses a couple of my dresses onto the heap at the floor.

I clench my teeth. "Were you *dragging* those? On this filthy floor? Do you have any idea how hard it was to find a girl my size to steal those from?"

"Shut your trap, Alosa," Draxen commands. "I'm still of half a mind to toss this lot overboard, my word be damned."

Kearan pulls a flask from his many-pocketed coat. He takes a large swig. "Might keep us from sinking, Cap'n."

"Oh, hush," I say. "It's not too late for me to kill you."

He has the decency to look troubled before taking another drink.

Draxen turns around. "Gents, go above and make ready the

ship. I want to leave immediately. Kearan, to the helm with you. Await my return."

As they depart, Draxen strolls up to Riden and slaps him on the back. "How did it go, brother?"

Brother?

Draxen's hair is darker, but his shoulders have the same broadness as Riden's. They have the same dark eyes, but Riden is more handsome. No, not handsome. Rivaling pirates are not handsome. They're bilge rats.

"Well enough," Riden responds. "She's very much loyal to her father. She's confident in his ability to rescue her, since his reach upon the sea is so vast. Her words lead me to believe he'll be looking for us in open water, so I recommend we stay close to shore."

Hurriedly, I think back to our conversation, realizing the all-too-revealing mistakes in my answers.

Riden's more clever than he seems. He smirks at my startled expression, or perhaps at the look of death I send him afterward. Then he continues. "She's got a fiery temperament that matches the red hair atop her head. She's intelligent. I'd guess she's had some sort of proper schooling. As for her fighting and such, I'd wager she was trained by the pirate king himself, which means he truly cares for her and will agree to pay the ransom."

"Excellent," Draxen says. "So the blackhearted pirate king would indeed come for his daughter."

"Probably in person," Riden says.

I'm careful to keep my expression the same. Let them think my father will be looking for me, rather than sitting safe in his keep, awaiting my report. However, Riden's spot-on about my training. My father would only trust this mission with someone he had trained himself. And he's only ever trained one person.

"Anything else?" Draxen asks.

"She's a dangerous one. She should be kept locked up at all times. I also wouldn't let any of the men be alone with her, for their sakes." Riden says that part jokingly, but then he returns to seriousness, taking a deep breath while he collects his thoughts. "And she's hiding something. More than the secrets we already know she keeps. There's something she really doesn't want me to find out."

I stand from my chair and step up to the bars, my mind reeling. He can't know my darkest secret. Only my father and a select few know it. "How could you possibly know that?"

"I didn't."

Draxen laughs.

I ball my hands into fists. I want nothing more than to strike Riden's cocky face again and again until each of his teeth fall out of his smile.

But, alas, his face is too far away. So I settle for grabbing the sleeve of his long shirt. Since he's still sitting, he flies headfirst toward the bars. He braces his hands against the bars so his face doesn't connect. That's fine by me, because it gives me the time

I need to use my free hand to pluck the key to my cell from his pocket. Once I've got it, I place it in my own pocket and back up to the wooden wall of the cell.

Riden grunts as he stands.

"Perhaps you shouldn't be left alone with her, either," Draxen says.

"I can handle her. Besides, she knows that the longer she holds on to it, the longer she'll have to enjoy my company."

I remind myself that I'm on this ship by choice. I can leave anytime I wish. I just need to find the map first.

I unlock the door myself. The two men allow me to haul my bags into my cell. They don't bother to help. They wait as I make the three trips. Not that I want their help. I'm in a mood to break bones. Riden's, mostly. Father would no doubt admire my restraint. I lock myself back in the cell once I'm done.

Riden holds out his hand expectantly. I hesitate for only a brief moment before tossing the key at him. He catches it effortlessly. A look of skepticism crosses his face. He grasps a bar of the cell and tugs. It stays firmly in place, locked.

"Can't be too careful," Riden says to Draxen. "Did you check through her things?"

"Aye," the captain says. "There's naught but clothes and books in there. Nothing of danger. Now, I think we've had enough excitement for one day. Let's go above and decide the best location to stall the ship. And it would be best not to tell the lass where we'll be. Don't need her gettin' any ideas."

Draxen makes for the stairs. Riden quirks up the right side of his lips before following.

Once they're out of sight, I smile. Riden isn't the only one to have gathered information during our little chat. I've learned that Riden and Draxen are brothers, sons of the pirate lord Jeskor. I'm still unsure as to what happened to Jeskor and his original crew for Draxen to inherit the ship, but I'm sure I will learn that later. Riden's a good shot, and he has his captain's confidence. How else did he manage to convince Draxen not to kill any more of my men? I wonder what he whispered to him back on the other ship and why he bothered to step in, in the first place. Riden's concerned for the men on this ship, not just with the normal concern that a first mate might have for the men he oversees. I think back to when he told me all the men on the ship are killers and how saddened he was by it. He feels responsibility for something. Perhaps it is tied to whatever happened to the original crew of the *Night Farer.*

There are many secrets aboard this ship, and I will have plenty of time to discover them all, starting tonight. I shake my right arm. I feel the metal slide down and slip into my hand.

It's the key to my cell.

Chapter 3

I HAD AMPLE OPPORTUNITIES to snatch the key from Riden. The trick was finding a way to lock myself in the cell before switching the key with another one I'd brought on board with me. I guessed that the key to my own ship's brig would be about the same size. Riden couldn't have noticed the difference.

He's not as clever as he thinks. And I am far more clever than he realizes.

Big mistake on his part.

Now that I'm alone, I rummage through my bags to find something suitable to wear. I can't stomach this sailor's outfit any longer. It'll take an entire bottle of perfume to rid my skin of the stench of the last owner. Who knows when I'll be allowed a bucket of water to wash? With Captain Draxen's cruel demeanor, I'm sure it will be quite some time.

I select a dark blue corset with wide sleeves that attach with thick ribbons. I place these atop a white blouse. The corset ties up the front, so I'm able to do it myself. I never had ladies to wait on me like land-faring noblemen's daughters. There are not many women willing to work for pirates. And the ones equipped for a life at sea are not wasted as maids. My own crew back at the keep is nearly entirely composed of women. A fact I am proud of.

I pull on a pair of black leggings and a pair of clean breeches atop that. My boots, perfectly snug and comfortable, go on next, extending all the way up to my knees. I sigh in contentment once I'm done. Looking good certainly helps to make one feel good.

Humming as I work, I grab a book titled *Depths of the Sea* from one of my bags. It's an index of all the creatures known to live in the ocean. I memorized each entry long ago, and I've spent so much time at sea that I've seen more creatures than charted in the work itself. That's why I had no problem hollowing out the binding of the book and hiding a small dagger inside.

Voices and footsteps reach my ears. I quickly place the dagger into my right boot and drop the book back with my other things. I sit down in what I hope is an inconspicuous manner as three men enter the brig.

"She don't look like much," one says to the others.

"But did you see what she did to Gastol and Moll?" another asks. "Dead as rocks."

The third man remains quiet, watching me as the others do.

"Have you finished ogling?" I ask. "Or are you hoping I'll perform tricks for you?"

"Don't mind us," the first pirate says. "It's not every day you get to see the pirate king's own flesh and blood."

"And am I what you were expecting?"

"They say the pirate king is as big as a whale and as fierce as a shark. We weren't expecting a tiny little thing."

"I must take after my mother," I say. I've never met my mother, so I couldn't say for certain, but my father tells me I received my red hair from her.

The rest of the day is much like this. Pirates come and go, taking whatever chance they can get to see the pirate king's daughter up close. After the first bunch, I stay mostly quiet.

It's close to nightfall when my last visitor shows up. Whereas all the other pirates arrived in groups, this man comes alone.

He's not much to look at, this one. Medium height and build. Brown hair and beard. He does look older than most of the other pirates on board. Maybe not quite thirty, but it's hard to tell with the beard hiding the bottom half of his face. He's got a gold coin in his right hand, which he moves over his knuckles with ease.

"Hello, Alosa," he says. "Name's Theris."

I'd been leaning back on two legs in my chair, but now I swing forward, straightening myself. "I must have seen every man on board pass through here at least once today. Why should I remember you? Or care what your name is?"

"You shouldn't," he says, reaching a hand up and scratching his forehead. His fingers move fast, but the movement is unmistakable. He draws the letter *K*. "I'm not a very interesting man to know."

The *K* is for Kalligan. It's the signal men under my father's employ use to identify themselves. Theris must be the man on the ship working for my father. He would have been the one who let my father know that the crew of the *Night Farer* wanted to kidnap me in the first place.

You never know when unfriendly ears are listening in, so I keep the conversation casual. "So it would seem."

"Just wanted to catch a glimpse of the pirate king's daughter."

"And let me catch a glimpse of you?"

"Precisely. Sometimes survival isn't about what you can do, but who you know."

"Noted," I say icily.

Theris nods before retreating.

I wasn't expecting my father's man to make himself known to me. We have different jobs on the ship. Theris's is to provide my father with information about this ship and its captain. Mine is to play the role of thief. We shouldn't need to help each other. In fact, we're expected to be able to perform our tasks alone.

But my father is counting on me not to fail. Perhaps his desire to find the map is so great that he's ordered Theris to keep an eye on me. On the one hand, I can understand why he wouldn't want to take any chances, but on the other, I'm deeply insulted. I can handle this mission on my own, and I won't be calling on Theris for help.

I have to wait until nightfall before I can start. I can tell when the sun sets because most of the pirates retire below. I can't see them from the brig, but I can smell them. They can't be far. I can imagine them sleeping in hammocks or on a straw-strewn floor. Whatever it may be, it's bound to be better than the brown-caked floor I'll be sleeping on. I cringe at the thought.

I start humming again as I shrug on my coat, which is fashioned similarly to the justaucorps men wear, but mine was made for a woman's figure. Mandsy made it for me. She can wield a needle just as well as she can wield a sword, which is only one of the many reasons why I made her part of my crew.

Though the coat will help me look like any other sailor if I'm seen from a distance, I hope I won't have much need to blend in once I'm above deck. I'm counting on the cover of darkness to mask me.

Once I've got my cell unlocked, I silence my humming. I drift around the lower areas of the ship, getting a feel for the shape of it. A storage room for food and supplies, a treasury for the pirates' plunder, a modest kitchen, and the main crew's sleeping quarters make up the space belowdecks. Easy enough to remember.

Now I need to make it into the captain's quarters without being seen. I don't have Draxen figured out yet, but if I were trying to hide something important, like a map, I'd keep it close.

There is a possibility, however, that Draxen doesn't even know the map is on board. It belonged to his father, who is a descendant from one of the three ancient pirate lord lines. (I am, of course, descended from one of the others.) Lord Jeskor may not have even told his sons about the map. No matter. The map has to be on board. Jeskor would have had it here when he died, and Draxen's quarters used to be his own. They're most definitely the first place I should look.

I peek up over the last step of the stairs, observing the deck. It's hard to see, as the moon is almost new. Naught but a sliver of light shines down upon the dark deck of the *Night Farer*. The ship was once a standard caravel ship, a type of vessel used for maritime exploration. Most pirates steal them from the land king's own armada. Then we make adjustments to fashion the ship to our own liking. I can see that Jeskor has had the rigging redone. He's exchanged the traditional lateen sail on the mainmast with a square-rigged sail. Smart, as it'll give him more speed. I also noted, while I was back on my father's ship and watching the *Night Farer* approach, that Jeskor's added a figurehead below the bowsprit. I doubt the land king has ever had large carvings of women fashioned to the fronts of his ships. He's much too practical for that.

There are only a few men above deck. Someone's at the helm, a man sits in the crow's nest, and a couple of others roam the deck to ensure all is well. I can tell exactly where they are, because they hold lanterns out in front of them.

Draxen and Riden will already be in their quarters. Assuredly sleeping. They just made an impressive capture—they will have celebrated. Now they're likely sleeping off their drink. I anticipate tonight's venture going over smoothly.

There are two separate levels above deck at the stern of the ship. The lower level likely holds Riden's quarters. The captain's will be off the aftercastle.

All I need to do is get past the man at the helm. Luckily for me, the man seems drowsy. He lazily leans against the railing while holding the helm with one hand.

Draxen's doors are likely unlocked. He wouldn't need them locked while he's in there. Unless he's paranoid or mistrusting of his crew. He didn't seem to be either sort to me, so I should be able to get right in.

I crouch on the deck beside the stairs that lead up to the second level. I wait for the man's head to loll to the side. Standing on my toes, I carefully creep up the companionway. All is well until I get to the last step, which creaks out a sound so loud in the silence, it feels as though I could have heard it from belowdecks. I feel my body go rigid at my mistake.

The sailor at the helm jerks awake fiercely, turning his head toward the sound. Toward me. "Blast it all, you gave me a start! Please tell me you're here to relieve me, Brennol."

He's too tired, and the sky is too dark for him to tell who I really am. Quickly, I play along, lowering my voice as much as I can. "Aye." I keep my response short. I've no idea what Brennol sounds like, and I can't risk my voice being off.

"Thank the stars. I'll be off, then."

He heads belowdecks while I stand there. I need to hurry before the real Brennol shows up for his shift. Without another thought, I slip inside Draxen's quarters.

I spot him instantly, lying on the bed. His face is turned away from me, but I can see the steady rise and fall of his chest. He's out. A candle burns softly near the bed, offering the room a little light and warmth. The place isn't filthy, but neither is it exactly tidy. This is a small blessing, at least. It's much harder to mask thieving when tossing a clean room. It's easier for the owner to tell if something's been touched.

Now I get to work, starting at the desk, where he has various papers and maps strewn about.

The map I seek will be different from the others. For one, it's older. It'll be fragile and darkened with age. Also, the map will not bear the language of the common tongue. Its language, too, is more ancient. There are few who know it. Lastly, the map is not complete. It is one of three pieces, separated long ago and dispersed to the three pirate lords of the time. With the three pieces united, the bearer will be able to find the legendary Isla de Canta, an island heaped with untold treasure and protected by its magical occupants, the sirens.

It's not anywhere on the desk or near it. I checked each drawer for false bottoms and hidden compartments. I move on to the cupboards where he keeps his clothes, rifling through every pocket in each garment. I feel a desperate need to wash my hands afterward, but I squelch the urge.

Instead I continue to scour the place. I pick at each wooden panel in the floor to see if anything is hidden underneath. I lightly tap the walls, listening for irregularities that hint at secret openings. I strike the last wall a bit too harshly, and Draxen rolls over in his sleep. Thank the stars, he does not wake.

Deep sleeper, that one.

Lastly I check under the bed. He's got a few things here. Thick woolen stockings, a broken sextant, a telescope.

When I want to sigh in exasperation, I swallow instead.

It's not here. It's not anywhere in this room or the adjoining washroom and sitting room. And that means it's somewhere else on the ship. But the ship is *enormous*. There are countless hiding places. And I will have to check them all until I find the map.

I'm going to have a miserable time of it.

Opening the captain's door quietly, I peek my head out. I've spent over half the night. No point in doing any more searching now. Might as well return to my cell for some sleep.

Brennol seems to have made his appearance, and he looks wide-awake. He has both hands placed firmly at the helm. How to get past him? If I simply walk out, he'll notice I'm not the captain. I'm too short.

If I could just make it down the companionway, he probably wouldn't take notice of me. But it's a good ten feet away. I tiptoe back into Draxen's quarters and search for something to use.

Eventually I find a copper coin. Perfect. Back at the door, I place the coin over the top of my thumb and flick it toward the port side of the stern. Brennol turns his head in that direction, leaning forward and squinting. Quickly, yet silently, I make for the stairs on the right and descend them, remembering to skip the step at the top.

When I hit the deck, I slam my back into the wall behind the companionway, ducking out of sight. I think I took the final step too loudly. And Brennol is bound to be even more alert now. I should wait a couple of beats before heading belowdecks.

A door to my left opens.

The door to Riden's quarters.

He looks first to his left, then to his right. "I thought I heard something. 'Fraid I'm a light sleeper. Didn't expect you, though."

I have only a moment to register the fact that all he has on are a pair of breeches before he reaches for me.

I have nowhere to go. Between the walls and the stairs, the only way out is through him. And I suppose it makes sense to simply let him catch me, even though my instincts scream at me not to.

I want to be here. I have a job to do. It's okay to let him catch me.

"How did you get out of your cell?" he asks. Not an ounce of sleep traces his words, though he had to have just woken. He grabs me by my upper arms, holding me in place.

I say, "I stopped the first pirate I saw and asked really nicely."

His face is cloaked in shadows, but I swear I can hear his smile. "I'm the only one who has a key."

"Perhaps you dropped it, then. That was careless of you."

He touches his side as if to grab a pocket, then remembers he's not wearing a shirt. A fact I haven't been able to forget.

It wouldn't be so bad if he didn't smell so good. Pirates are supposed to stink. Why does he have to smell like salt and soap?

He yanks me forward, and I realize I should probably be putting forth at least a little resistance. So I place my hands on his chest and shove. The night air is brisk, but Riden is still warm from being wrapped in bed. Warm and solid and good smelling.

With iron-gripped fists. If he bruises my other arm, I will have to retaliate.

He hoists me to the door he came out of. It's as dark as the end of a cave in here, but Riden seems to find whatever he's looking for just fine. He pulls me back outside with him and holds something up in the air for me to see.

"This would be the key I so carelessly dropped," he says.

"Strange, that."

He sighs. "Alosa, what are you even doing out here?"

"You've kidnapped me. What do you *think* I'm doing out here?"

"The rowboats are over there." He points to the opposite side of the ship. "So why would you be lollygagging around my door?"

"I wanted to kill my captors before I left."

"How'd that work out for you?"

"Still working on it."

"I bet."

Down the stairs we go, past the sleeping crew, and into the brig. Riden shoves me back into my cell. Then he tries the key.

Obviously, it doesn't fit.

Riden observes it more closely. Surprise takes over his face. "You switched them."

"Hmm?" I ask innocently.

He comes into the cell with me. "Give it to me."

"What?"

"The key."

"You have the key in your hand."

"It doesn't fit."

"You can hardly blame me if you broke it."

I don't expect him to buy any of what I say. I'm learning that I enjoy toying with him. I like the surprise and . . . not respect, but something close to it, that shows on his face when he learns something new about me. But I can't let him discover too much about my true nature. That'd be dangerous.

For him.

Because I won't fail. I can only imagine what my father would do to me if I did. But I'm not afraid. I'm doing this not only for my father but also because I want to. Because I'm a good pirate and the hunt is thrilling. Because I want to reach the siren island as much as any other pirate. Perhaps even more so. I'm determined to do *whatever* it takes to get the map. If Riden becomes too difficult, I will remove him from my path by any means necessary.

"I'll give you one more chance to hand it over, princess."

It's brighter down here. Several lanterns are lit outside the cells. I can see Riden's face perfectly. In the getup he's wearing, I can see a lot of him perfectly.

"I don't have anything," I say again.

He steps toward me slowly, keeping his eyes on mine as he does so. I back up until I hit the wall, but he continues to advance. His face is too close. I can see flecks of gold in his eyes. They're lovely eyes. I'd like to study them longer.

But suddenly his hands are on my hips.

I think I might stop breathing, but I'm unsure. I'm startled, certainly; am I supposed to slap his hands away or stand still?

He moves his hands up my stomach, never taking his eyes off me. Now I know I'm breathing because I think I might have just gasped. I'm pretty sure I should slap his hands away.

But I don't. Once he reaches my ribs, he moves his hands to my arms, running them up to my shoulder.

"I don't know what you're wearing," he says. "But I like it."

"Custom-made," I say.

"And then stolen by you?"

I shrug. "What are you doing?"

"What does it look like I'm doing?"

"You're touching me."

"I'm trying to get my key back."

"Sounds like an excuse to touch me."

He smiles and leans forward so his mouth is at my ear. "I don't see you stopping me."

"If I had, I wouldn't be able to do this."

His eyes shoot up in alarm, but he doesn't have enough time to guess what I'm about to do until I've already done it.

Yes, I knee him. Right between the legs.

He takes some time to recover. Enough for me to exit the cell and lock him in.

He stares at me levelly. "That was low."

"I thought it was rather brilliant, actually. Besides, you said you wouldn't touch me. I can see your word does not mean much to you." I throw at him the same words he used on me.

"And you said if we brought your blasted luggage on board, you wouldn't put up a fight."

"I didn't put up a fight. I got out of my cage fight-free."

"Lass, let me out of the cage."

"I think you're more suited for it than I am."

He bangs a fist against one of the bars. "Let me out. You know you won't get far. All I have to do is yell, and over half the crew will be upon you."

"And I can't wait to see the looks on their faces when they find their first mate trapped in the brig."

"Alosa," he says, a hint of warning in his voice.

"Answer something for me, and I will spare you the embarrassment of your crew finding you."

"What?" He's clearly agitated. I suppose I would be, too, if I had been duped by a pretty face.

"When we first met, and I was bargaining for the lives of my crew, you whispered something to the captain. Something that made him stop killing my men. What was it?"

Riden appears perplexed, but he answers. "I told him that if he wished to keep the support of his crew, he would be wise to stop encouraging you to kill them off."

"Did you care for them? The men who I killed?"

"No."

Hmm, perhaps I was wrong about how much he cares for the members of this crew. "Then why bother?"

"I answered your question. Now let me out."

I sigh. "Fine." Though I wonder why he doesn't want to talk about it. Perhaps I've hit on something there. If it wasn't to do with the men I killed, then wouldn't it have to do with his brother?

The cage sings as it unlocks, and I hand the key to Riden. "You and the captain are brothers."

"I'm aware of that."

"What exactly happened to your father?"

Riden locks me in soundly. Then he pockets the key without taking his eyes off of it. He turns to leave.

"I killed him."

Chapter 4

THE FLOOR IS DISGUSTING, but somehow I manage to sleep. When I wake, a face is inches from my head.

I shriek and roll away. Even though I realize now that he's on the other side of my cell, my heart still races.

"No need for that," the pirate says. "Just needed a lock of your hair is all."

My hand flies to my head. Indeed several strands have been cut. "What are you doing? I'll kill you for that."

"It's best to leave the lass alone, Enwen," another man says. It's Kearan. "Has a thing about people touching her."

"It needed to be done," Enwen says. "I tell you, red hair's good luck. Keeps you from getting diseased an' all."

I recognize now that Enwen is the tall man who helped carry my things down yesterday.

"That's the most ridiculous thing I've heard," Kearan says. "I hope you get sick tomorrow. You need to set your head right."

"You just wait. Next time a plague hits, I'll be strokin' this hair while you all will be coughin' and dyin' and such."

"I need a drink."

"Nah, Kearan. It's too early for that."

"If I'm to survive the day, I'll need to start early." He pulls out his flask from one of his pockets.

"What is this?" I ask as I stand and stretch out my neck. I can feel a couple of cricks in it. And I smell worse than I did yesterday. Blasted floor.

"We're your guards, Miss Alosa," Enwen says. "First mate says it's wise to have someone watching over you at all times."

I eye Kearan. "And I take it that neither of you volunteered."

"That's the truth of it," Kearan says.

"Oh, I was happy to do it," Enwen says. "Ever since I saw you yesterday, I've been wantin' to get my hands on that hair of yours. Very rare, it is."

"I can assure you, it has no magical properties," I say, angrily fiddling with the patch of hair that is now shorter than the others.

"Not magical," Enwen says. "Just good luck."

"I get sick as often as any other person."

"What?"

"You said red hair wards off disease. I've got a whole head of it, yet I get sick."

"Oh." Enwen looks troubled for a moment. He hunches over my lock of hair, staring at it. "Well, I suppose it doesn't work on you because it's your own hair. It's got to be taken from someone else for the luck to work."

"So if I steal it back from you, will it work for me?" I say sarcastically.

Kearan laughs, choking on the rum in his mouth. A few drops fall to the floor as he coughs. He sighs. "Bloody waste, that."

I sit on my chair, all too aware of the grime and slime that coat everything in the cell, including me. I need to change, and I need some water to clean myself off. I'm about to ask for the latter, when I hear someone coming over.

It's Riden, of course. He carries with him a tray of food and a dangerous smile. At the sight, I feel my stomach growl. I'm fairly certain that's a response to the food and not the smile.

"Enwen, Kearan, you're relieved while I question the prisoner. But you will return to this post once I'm done."

"Aye, Master Riden," Enwen says. Kearan nods, looking bored. The two leave.

"Hungry?" Riden asks.

"Starving."

"Good. I managed to swipe you some eggs." Riden unlocks

the cell and puts the tray on my table, keeping a close eye on my legs. I'm certain that's because he's wary of me kicking and not because he simply wants to stare. He shuts me back in, standing safely on the other side of the bars.

I start eating at once, cracking the boiled eggs and adding a bit of salt before chewing. I wash each one down with some water from the cup on the tray.

Riden seems to be in high spirits once again. It appears that there are no hard feelings for last night.

"So, what's it to be today?" I ask. "More talk of my father?"

"Yes."

"Hoping I'll unintentionally reveal where the keep is? You're wasting your breath."

"What you unintentionally reveal is up to you. What I wish to discuss is your father's reputation."

"Whatever you've heard, it's probably all true."

"Nevertheless, let's discuss it anyway."

"I want some water," I say, wiping at a spot of dirt on my arm.

"I'll refill your glass when we're done."

"No, I want a bucket for washing. And a rag. And soap."

"Don't you think that's asking a bit much for a prisoner?"

"And," I say, practically singing the word, "I want a new one of each every week."

He scoffs at first. Then he thinks it over. "We'll see how our conversation goes today. If I like what I hear, I'll make the proper arrangements."

I cross my legs and lean back in the chair. "Fine. Let's talk."

Riden pulls a chair out and sits. He's wearing a hat today. A tricorne with no feather. His hair is bound at the nape of his neck. His shirt and breeches fit nicely. White on top, black on bottom.

"I've heard rumors of Kalligan's dangerous deeds. He's said to be able to take on twenty men at once in battle. He's traveled every inch of the sea, fought off all manner of sea demons, including a shark, which he fought underwater with his bare hands. He makes deals with the devil and encourages evil in others."

"So far, you're not wrong," I say.

"He's even said to be the only man to survive an encounter with a siren."

I snort at that.

"He even bedded her," Riden continues. "Used the creature's own tricks against her. Now it sounds to me like our dear king is, at best, a manipulator and a wild storyteller. Perhaps he's not as honest as his new laws demand."

"He can hardly help what other people say about him."

"And what would you say about him?"

"He's my father. What more needs to be said?"

"There are different kinds of fathers. Those who love unconditionally, those who love on condition, and those who never love at all. Which would you say he is?"

For the first time, I feel Riden touching at something I'd

rather leave alone. "I hardly see how this line of conversation is helpful to you."

"Hmm. You're deflecting the question. On condition it must be. For if he never loved you, you wouldn't hold him in such high regard. So tell me, Alosa. What sorts of things have you had to do to earn your father's love?"

"The usual. Cheat. Steal. Kill." I throw each response out offhandedly. I hope he doesn't detect the distress I feel.

"He's turned you into something. Trained you to become something no woman should ever have to be. You—"

"I am what I choose to be. You speak ignorantly. I think we're done talking."

Riden stands, comes close to the bars. Then, thinking better of it, he backs out of my reach. "I meant no insult, Alosa. Consider yourself lucky. It is better to have a little love than it is to have a father who never loved you at all."

I know Riden speaks of himself now. But I'm still irritated. I feel as though I need to set him straight. "Everything my father did, he did out of love. He made me strong. He made me something that could survive in his world. Doesn't matter what he did to get me here. I'm a fighter. The best."

I don't need to block the memories. That's all they are. Memories. They can't hurt me. They're done. It doesn't matter that my father would have me fight boys older and stronger than me every day while I was growing up. Now I can beat them all. It doesn't matter that he shot me once to show me the pain of a gunshot wound, to have me practice fighting while injured. Because now I can do it. It doesn't matter that he would starve me and weaken me, then give me tasks to complete. He taught me endurance. Now I can handle anything.

"What about you, Riden?" I ask. "What has gotten you to where you are? You claim to be the one to have killed your father, yet Draxen is captain of this ship. Was Draxen your father's favorite? Or was he simply the oldest? Either way, why would you let him take something you earned?"

Riden's face hardens. "Draxen is older. And he was Father's favorite. Not that it matters now. You were right earlier. We should have stopped talking. I don't suppose you wish to tell me where your father's keep is now?"

"No."

He nods, unsurprised. "A storm's coming, and we haven't quite reached our destination. Be prepared for a rough night."

"I always am."

I clear my mind rather than replay our conversation. I'm exhausted from being out so late, so I return to the floor and doze. It's not as though I have anything better to do.

A loud ringing sound jolts me awake, sending my heart racing for the second time today. Someone kicked at the bars of my cell.

When my eyes focus, I spot Draxen standing before me, hands at his belt, plumed hat upon his head. He watches me as though I'm some prize he's won. Or some new tool he's received.

I suppose he sees me as both. But I don't care. In the end, I will be the tool that ends his life.

My father couldn't simply take the *Night Farer* by force. The map could easily get ruined in the struggle should he gun the ship down. He had to send one person aboard to search it. But when this is all done, I will lead this ship straight to my father so he can kill them all. The pirate king wants no competition when searching for the Isla de Canta.

"How are you liking your accommodations, Alosa?"

"The floor's rough and the cell stinks."

"Fit for the princess of thieves and murderers, don't you think?"

"Still could do with a bed."

"You're welcome to ask one of the crew to share. I'm sure any of them would volunteer."

"If I'm sleeping in anyone's bed, it'll be because I've killed him and taken his property as my own. Haven't you lost enough crew members, Draxen?"

"You're too sure of yourself. I think I should order Riden to add some beatings into his sessions with you. Might do you both some good. Stars know, he could use it."

Since I doubt I'll be able to finish my nap, I rise and take the chair, though I'm far past bored with the confrontation. Draxen has nothing interesting to say. He's hoping to see me squirm with fear. He's a man who feeds off of others' pain. So far, none of his intimidations have worked.

"I've granted Riden permission to work on you, but should you continue to be uncooperative, I'll give someone with less charm a chance to question you. Keep that in mind while you sit down here."

"Better hope he doesn't get soft on me. I'd hate to turn one of your own men against you."

"Princess, Riden's dealt with hundreds of women already in his life. He's never had trouble leaving one of them. You will be no different." His boots echo through the empty room as he leaves.

Draxen's a real piece of work. So is Riden. They operate in different ways, but their goals are the same, which makes them both equally stupid. What morons would think to steal from the pirate king? Especially without sufficiently checking their crew for spies? It was easy to arrange my "kidnapping" once Theris provided all the information we would need.

I'm surprised when Riden comes to visit me again, this time carrying a bucket of water, a bar of soap, and a few clean rags.

I was certain I had angered Riden past the point of kindness. I almost feel bad for all the terrible things I've thought about him.

Almost.

"You have ten minutes before I send the men back to watch over you."

"I'll only need nine," I say to be difficult.

He shakes his head before leaving.

The boat rocks a little higher at that moment. Storm's coming indeed. I've got a good pair of sea legs on me. I feel sturdier on the sea than I do on land. I'm used to her movements, her language. She'll tell you what she's going to do, if you listen.

I'm clean and dressed in a fresh corset, this one red, when Kearan and Enwen return.

"I'm telling you, it's bad luck to twist left. You should always thrust and turn right. Good luck, that is."

"Enwen, if I'm stabbing a man in the heart, it doesn't matter if I twist the knife right or left. Either way, I've managed to kill the bastard. Why would I need any luck?"

"For the next man you kill. Suppose it causes you to miss the heart the next time? Then you'll be wishin' you took the extra time to twist right the time before. You can't kill a man good and proper if you miss the heart."

"I'm starting to think that my 'next time' is very soon."

"Don't be like that, Kearan. You know I'm the only friend you've got on this ship."

"Must be doing something wrong." Kearan already has his flask out, but as he raises it to his head, he frowns. Empty. So he reaches into his pocket and pulls out another one. Now I understand the reason for all the pockets on the coat he wears. I would've suspected they were for a thief to put his finds. No, they're for holding multiple flasks of rum. I wonder how many he has in there.

"How do you fare, Miss Alosa?" Enwen asks, turning toward me, unfazed by Kearan's words.

"For stars' sake, Enwen," Kearan says. "The woman's a prisoner. How do you think she fares? Shut your trap for one blasted moment, would you?"

"The woman can answer her own questions," I say.

"You shouldn't be talking, either," Kearan says. "Don't need no noise from the both of you."

Enwen rubs his temple. "Master Riden only said I 'probably' shouldn't speak to her, on account of beautiful women have a way of playing tricks on a man's mind. But it wasn't a direct order."

"He said I was beautiful?" I smirk at the thought.

Enwen looks troubled. "Probably shouldn't have said that."

The ship rocks faster and faster as time goes on. Coming up on a storm is like getting into an argument. There are a few warning signs. Things heat up. But then there's a jump. The storm hits you before you're ready. And then you're too far in to do anything about it except get through it.

Everything is loud. There's nothing to hear except the wind and waves. Nothing to feel except the bitter cold. I put on the heaviest coat I own to ward off the bitterness. Every once in a while, I think I catch a shout from above deck. But that could easily be an echo of the wind.

I have to resort to sitting on the floor. My chair can't be

trusted not to tip. Enwen sits as well. He pulls something out of his pocket: a string of beads. Maybe pearls.

Kearan starts snoring. I know he must have some affliction of the sinuses, because I can hear him over the storm. He jerks awake suddenly. "Give that back."

Enwen must see the strange look I shoot Kearan. He explains, "He talks in his sleep a lot."

Kearan rubs at his eyes. "This is a nasty one. Might tip us over."

Enwen extends his pearls. "No, it won't. I've got our protection right here."

"I feel so reassured."

"You should. Storms are a dangerous time to be about. Some men say this is the time when the unpleasant seafolk come roaming out of their underwater domains."

"You mean the sirens," I say.

"Surely, I do. They like to hide in the waves. You can't see them in the water when the sea is boiling and tumbling and all, but they're down there. Kicking and pounding at the boat, helping the storm take us under. They want us. Want to eat our flesh, make necklaces out of our teeth, and hollow out our bones to make instruments to aid their song."

"Bloody poetic," Kearan says. "And a load of rubbish. Anyone ever tell you, you can't be hurt by something you don't believe in?"

Realization lights up Enwen's eyes. "That's why everything is out to get me."

I hide a smile behind one hand while Kearan tugs a flask out.

Sirens have worked up quite the reputation throughout time. They are considered the deadliest creatures known to man. Storytellers in taverns share tales of women of extreme beauty who live in the sea, searching for ships to wreck, men to eat, and gold to steal. A siren's song can enchant a man to do anything. The creatures sing to sailors, promising them pleasure and wealth if they will jump into the sea. But those who do, find neither.

Once a siren has a hold upon you, she will not let go. She carries her sailor with her all the way to the bottom of the sea, where she has her way with him. Then she steals all of his valuables and leaves him to float in the abyss.

There are many myths surrounding sirens. Most no one knows fact from fiction. But this part I do know. All the sirens throughout the centuries have carried their stolen treasures to an island, Isla de Canta. There can be found the wealth of history, treasures beyond imagination.

This is what my father seeks. This is why I'm here. This is what I've been prepared for: stealing another piece of the map.

Each of the three pieces was passed down from father to

son for generations. One traveled down the Allemos line, eventually falling into Jeskor's hands, possibly now Draxen's. Another down the Kalligan line, now safeguarded by my father. And the last belongs to the Serad family. Vordan will be in possession of that one.

With the three pieces united, the bearer will be able to find the legendary Isla de Canta. Island of Song. Also called the Land of the Singing Women.

"There aren't any sirens out there," I say to Enwen. "If there were, you'd already be enchanted to jump overboard. Do you hear any music?"

"No, because the storm's blocking it."

"So the storm's a good thing?"

"Yes—no. I mean . . ." Enwen wrestles with that for a moment.

Enwen and even Kearan seem too anxious to sleep tonight. Even a man who's spent his whole life at sea has reason to fear her when she's angry.

But not I. I sleep soundly. Listening to her music. The sea watches over me.

She protects her own.

Chapter 5

THE NEXT FEW DAYS and nights pass in much the same way. During the day, Riden comes down to question me. We poke and prod at each other, trying to get answers. Rarely does anything come of it. He also brings me my meals, but aside from that, I'm always left alone in my cell, a couple of guards watching over me. The guards get switched out every so often, but Kearan and Enwen are by far the most entertaining.

Unfortunately for Riden, guards are not the deterrent I'm sure he was hoping for. Even they have to sleep, and once they do, I creep from my cell and poke my nose around the ship. Since the map didn't turn up in Draxen's quarters, I decide to start my search belowdecks from stern to prow and then make my way above. I chose this order because I assumed I would be starting with the easiest places to search and making my way toward the harder ones.

But nothing proves to be quick or easy.

When there's nigh forty men belowdecks, sleeping, there's always at least one every hour who needs to piss in the night, no doubt due to heavy drinking before bed. I spend half my time ducking out of sight, squeezing between tight spaces, or holding absolutely still while they rush over to the ship's edge and then return to their beds.

My search is tedious and unfruitful, and each night I manage to finish only a small section of the ship.

On my fifth night aboard the ship, Kearan is snoring loudly while Enwen counts gold coins out of a small purse.

"Have you been gambling?" I ask.

"No, Miss Alosa, I don't like to gamble."

"Then where does your money come from?"

"Can you keep a secret?"

I look pointedly around my cell. "Who would I tell?"

Enwen nods pensively. "I suppose you're right." He looks down at the coins again. "Well, this one I got from Honis. This one's from Issen. This one's from Eridale. This one's from—"

"You're stealing them." I smile.

"Yes, miss. But only one from each man. If a man sees his whole purse gone, he'll know someone's taken it, but if he's only missing one coin—"

"He'll assume he's lost it," I say.

"Yes, exactly."

"That's brilliant, Enwen."

"Thank you."

"You're much smarter than you let on. Do you only pretend to be a superstitious fool so the crew will remain unsuspecting?"

"Oh no. I'm as superstitious as you can get."

"And the part about being a fool?"

"I may overdo that one just a bit."

I laugh lightly. This is the kind of man I would allow to be on my own ship, if he could manage to reserve his stealing for people who weren't his crew members.

"And what about Kearan?" I ask. "What's his story?"

Enwen looks over at his snoring companion. "Not much is known about Kearan. He doesn't talk about himself, but I've gathered quite a bit from his sleep talking."

"What have you learned?"

"Why do you ask?"

"Simple curiosity and boredom."

"S'pose it wouldn't hurt to tell you. Just don't tell Kearan I was the one who told you."

"I promise."

Enwen starts dropping his coins back into his purse. "Kearan has been all over the world. He knows the Seventeen Isles inside and out. He's met all kinds of people, performed all kinds of jobs and such. He was an adventurer."

So Kearan not only knows his way around the ocean, but on land as well. Unusual for a pirate. Our little isles are so close together that everyone travels between them. Each is rich with different food sources. Trade is frequent and necessary between the isles. As such, whoever controls the sea, controls the money of the realm.

Father tolerates the existence of a monarch over the land because he has no wish to rule over landlubbers. He prefers to keep company among the brutes of the sea. The land king pays tribute to my father yearly in exchange for letting his explorers search through the sea for new lands.

No one has ever managed such a total monopoly over sea travel until my father established his ruling. And someday all that control will be passed down to me, which is why I wish to prove myself again and again to my father. My current task is one on a large list of feats I've completed for him.

I look over at Kearan's fat body, ugly face, and overall unkempt look. "You certain he's not just adventuring in his sleep?"

"Oh yes. He might not look like much now, but that's because he's turned into a man who has lost much. Imagine if you were never satisfied with your life, Miss Alosa. Imagine that you traveled all over the world, looking for happiness, looking for thrills to pass the time. Imagine seeing everything there is to see and still not finding happiness. Well, that would give you a very bleak outlook on life, would it not?"

"I suppose it would."

"There's not much to do after that. Kearan makes his living on this ship. He's an ugly drunk because it takes away the pain. He has no desire to live, yet no desire to die, either. It's a tough spot to be in."

"Yet you're his friend. Why?"

"Because everybody needs somebody. And I haven't lost hope for Kearan. I believe he will eventually come into his own, given the right amount of time. And the right motivation."

I honestly doubt that, but I'm humoring him. "Why do you assume he's lost much?" I ask.

"I hear him calling out a woman's name at night. Always the same woman. Parina."

"Who is she?"

"No idea, and I don't intend to ask."

Enwen spreads out on the floor, ending the conversation. He's given me much to think about while I wait for him to sleep before starting my nightly search.

Everyone has something dark in their past. I suppose it's our job to overcome it. And if we can't overcome it, then all we can do is make the most of it.

"Feel like a stretch?"

Riden stands in front of my cell, tossing the key up in the air and catching it. I've been aboard the *Night Farer* for six days now. This is the first he's offered to let me out of my cell.

"Do you like flaunting my freedom out in front of me?" I ask, eying the key.

"You know, I do get a strange sense of amusement from it."

"Can't be too easy for you to feel amused when you know I can get out all on my own." Of course, I'm referring to the night he caught me sneaking out and not all the nights I've snuck out since then.

Riden steps closer, dropping his voice. "I've been taking excellent care of the key ever since. And if I were you, I wouldn't mention that little mishap to anyone else. Captain'd get an idea in his head if he knew. And you won't like his ideas."

I tilt my head to the side. "You mean you didn't tell him I tried to escape?" Best to reinforce the notion. The more Riden doesn't tell his captain, the more of a wedge I put between Draxen and the crew. Might be able to use that distance later. Who knows what else will happen while I'm a "captive" at sea?

I add, "Perhaps you should get some ideas about what he would do to *you* if he knew."

"Guess I'm counting on the fact that you'll be more worried about your own skin rather than harming mine. Now, I'm giving you a break from your cell. Do you want it or not?"

I appreciate the gesture, but I can't say that I trust it. "Where are we going?"

"We've come across a ship that appears to have been

abandoned after the storm. The vessel is a little worse for wear, but we may find some salvageable goods on board. We're in the middle of the sea with nowhere for you to go should you try to escape. The captain has granted me permission to bring you aboard for the search."

I realize he could be telling me we're in the middle of nowhere, when in reality we're only a day from land. Impossible to tell. Though it doesn't matter either way. Still, I like knowing where I am. The uncertainty makes me a bit uneasy.

"I'm always up for some thieving," I say.

"Somehow I knew you would be."

He lets me out. Then he pockets the key, this time putting it in his breeches rather than his shirt. "I'll be keeping a close watch over this, so don't get any ideas."

"I've no idea what you're on about."

He grabs my upper arm and leads me toward the stairs.

"Must you?" I ask. "You've already stated I've nowhere to go. Can't I have the freedom to walk without your aid?" I can't help but add, "Or can you simply not keep your hands off me? Enwen informed me you're helpless against my feminine charms."

Riden looks unworried. "If you've been talking to Enwen, lass, then I'm sure you've learned that half of what he says is squid brain."

I smile and lean in his direction. "Perhaps."

"Quit your smiling and get your arse up those stairs."

"I wouldn't dream of giving you such a view."

Now it's his turn to smile mischievously. "You don't get the option to walk behind me. Don't trust you. Now, up with you."

On deck, men are tying down ropes, grabbing their weapons, scurrying about. Excitement for the upcoming adventure is almost tangible upon the air. I myself can feel the anticipation of the hunt. I am not immune to the prospect of some good fun. No pirate is. It's why we choose this life. Because we're good at it.

And we have no morals.

"Ah, Her Highness has decided to honor us with her presence," Draxen says. "What do you say, gents? Should we have the lady go first?"

A few ayes and a good deal of laughter are their responses. I look around the crowd of men and spot Theris blending in with the rest of them. He glances at me but doesn't spare me any special attention. He's good at his job, that one.

Riden says nothing from beside me. He doesn't look bothered either way. Not that he should. He is not here to look after me, and I don't need him to. He's here to make sure I don't escape, which he might be doing too good a job of at times. Not to fear. I've still got a few tricks up my sleeve.

"If your men are too cowardly to venture over by themselves," I say, "then by all means, I'd be happy to teach them how to properly secure a ship." A challenge and an insult all wrapped into one. My specialty.

"I'd rather risk your life than theirs. Be off with you. Riden, go with her."

I think it strange that Draxen would risk me when he knows he needs me as leverage. I suspect he's trying to make up for what happened back on my ship. He placed teaching me a lesson over the lives of his own men. Now he's showing that he's putting me at risk before them. It's a clever play. Especially since it's very unlikely that anyone would still be over at the ship. And, as a last precaution, he's sending Riden over with me.

We secure the gangplank between the two ships. The damaged ship before us appears to be a cargo vessel. There's bound to be lots of food and water aboard. It's its own kind of treasure out here.

The gangplank is plenty big to walk across without having to try to balance. I could probably do it with my eyes closed. Still, its width is small enough that I'm tempted to give Riden a slight push.

As if sensing this, he says, "Don't even think about it."

"I already did."

"I could have you shot."

"Your gun would have a hard time working once it's wet."

"I didn't say I had to be the one to shoot."

"But let's face it, you'd like that pleasure for yourself."

He smiles.

The ship's mainmast has broken clean off. It lies at an angle on the ship, supported by the railing on the starboard side.

That'll lock the ship in place for sure. All the rowboats are missing from the ship, which leads me to wonder how far from land we could be. The ship still floats. It would hold the men steady for as long as their food and supplies lasted, so why row away if there's nowhere to make it to in time?

The deck is one scattered mess. Ropes lie haphazardly, some in knots, some in coils. Articles of clothing sit here and there, likely having fallen out of their owner's bags in the confusion. The wood's still wet. Everything's wet. We have to be extra alert not to trip or slip.

"Anything valuable will likely be belowdecks," Riden says.

"I know."

"So, what are you waiting for?"

I raise an eyebrow. "You're going to make me go first?"

"Can't risk you trying to jump me from behind."

"But I don't have a weapon."

"That hasn't stopped you before."

I can't help but smile. "I meant, how can you expect me to go below first without a weapon?"

"I'll be right behind you."

"That's not the comfort you think it is."

"I know." His brown eyes are alight with merriment. I think he enjoys our little spats. I think of them as part of my act. I'm playing a part. If I keep too much of myself hidden, he might be suspicious that I'm planning something. So I give him the resistance he expects. The enjoyment I get out of toying with him is an added bonus. I could have been stuck with a worse questioner. Why he's not captaining the *Night Farer*, I'll never know.

"Go now, Alosa," he says.

Water drips from everywhere it seems. Today is the first day after the night of the storm that the rain's let up. It's dark below, further suggesting that no one's belowdecks.

Riden, ever prepared, brought a lantern over with us. He lights it. Then he hands it to me. "Lead on."

We find the kitchens, where dried meats, well-stored water, crackers, pickled vegetables, and other seaworthy foods are safely secured in their cupboards. These will all be taken over to the *Night Farer*, no doubt.

We pass through the sleeping quarters. Some blankets remain. The smell is much better here than back on the *Night Farer*. Why couldn't Draxen's men show more aptitude for personal hygiene? Truly, it benefits everyone on board.

We're about to pass into the next room when the candlelight catches something on the floor.

That would be a sword. Good to know it's there. If only I could grab it without Riden noticing, but that's all but impossible. A sword would be much harder to hide than a dagger.

There is nothing else of interest on the ship. At least not anything that's visible right away. There may yet be some nooks and crannies that remain hidden. But it's also just as likely that the crew members took anything valuable with them. It's been my experience that when a crisis strikes, the first thing that men think about are all the treasure they can take with them. Thoughts of their friends and shipmates usually come second, if at all.

"Looks all clear," Riden says. "I'll start looking deeper. Kindly go and hail the rest of the crew over."

"Oh yes, I'll just go hail the crew over. Truly, I enjoy helping the men who've kidnapped me."

"Can't leave you down here by yourself while I go fetch them. Would you rather I hauled you all the way up the deck with me? I know how much you like it when I have my hands on you."

I huff and head up the stairs. He's difficult to figure out, that one. One instant he seems to try to distance himself from me. The next I swear he fancies me. He's probably keeping me on my toes, just as I try to do to him. The game of predator and prey can be a fun one. When you're the predator, of course. It's fun to rub the victory into your prisoner's face. You beat them. You captured them. It's your right. Father said once that if you can catch and imprison a man, then his life is yours to take or do with as you please. His philosophy is that if you have the power to do something, then you *should* do it.

Once on deck, I wave at the pirates, signaling that everything is all clear.

With nothing else to do, I return belowdecks. Might as well continue to walk and stretch before I get shut into my cell again. Not that I don't intend to spend tonight moving about anyway.

"They're on their way," I say as I enter the room Riden and I last checked: a storage room.

That's when they grab me.

Riden's shoved face-first against the wall, a sword point pressed against the middle of his back while the bearer's free hand pushes against his shoulder. I can see now that a few panels have been removed from the wall straight ahead. A hidden room. Three men stand in the room with Riden and me: one keeping Riden where he is, and now two holding me.

"Blast it," I say. "You couldn't have shouted out a warning?"

"When a sword's pointed at me?" Riden asks. "I think not."

"Shut up!" one of the men holding me yells. "How many are in your crew? How many will come?"

"Sixty," Riden says, exaggerating the number by twenty.

"Stars," the man holding Riden at sword-point says. "We can't hold them off. And we can't count on the others returning in time."

"Then we'll use 'em as hostages," the last man says. "We'll tell 'em we'll kill the members of their crew unless they stay back. We can buy time."

"But will it be enough?"

"It'll have to work."

"But do we need them both? The man looks like too much trouble to deal with. I say we gut him and deal with the girl."

Being underestimated always works to my advantage. But sometimes I find it offensive. That often makes me violent. It makes me question whether I should allow them to kill Riden, just so I can beat the hell out of all three of them without Riden watching. I couldn't let him see what I'm capable of doing to them. I hate that I have to hold back now.

The men continue to argue among themselves as I decide what to do.

Riden interrupts my line of thinking. "Now, Alosa, would be a good time for you to employ that same tactic you demonstrated when we first met."

"Are you certain you wouldn't like to handle this one yourself? I'm just 'the girl.'"

"Stop talking!" a sailor shouts.

But I'm not really listening to them. My eyes are on Riden. His eyes widen meaningfully, frustratingly. Then he relaxes. "Please."

"I said—"

Perhaps it's the fact that Riden remembered exactly what I did to those two crew members when they stole me from my ship. Or perhaps it's that I like the sport of it. Or it's the idea of showing these sailors exactly what I can do.

But if I'm being honest . . . it's because he said please.

This prompts me to action in a way I can't explain.

I slam my heel into the foot of the sailor on my right. Then my free hand goes to the other sailor's throat. I place one hand at the back of each man's neck. With one choking and the other stumbling, it isn't difficult to connect their heads. Hard.

That wasn't part of my routine back on the ship. But a little improvisation goes a long way. This situation is a bit more dire. For one, it isn't one I had planned for.

There's only the man with the sword left. He stays right where he is, though his eyes have widened significantly. "Stay where you are or I'll kill him."

I roll my eyes. "Go right ahead. You'd save me the trouble."

I'm not sure whether I should laugh or not at his confusion. "What?"

"I'm being held prisoner by pirates. If you say more of your men are coming, then you can help me. We can use him as leverage as was suggested before."

He looks to his fallen shipmates.

"Sorry about that. I don't like being held against my will. Now please. Say you'll help me."

The sailor focuses on Riden, which gives me the distraction I need to reach for my boot. "Is what the girl says true?"

"Trust me. The girl's more trouble than she's worth, and you can't believe a thing she says. You'd be better off killing her now."

I see sweat drip down the sailor's face. The hand on his sword trembles. "That's enough." He turns his body toward me while keeping his sword on Riden. "I'm—"

The dagger flies straight and true, finding its place in the sailor's chest.

Thank the stars I still had it on me. The dagger-hidden-in-book trick is one I will never take lightly should I ever need to intentionally get kidnapped again. And it was a wonder Riden hadn't checked me for weapons when he found me sneaking about the ship that night.

Riden stands up straight. His mouth is slightly ajar, his eyes wide. "I thought you . . . I thought—"

"You thought I'd really turned on you. Probably should have, but oh well. Too late for that now."

I walk over to where Riden stands when others enter the storage room.

"What happened here?" Draxen asks. He looks neither worried nor upset by the bodies on the floor.

I wait for Riden to sell me out to save his own skin. He could easily tell Draxen that I left him to die, telling the pirates to come aboard when an ambush was in place. It would be a little farfetched, considering there were only three men on board. But still plausible.

"It was my oversight," Riden says. "I thought the ship was clear. I told the lass to go above and bring you over. Then they came out of a hidden room. I handled them."

"Excuse me?" I say. He is *not* taking credit for my kills. Not that I need Draxen to know I'm capable. In fact, it's probably best that Draxen thinks I'm not.

Riden ignores my outburst. "I think you'll be pleased with what else awaits in the hidden room."

That distracts me. I look over Riden's shoulder and see three chests filled with coins. There could easily be more behind other panels.

Draxen's eyes are on fire as he stares. He alone advances, taking stock of it all.

"They're smugglers," Riden continues. "Looks like they've just delivered their cargo, whatever it may have been. I suspect that after the storm, most of the crew left to go get a new ship and return here. They weren't about to leave all this wealth behind. These men were left here to guard it. I probably wouldn't have found them if I hadn't heard one of them moving through the wall."

"Yes, yes," Draxen says. I doubt he heard a word Riden said. He's still staring into the wall. "Take the girl back over. The men and I will handle this. We need to be quick before the rest of their crew returns." Almost as an afterthought, he adds, "Well done, brother."

Riden nods.

And just like that it's back to the brig I go.

Riden opens my cell and thrusts me inside.

"What are you doing?" I ask.

"Following orders."

"I thought we were past you hauling me around. Haven't we established that I can walk on my own?"

Riden stands at the opening of my cell. He hasn't shut me in yet, but he's not looking at me. He's looking at the ground. "Why did you do it?"

"Do what?"

"You saved me."

"Yes, and then you took credit for it. What kind of thanks is that? That was damned insulting. I ought to—"

"That was for your benefit."

I'm too full of energy to sit. I usually am after a fight—should I not exhaust myself to the point of passing out. Father did have me do that on several occasions so I would know what it feels like to be worn thin, so I could be mindful of my own strength. It's important to know how much energy I have, in case running becomes the better option. But so far no one except my father has been able to wear me out to the point of losing consciousness.

"Just how exactly was that for my benefit?"

Riden grows very serious. "I don't know what you're doing. I do know you had an opportunity to escape from us back there, and you didn't take it. And you stopped them from killing me when you had no reason to. Now that leaves me with two notions. Either you're not so despicable and heartless as your prior actions would suggest. Or you have some sort of ulterior motive for keeping me alive and staying on this ship."

"I'm still not seeing how you claiming my kills is a kindness to me." Riden thinks I'm up to something, eh? Guess I will have to up my act. I need to rid him of the idea.

74

"You don't know my brother. So allow me to explain something to you. If he thinks you're up to something, he'll kill you. Now I owe you my life. So consider my silence part of my repayment."

"There's nothing to be kept quiet. You're overlooking a third option, Riden."

"And what's that?"

"I was looking out for myself. There was no guarantee I could trust those men. If they found out who I was, they could try to use me for leverage just as you do, especially if they're smugglers, as we suspect. And if something were to happen to you, Draxen would have someone else question me. And there's a good chance I'd hate him more than I do you."

Riden watches me. No amusement. No gratitude. No anything.

What is he thinking?

Finally, he says, "I suppose I didn't think of that. Of course I should have considered that your only concern was for yourself."

"I'm a pirate," I remind him.

"Yes. I just can't figure out if you're a good pirate or a *really* good pirate."

"I'm not sure I know what that means."

"Just know that whatever it is that you're hiding from me, I *will* figure it out."

Clinking metal beats a steady rhythm. Not that of swords,

but of chains. I know the sound well, as I've spent much time practicing how to get out of them.

At the sound, Riden goes ahead and locks me into the cell. Did he decide that our conversation was over, or does he not want Draxen to see him talking to me through an open door?

Draxen and two pirates—one who I've never seen before and the third pirate who helped bring my things down with Enwen and Kearan—lead two of the smugglers, who are clad in manacles, down the stairs. The conk to the head I gave them must not have been enough to kill them. 'Tis a shame for them, because death likely would have been better than whatever the pirates could have in store.

I may also be a prisoner, but they need me alive and in good health if they expect a ransom from my father. These two smugglers, however, do not need to be traded. Nor do they need information from them because the gold has already been found. The fact that they were brought on board alive, then, spells disaster for them.

"What is this?" Riden asks.

"Ulgin's getting a bit restless," Draxen says. "I thought he could use this."

Riden nods, though he doesn't look happy about what he knows will happen next. Yet he opens a new cell far away from mine. The pirate I assume is Ulgin leads the smugglers inside.

"And I came down to collect you," the captain continues. "What with our fortunate find and all, I figure the men could use a payday on land. There's lots of gold to be spent. I want you to oversee the distribution of each man's share. We should be upon the shore by nightfall."

I knew we were close to land, despite everyone's misleading. The smugglers who left their shipmates aboard their broken ship would have had to take the time to find a new ship and then find where their old one had drifted off to. It's no wonder they haven't come back to it yet. And rather fortunate for Draxen and his crew that they happened to stumble across it.

"What are we to do with the princess?"

"Nothing at all. That's why I brought Sheck down here. He'll be guarding her until we reach land."

"Is that really such a good—"

"I think she's been having too good a time of it, Riden. It's time we remind her who we are. Don't know why you chose Kearan and Enwen, of all the crew, to primarily oversee her. If they didn't have their particular talents, I would have tossed them overboard long ago. Almost bloody useless."

Riden looks like he wants to argue. Very badly. But he doesn't. "Let's see to the gold, then," he says instead.

For the first time I turn my attention to Sheck. And nearly jump away.

He's pressed up to the bars, staring hungrily at me. I feel as though rats crawl across my skin. Actually, I think I would prefer it if rats were crawling against my skin.

When I was little and faced with a new challenge each day,

I would look to my father for help. He would instruct me and then send me into the fire pit—figuratively speaking. I always got burned. And I learned quickly that turning to him for help was useless. He never assisted. I either succeeded or suffered the consequences of failing. There was no relief. Long afterward, I might be given some advice and encouragement. Sometimes even comfort. But in the moment, there was no aid. It wasn't long before I learned to stop turning to others for help. It's never an option, so I don't even think about it.

Which is why when I am faced with the hot-blooded pirate, my first response is not to look to Riden. Or to ask Draxen to have someone else guard me. No, I handle my problems alone because that is the way things are.

"There isn't a problem, is there, Alosa?" Draxen asks. His sneer is full of poison.

I say, "I've never had a problem I couldn't handle myself."

Chapter 6

THOUGH MY TIME SPENT with Sheck and Ulgin was only a few hours, it felt like much, much longer.

It started with Sheck walking back and forth in front of my cell, never taking his eyes off me. Occasionally he would reach through the bars, as if he could grab me. He was trying to get a response from me. To see me afraid. I never gave him the satisfaction. I stayed to the far end of the cell the whole time. Though I was tired and could have used a rest before I sneak out of my cell tonight, I didn't nap. I couldn't risk rolling over in my sleep, coming within reach of Sheck's searching hands.

But that was not all that prevented me from sleeping. There was also the screaming. Ulgin, like Sheck, is not a complicated pirate to figure out. Each pirate has their vice. For some it is drinking, for others it's gambling, for those like Sheck, it is deriving forced pleasure from a struggling woman.

But Ulgin—his is seeing pain in others. So I sat, facing away, while Ulgin tortured those smugglers to death.

Draxen keeps vile men in his company, but I am neither surprised nor terribly bothered by it. My father has much worse men at his disposal. Some of them I know enjoy the taste of human flesh, right off a living body.

I have no such creatures within my own crew. I value other traits above an affinity for torture and power over those weaker than oneself. I value brilliant minds, honest souls, and those with long endurance. I forge relationships based on trust and mutual respect, not fear and control.

Empathy for human life is something my father tried to beat out of me. He thinks he succeeded. Most people do. And while I can kill evil men without guilt, the suffering of others pains me as well as it does them. It hurts, but I can handle it. Bad things happen to people who may not be deserving of such punishment. The world continues on. I continue on. Because if nothing else, I'm a survivor.

So it is with relief that I look upon the dead smugglers. Their pain is gone at last.

Shortly after, Riden comes below with two pirates I haven't met.

"You're relieved, Sheck. Go ashore with everyone else. You

may, too, Ulgin, once you've cleaned this up." Riden's posture is stiff, and he looks at Sheck with such disgust, I'm surprised his tone doesn't reflect his feelings.

Sheck hasn't said a word during the whole time he's been down here. I wonder if he can talk at all. He looks me up and down one last time, as if memorizing every part of me. Then he races out of sight.

Riden turns to me next, his face blank now. "This is Azek and Jolek. They will be watching over you while I go ashore as well." Riden steps right up to the bars, trying to get out of earshot of everyone else. "I know to expect some sort of attempt at fleeing from you, what with us being so close to shore and all. So let me save you the trouble. There are five men guarding the ship above deck. They know to watch out for you."

There's a slithering sound; Riden and I turn to see Ulgin dragging a sheet topped with the bodies of the smugglers out of the brig.

Riden looks at me then, and it might be the poor lighting, but I swear his eyes are wetter than usual. He is not anywhere close to tears, but he might be feeling . . . something.

"I'm sorry," he whispers.

And then he's gone.

He's apologizing as though Sheck and Ulgin are somehow his fault. Or maybe he's apologetic for some other reason. I never know with Riden. Sometimes it feels like he's trying to help me. Other times, he's obviously doing the complete opposite.

He subjected me to Sheck and Ulgin, yet he never ordered me to give him my dagger. I know he saw me take it off the dead smuggler back on the ship. Did it slip his mind? Or did he want me to have it while I was belowdecks with those two?

Either way, I still don't know what to make of Riden.

Doesn't matter at the moment, anyway. I have a more pressing problem. Riden assumes I will try to escape this ship in some way. He already suspects me of being up to something. Of being more than just a prisoner on this ship. He knows I'm hiding something.

Which means if I'm to keep up appearances, I'll have to escape the ship.

Then get caught on purpose.

Oh, the ridiculous things one has to do when one is a pirate.

The two pirates ordered to guard me sit in front of my cell, playing dice. I suppose that since they're not permitted to go ashore and spend their money, the next best thing is to gamble. I myself like to gamble as well, just not with money.

"Sixes beats sevens, don't it?" asks Azek.

"Sures do. But nines beats them all," Jolek says.

"Then how comes you have more points than me?"

"Because I'm better with numbers."

Honestly, it doesn't look like either of them can count very well. But each time the other starts to get ahead, a similar argument will break out.

They're both so focused on the game that they don't pay any attention to me, which works perfectly to my benefit.

I return to one of my bags, the one holding the books, and take out a book on sailing, another subject I have mastered. The spine of this book holds my lockpicks.

The simple fact is that each time I break out of my cell and get caught, Riden will be determined to learn how I managed it. My key-swap trick was bound to work only until Riden tried to use the false key. Now I have a second method for getting out of my cell, which I've been using for the last several days. It's actually been quite easy, since Kearan and Enwen fall asleep quickly, and Kearan's snoring masks the clicking of the lock.

Azek and Jolek don't look up until the door creaks open. They stand from their chairs and stare at me.

"Didn't thinks she could do that," Azek says.

"You don't think," Jolek says. "You just pretends to."

Rather than let them make the first move, I grab each man by the collar at the back of his neck. *Easier to strike than to dodge,* Father says. I use the same head-bashing trick I performed back on the smuggling ship. I take care not to break either man's neck—if for no other reason than the fact that they didn't leer at me as Sheck did.

The deck is nearly empty when I get up top. There might be a couple of men leaning against the railing near the bow of the ship. I wonder if Riden merely exaggerated the number of men who would be guarding the ship or if some of the pirates abandoned their posts. Being left behind is never a pirate's first choice when there's gold to be spent.

I can see the shore ahead. It's not far, but I still need a boat.

"Abandoning your mission?" a voice asks me from behind.

I spin around and find Theris standing casually, a coin between two of his knuckles. Glancing over at the bow of the ship, I note that the other men on deck haven't noticed me yet.

"I have business on land," I say quickly.

"Did you finish what you were sent here to do, then?"

It's a struggle to keep my voice quiet when all I want to do is lash at him. "No—not that it's any of your business. I'll be back shortly."

"I have my orders, and making you part of my business is one of them."

Blast my father. Can he not trust me to do this alone? "That's nice, but I don't need or want your help, so stay out of my way."

"I'll do better than that. I'll distract the men so you can go ashore without being noticed."

"That's not necessary—"

"I'll do it anyway."

I glance heavenward. Then I reach for the pulley to lower down a rowboat.

"You're not going to swim it?" Theris asks.

I look over my shoulder, narrowing my eyes. "Why would I?"

"I would have thought it would be easier for you. Is it not?"

Just what does he know or think he knows about me? How much did Father tell him?

"I thought you were distracting the men for me."

"And I thought you didn't need my help."

I ignore him once I hear the light splash of the boat connecting with the sea. His footsteps finally recede as I lower myself down with another rope. Putting Theris out of my mind, I start rowing. 'Tis not my favorite activity. When going ashore with my crew, I always make someone else do it.

Such are the privileges of being captain.

Can't be more than a few minutes when I reach shore. It's night, and no one is patrolling the dock. Good thing, because I haven't any money on me.

Not that I can't just procure some. But that takes time and a little planning.

I pull my coat around me more tightly. The night air is brisk, as is typical during the fall. Some of Maneria's more southern isles experience warm temperatures year-round, but here in the northeast, the winds and waters are always cold, save when it is the heart of summer.

I travel farther inland, trying to get a sense of where I am. I know that when I was taken, I was over a two days' ride from the south side of Naula. We've been on the sea for only about seven days. We could have just gone around to the other side of the isle. Clever, that. Most would assume that after a kidnapping, the perpetrators would want to get as far away as possible from where the crime took place.

Word must have gotten around to my father that I succeeded in getting aboard the *Night Farer*. I'm sure he'll want a report soon. I might as well write him now since I'm on land. Who knows when I'll have such an opportunity again? Besides, it's best to wait awhile before I let the pirates catch me attempting to "escape." Can't make it seem like I got away too easily.

I didn't want to let Theris turn me in. I know the whole point of this little side venture is getting caught, but letting Theris do it would feel like using his help. And I won't be doing that.

I continue heading inland. There will be someone working for my father in the pirate quarter of town. There always is. Father has a man in each major port city in all the Seventeen Isles. The trick will be figuring out who he is. I can use the signal that men in my father's employ exchange. But how I'll be able to signal my father's man without getting caught by all the pirates from Draxen's crew, who are also likely to be there, first will be the tricky bit.

As I walk the city streets, I start to feel a tingling at the back of my neck.

I'm being followed.

Is it a member of Draxen's crew? I would hate to be caught already. But it wouldn't be the worst thing in the world if Father didn't receive a letter from me.

So long as it's not Theris trying to keep an eye out for

me. I will start retaliating with violence if he becomes too meddlesome.

I look behind me casually, as if I'm only observing the night sky or something else that's caught my fancy. There is definitely a figure in the shadows. Maybe more than one.

We're stopped between two town homes. I'm not on the street, just a grassy area that separates the two houses. The grass is wet, softened by the rainfall over the last several days. I've no weapons on me, save the dagger in my boot.

There can't be too many of them, otherwise I would have spotted them earlier. It's likely that I can take them. Might as well risk it.

I pat my pockets, as though I realize I've just forgotten something. I spin around in the wet grass, making a light squeaking noise with my boots. This emphasizes my casualness. I'm not trying to be quiet. My followers won't think I've found them out.

I start walking back in the direction I came from. When I reach the corners of both homes, I leap forward into the shadows on the left. Right where the sparse moonlight is blocked by the roof of the home there.

"Ah!" a woman's voice calls out. I put my hands to her mouth, stopping the cry. We can't have everyone in this part of town waking and spotting us.

"Mandsy, is that you?" I ask.

"Hello, Captain."

I sigh and look heavenward, though no one can see the motion. "All right. Come out. All of you."

There are three of them—the three members from my crew who I saw not long ago: Mandsy, Zimah, and Sorinda. I'm relieved they made it safely to land, but I don't let it show.

"I told you she was going to see you," Zimah says to Mandsy. "You're terrible at staying hidden. And quiet." She meets my gaze for only a moment before looking at the ground, ashamed to have been caught on land when they're supposed to be on the ship.

"What are you doing here?" I ask.

"We've been following you," Mandsy says, smiling widely. Her teeth shine now that she's stepped into the moonlight. "Zimah has been tracking you. We were worried, Captain. Just wanted to make sure you're all right. I hate the thought of you being stuck on board with that lot."

"As you can see," I say, "I'm fine. Really, this was reckless of you. What if you were seen by Draxen's men? You could have blown my cover."

"We were careful. No one spotted us, what with Zimah here."

"*I* spotted you."

"That's because we weren't trying too hard to hide from *you*," Zimah says defensively, as though her skills are being brought into question. "We wanted to talk with you. Ship's lonely without you, Captain."

I can't help but smile. "I suppose I should have expected this from you two. But, Sorinda, what in all the seas of Maneria are you doing here?"

Quiet as death, Sorinda finally speaks. "Niridia ordered me to come with them."

Sorinda is the best swordswoman on my crew. She's an excellent killer. And since she's been in my crew, an excellent protector as well.

"Which means that Niridia's with the ship nearby?" Niridia is my first mate and trusted confidant. I made her temporary captain of my ship while I went on my mission aboard the *Night Farer*.

"Aye."

I put my head in my hands. "I'm perfectly fine. You're all being careless."

"What's it like, Captain?" Mandsy asks. "Being on that pirate lord's ship? Are they treating you well? No one's laid hands on you, have they?"

"No," I lie. "And there will be plenty of time for storytelling later. For now you're to report back to the *Ava-lee*. And you tell Niridia that I order her to take the ship to the checkpoint and wait for me there. No more following me. I mean it." I look each one squarely in the eyes. Mandsy nods feebly while Zimah looks disappointed. Sorinda looks as though she really couldn't care either way. But she always wears that face.

"Aye, Captain," Mandsy says on a sigh, "but what are you

doing here anyway? Why aren't you on the ship? Is there something we can help with?" She can't hide the eagerness and enthusiasm in her voice. That's Mands. Always optimistic and ready to help. Drives the rest of the crew bloody insane sometimes.

"No, I'm f— Wait. Actually, you can. I need to get a message to my father."

"What is it?" Zimah asks. She has a perfect memory. She can recite back to me minutes of overheard conversation at a time.

"Tell him our plans for getting me on board the *Night Farer* went perfectly. I've begun my search for the map. No one suspects me. It's my belief that Draxen doesn't even know the map is aboard his ship, since he doesn't hide it in his quarters. Searching the rest of the ship shouldn't take me long. Be ready at the checkpoint. I'll bring the ship to him soon."

"Got it," Zimah says. "Anything you'd like us to pass along to the crew?"

"Tell them I miss them all, and I'll be home shortly."

"Glad to hear it," Mandsy says.

"Yes, yes, now go. And be quick about it."

"Aye," they say at once, and hurry back toward the shore.

Part of me wishes I could go with them. Another part is still eager for the hunt, for the game of finding the map. I long for the victory of finding something so important for my father. He will be quite pleased when I return.

And I am pleased that getting word to my father became easier than I expected.

Now I get to skip ahead to the getting caught part. Should be simple enough once I find Draxen's crew. The difficult bit will be making it look like an accident. They'll surely be suspicious if I simply hand myself over to them. The last thing I need is Riden getting more curious about my intent. I'm not too worried, but I'm also not careless. I may have lied to my father in my message about no one being suspicious of me, but Riden is simple enough to deal with. Father doesn't need to know about him.

I pass by the large estates where the rich live, and have to stomp out the urge to go snooping around their valuables. For one, they'll have many men inside, guarding their riches from all the pirates currently at this port. (Thanks to my father's regime, there are always several crews in each port city, stopping to spend their plunder.) Such discouragement has no effect on me, save that I know the steal will take more time and planning, which I don't have.

And secondly, I wouldn't have a place to hide such valuables after I took them. Riden would be sure to notice and steal a new gem from around my neck.

Eventually I make it to the raucous section of town, the one that wakes once the rest of the city sleeps. You can tell it's for the more unsavory sort, because it's so very loud. Music pours out the windows onto the streets. Gunshots sound. Men and women laugh. Tables overturn. The streets are filled with the light of lanterns.

Any crime at all can be committed here, and the law of the land cannot touch us. It's part of the deal my father has with the land monarch. The pirates get a district on land, free from the burdens of the law, and my father won't blow excavating ships out of the water.

I know instantly when I'm in the right place. There's a tavern on one side of the street, a whorehouse on the other. This is where most pirates go to spend all their spoils. They are men of simple pleasures. I, too, enjoy a good flask of rum from time to time, but I also take pleasure in longer-lasting rewards. I spend my earnings on good clothing and face paint. Appearance is important. I pay for information on big players on different islands. I enjoy meeting new people and learning their stories. The really interesting ones become members of my crew. But ultimately I always seek to win my father's approval, to solidify myself as his heir and become the queen of sea thieves. I can't imagine anything more fun than humbling stuffy land nobles as they cross the ocean. *My ocean.*

I approach the tavern first, since the men at the whorehouse are far less likely to notice me while engaged in their activities. Now, how to get caught without making it too obvious?

I go around to the side of the tavern and peer through a grime-covered window. It's packed, and I can see several members of Draxen's crew. They sit at tables, drinking and gambling and talking. I note that Draxen himself is not here. He's probably over at the whorehouse. Riden must be over there, too— Wait, Riden's in here.

I spot him in the back, at a table with a bunch of men. He has one hand full of cards, while the other is draped around some woman seated on his lap.

A snort escapes me. And he said he didn't pay for female companionship. Although—I squint, getting closer to the window without actually touching it. She's not dressed like a whore. Her face isn't extravagantly painted—

The tavern doors groan as they open wide. Stars, I should have been paying attention to the door.

A body comes walking around to the side of the tavern where I stand. After a few moments, I recognize it as Kearan.

Perhaps *walking* had been too generous of a term. *Stumbling*'s more like it. The big oaf zigzags right past me. Then he stops, bracing himself against the wall.

Time to act.

I pinch my cheeks to bring red to them. I flick my head downward, rumpling my hair. Adding a slight tremor to my whole person, I rush forward, leaning against the wall right next to him.

"Kearan. You have to help me. Please. Help me get away from here."

He turns his head slightly in my direction but says nothing.

"Please," I say again. "I know deep down you're not a bad man. Please get me out of here."

My intention is for him to assume I misplaced my trust. He's supposed to haul me back to the ship.

Instead he vomits and collapses to the ground.

I shouldn't be surprised.

That's when I'm grabbed from behind. Oh, excellent! I was worried I'd have to—

I feel hot breath at my ear. It smells of rum. The chest at my back rises and falls rapidly. Then my hair stands on end as a wet tongue starts at the corner of my chin and rises up my cheek.

Stars, it's Sheck.

Why does he have to be the one to catch me?

He's got both arms around me, holding my own arms flat against my sides. I wait for him to turn me around, to carry me over to Riden or Draxen. But he does no such thing.

He shoves me against the wall of the tavern. I feel a hand at my lower back, dipping lower.

Sheck has no intention of taking me back to Riden—not right away, at least. And I have no intention of waiting around until he's ready.

"You're going to want to let go of me now," I say, giving him a chance to walk away, even though he doesn't deserve one.

He doesn't speak. And why should he? He's more beast than man.

I hop into the air and press my feet flat against the wall, giving it a good push. Sheck tries to catch himself. But his choices are to let go of me or fall on his arse.

Surprisingly, he chooses the second.

My body is not enough weight to knock the breath from him, but I'm sure the fall had to hurt. I take some comfort in this.

I try to roll away from him, but his grip is too tight. I can tell he's done this many, many times before.

The thought spurs me on. I bring my head up as high as it will go, straining my neck. Then I send it flying backward. I can feel his nose connect with the back of my head in a loud crunch.

That is what finally prompts him to loosen his hold.

I stand an instant later, but before I can take a step, Sheck wraps a hand around my ankle.

I turn and kick him in the face with my free foot.

His face is a bloody mess now. I cannot make out his nose, eyes, or mouth. He can't still be feeling the heat of desire in his condition, can he? I hope not, but I have to assume the worst of people in my line of work. Besides, some men get a reaction from pain. Sheck is likely one of those.

Kearan moans from where he lies on the ground, passed out in his own vomit. He smells nastier than Sheck. But I don't need to touch him, just the grip of his sword. I could grab the dagger from my boot, but using it at this point requires close contact, and I don't want to be near Sheck ever again.

I hear a growl from behind me. It's the first sound I've ever heard Sheck mutter. It's an ugly, foul sound that makes me want to run, but I've fought that impulse my whole life. I've had to. It's been the only way to impress my father.

Besides, this man deserves to die, and I'll gladly be the one to do it. I grab the cutlass and turn. Sheck doesn't have his sword drawn. He's probably not used to women fighting rather than trying to run away.

I don't think he even notices there's a weapon in my hand until I stab him in the stomach with it. He cries out, still moving. It's not half the pain he deserves for the type of life he's lived, but it's enough to make me feel a little better. I don't wait more than a couple of heartbeats before dislodging the weapon and stabbing again, this time higher, toward his heart. He tries to squirm under its weight, but that only makes his blood run out all the more faster. He's dead in seconds.

I take a few deep breaths before setting the sword beside Kearan. One less monster in the world.

But I still need to get caught. It should not be this difficult to stay a prisoner on a pirate ship. This is the second time I've had to stage my own capture. Ridiculous.

I turn toward the tavern, wondering how I'm to get someone inside to catch me without making it look too obvious, when I notice someone standing in the opening between the tavern and the next building over.

It's Riden.

Chapter 7

HIS ARMS ARE CROSSED, one leg hooked over the other.

I suppose I should run now to make it look like I'm trying to escape, but why bother?

"How much of that did you see?" I ask instead.

"All of it."

I'm not sure what I should feel after hearing that. Anger that he'd let Sheck try to take me. Confusion that he let me kill him without helping his crewman. Worry that he saw the acting routine I tried on Kearan. Does he know I'm trying to get caught? There's no way to tell. His face reveals nothing in the lit street.

I need to do something. I can't just stand here and let him

take me. It's inconsistent with the character I've been playing for him. So I reach over and pick up Kearan's cutlass again.

"You want to fight?" he asks.

"I am not going back on that ship," I say.

"I'm sorry, Alosa, but you have to." He pulls his own sword from its sheath.

All right. I'll go easy on him. Let him disarm me quickly and get this night over with.

"You really want to do this?" he asks. "I was in the middle of something back there when I heard a struggle going on outside. You've put me in quite the mood. I wouldn't test me."

I snort. "I saw your lady friend. It looked like you were already in a mood."

"One night on land after months at sea, and you have to go and ruin it."

"And what about me? I was carrying out a very important mission for my father when you caught me. You've ruined my entire week. I should take an ear for that."

"You wouldn't take my ear. It would make it difficult for me to hear your whining. And I know how much you love that."

Never mind. I shall not make this quick. I want to hurt him a bit first.

I lurch forward, slashing at his stomach. Riden deflects the blow and reaches for my legs with his sword. But I leap backward.

"Why didn't you stop me?" I ask, sending a volley of strikes at him.

"Stop you from what?" He quickly defends himself against each strike, but I keep them coming as we talk.

"You saw me fighting him. You know your captain doesn't want me mistreated in any way, yet you let him try to take me. You just stood there. And—oh."

He gets his bearings and puts himself on the offensive. I like learning how he moves. It will let me know how to beat him. Later, of course. Tonight I have to let him win.

"You wanted me to kill him," I say. "Of course. You hate what he does. What with you being so *honorable* and all. But you can't kill him yourself because for some reason you're loyal to your brother, and you can't be seen killing a member of his crew. I'll never understand this loyalty; you seem to hate everything Draxen does."

I cut him on his arm. Riden is going a bit easy because he doesn't actually want to hurt me. It definitely gives me the advantage. Of course, I don't want to kill him, either—hurt him, though, yes. Part of what I told him the other day is true. I don't want Riden dead, because he is my preferred choice for an interrogator. Draxen would assign someone even worse to watch me if Riden weren't an option.

"That's why you were angry on the day you captured me," I say as a realization hits me. "I brought out the worst in your brother by challenging him, by killing members of his crew. You had to step in and remind him of his humanity. But he always seems to have a hard time finding it, doesn't he? He's more like your father in that way."

I gasp as pain burns against my leg. He actually slashed me with his sword. I must have touched on something too personal.

"You ruined my breeches!"

"Lass, shut up," Riden says.

"But why do you do it?" I say, forgetting my clothes. "You're clearly miserable among the crew. You probably don't even enjoy pirating! Why do you stay?"

I get in another cut, this time at his side. I make sure it's shallow. A victorious smile tugs at my lips, but then Riden does the unthinkable. Instead of flinching away from my sword, he leans into it, grabs my wrist with his free hand, and raises his sword to my neck. Before I can blink, the hand at my wrist grabs my sword, and he's pointing both blades at me.

I stare at him, stunned. He let me cut him so he could take my weapon from me. It's a bold and stupid move.

I like it.

I'm so impressed, I can't even muster up the right amount of anger. I have underestimated Riden.

He sheathes his blade, tosses Kearan's back to his sleeping form, and then grabs me by my upper arm. "I stay because he's my brother. Because he is the only family member who loves me unconditionally. Something you could never understand."

I want to deny it, to defend my relationship with my father. But no words spring to mind. So with my free hand, I hit him where my sword struck him earlier. He winces with pain, then moves me over to the other side of him.

"It seems we both managed to uncover things better left buried. Now, let's get you back to the ship."

My leg throbs as we walk, but that's nothing compared to the fire in my chest that has ignited from his words. He keeps getting me angry. So very angry. I want to hit him some more. It takes every ounce of strength I have to let him take me back aboard that cursed ship.

I try to get out of the lifeboat once, but Riden kicks me, and I act as though the blow knocked the air from my chest. When a rope ladder is let down for us to climb aboard the *Night Farer*, I punch Riden in the face and try to jump into the water, but he catches me and practically carries me up the ladder. He's stronger than he looks.

These fake attempts at escape are the only satisfaction I allow myself for his daggered words.

Riden returns me to my cell. He ignores Azek and Jolek as they try to offer explanations for how I escaped. He simply orders them to leave.

Riden disappears from the brig for only a moment. Then he returns. I'm surprised when he locks himself into the cell with me.

"Have you decided that you deserve to be behind bars as well?" I ask.

"I decided that long ago, but that's not why I'm here."

I notice now the clean linens and bandages. A little while later, another pirate brings down a bucket of hot water before disappearing again.

"You want me to clean your wounds?" I ask with a snort.

"Of course not; I'm here to clean yours."

"I don't follow."

"Captain wouldn't like it if he knew I'd sliced you."

"I goaded you."

"Doesn't matter. I should be better than that."

"Pirate," I remind him.

"Still doesn't matter. Now . . ." He picks me up and sets me on the table so I'm sitting with my injured leg extended in front of me.

"I can sit all by myself," I say, completely off balance by the effortless way he lifted me.

"I know, but that was more fun. Now, take your breeches off."

"Ha. Not a chance."

"It's nothing I haven't seen before."

"You haven't seen *me* before. Nor will you."

Riden gives me his devilish smile. How quickly he can muster it up.

"I've a better idea," I say, reaching down. I grab the bloody rip in my breeches and tug. The cloth gives, ripping away from my thigh. I wince.

"And here I almost believed you couldn't feel pain."

"Shut your mouth, Riden."

He's quiet, and I know it's not because he listened to me. Instead I realize he's staring at my leg. No, not my leg. My scars. I have them all over my arms and legs.

"What happened?" he asks.

"I was born to the pirate king."

He reaches his hand out, about to trace one of the many thin white marks.

"Don't," I say. "I've just had to fend off Sheck. I don't need anyone else touching me."

"Of course," he says hurriedly. "Forgive me. But I wasn't going to—" He cuts himself off, ending the awkward moment. Instead he reaches down and brandishes a cleaning salve and clean rag.

"Give me those," I say. "I'd rather do it myself."

"And that is why I'll be doing it for you. You're a prisoner, and you tried to escape. You don't get to make any more demands."

"I could just hit you."

"And I could make cleaning this cut hurt more than it needs to."

I sit still, but I don't look at him as he rubs a foul liquid onto my leg. Bubbles come up from the cut, and the pain is searing hot. I grab Riden's arm and squeeze to keep from crying out.

"It's all right, Alosa. Almost done now."

I'm amazed at his soothing tone. It sounds a lot like the one Mandsy uses when she patches me up. Strange to hear it coming from a man.

He wipes the remaining liquid from the wound. The cloth becomes stained with pink. With steady hands, he cuts a bandage strip and ties it around my leg. His hands are warm in this freezing cell.

"It's over," he says. "It should heal quickly. It was a small cut."

"Yes, I know. As you can see, this is not my first injury."

"Why must you always be so defensive? I was helping you."

"Yes, and what a sacrifice it must have been for you. I'm sure you didn't enjoy every moment of it."

Smiling, he leans forward a bit. "You are by far the most enjoyable prisoner ever aboard this vessel."

"I assure you, I'm not trying to be."

His smile fades. Intensity takes hold in his eyes. "I know."

Riden's hand is still on my bare leg. His eyes capture my gaze. I swallow, lick my suddenly dry lips.

Riden places a hand at my cheek. "Alosa."

"Yes?"

Uncertainty flashes across his face. He lets his hand drop. "How did you get out of your cell?"

Instead of answering, I shrug, mostly because it takes me a moment to find my voice.

Riden takes a step back, observes me carefully. "You're

clever, Alosa, in a way that is uncommon for a pirate. And you're talented. There's no doubt about that. And I've always known you're hiding something. But now I'm starting to get the sense you want to be on this ship more than I do."

"Want to be on the ship?" I ask incredulously. "If that's your concern, then by all means, let me go."

"Why else would you go to the pirate quarter of town? You had to know we'd be there."

"You're joking, right? You locked me up and then sent Sheck and Ulgin down here. Do you know what I had to endure? I set out to find the two of them and kill them before I left. They aren't men. They don't deserve to live."

"I know. That's why I let you kill Sheck. Because I couldn't do it myself. But why risk it? You could have gotten away easily if you had just left."

"I have a hard time letting things go. I wasn't about to leave until everything sat right."

I can't tell if he believes me. He's still trying to read my face.

But then his eyes travel down to my bags.

I step in front of them protectively. "What are you looking at?"

"You know I'm going to have to search your things. Unless of course you want to tell me how you got out of here?"

"I just got out, all right? Leave me and my things alone."

"I can't do that. Now step back."

"No."

He steps forward and reaches for me, trying to physically move me out of the way.

I kick him square in the chest with my uninjured leg. The force is enough to knock him onto his back. Oh no. I put way too much into that one. I'm practically telling him all my secrets. He's the one most suspicious of me. I need to pull back. But he threatened my clothes! They're all I have on this ship, and I'm rather attached to them. I don't want his sticky fingers going through them. And I suppose it wouldn't be good if he looked too closely at my books.

When Riden stands, he looks at me with new understanding. "You've been holding out on me."

"It was a pretty decent shot, eh?" I try to make it sound like I got lucky, but I don't know if he falls for it.

"I don't want to hurt you, but I will if I have to."

Ha. As if he actually could if I were trying my hardest. That line of reasoning is dangerous, though. I relax my face, trying to add a hint of fear. And though it goes against every instinct I have, I step away.

Riden leans over my clothes in such a way that he can keep an eye on me as well. He's not about to let me get the jump on him from behind. He's learning.

He searches through my clothes. I notice him quickly scanning over undergarments, careful not to touch them. Interesting. The larger, pocketed clothing, he searches through most thoroughly. Unsurprisingly, he finds nothing except some rather sharp hairpins, which he pockets. He passes over the books quickly.

Until he comes across a volume titled *Etiquette: A Guide to Raising Proper Ladies.* I had no problems hollowing out that one. The entire concept is ridiculous. Unfortunately, Riden thinks so, too.

"What is this?" he asks.

"A book," I answer smartly.

"Am I to believe you would actually read a book like this? You're a pirate."

"And a lady, too."

"I don't think so." He flips through the pages. When that doesn't prove fruitful, he tears at the book, separating the binding from the spine.

Stars!

A small vial containing a purple liquid falls into his hand.

"What do we have here?"

"It's a tonic for seasickness."

"Then why would you hide it?"

"It's embarrassing."

"That's interesting, because this liquid is also the same color as a tonic used to help people sleep. When inhaled, the compound renders a person unconscious almost instantly."

"What a coincidence," I say.

"Yes, I'm sure." He starts tearing through the rest of the books, finding different weapons. Miniature throwing knives, wires for choking, more poisons, and many other things.

Pockets overflowing, Riden stands and moves for the door.

"Where are you taking those?" I ask.

"I'll put them in a safe place."

"Also known as the bottom of the ocean?"

He grins before disappearing.

I'm really starting to despise that man.

Chapter 8

ENWEN AND ANOTHER PIRATE come down to the brig not long after Riden leaves. I'm sure the replacement is necessary because Kearan is still passed out somewhere.

"This is Belor," Enwen says. "He's come to help me watch you. And a fine pirate, he is. He understands the importance of maintaining a healthy amount of superstition."

"No doubt," I say, though Belor seems to be more interested in watching the sack of coins that hangs from Enwen's belt.

The night is young. Most of the pirates will still be in town, sleeping off their drinks. Tonight is perfect for some sneaking about. I need to find that map. I'm ready to be rid of this ship and its cocky first mate. I still can't believe he managed to slice me. More than anything, it was a cut to my pride.

"The only amount of luck to be found is in cold, hard gold," Belor says. "You have that, and you can buy all the luck you need."

"Which is why I purchased these here pearls," Enwen says, pulling out his necklace.

Enwen relays the story of how he got the pearls. I doubt Belor hears a word of it, as he does naught but watch Enwen's purse. Neither pirate pays me any attention. They really are making it easy for me to escape. Not a soul on my own crew would ever be so careless. Not even little Roslyn, who is the youngest of my crew at six years old. Course, I would never have her watch over prisoners. She stays mostly in the rigging, where she climbs better than any monkey ever could.

As quietly as I can, I flip over the table and reach for the leg on the bottom left corner. I hollowed it out with my dagger and shoved the lockpicks in there after knocking out Azek and Jolek. It's a shame for Riden that he never thought to check here.

"You know, I might have something you'd like, Enwen." Belor pulls out of his pocket what looks like a leather string. "Man who gave me this told me it came from a siren's wrist. It's supposed to give the wearer protection on the sea."

Enwen looks at it with reverence, but I'm pretty sure Belor just pulled it off of his boot when no one was watching.

"I'll give it to you for three gold pieces," Belor says.

I've already got the door open. I stand before the two pirates. "It's a terrible trade, Enwen. The man's lying. He just wants your gold."

"But what if he's not? How can I pass up such a trade? No more harm at sea, Miss Alosa!"

"Then why in the world would he trade it for only three coins?"

"You're right. I should give him five for it."

Belor finally looks up from the sack of gold, the prospect of more money shining in his eyes. "Oi! What are you doing out of your cell?"

"Making sure you don't take advantage of poor Enwen, here." Although, now that I think of it, Enwen is probably intending to steal the gold back bit by bit over the next several days.

"Appreciate the help, Miss Alosa, but you best be getting back in your cell," he says as he reaches for his sword.

"Can't do that. Sorry about this, Enwen. I rather like you."

I knock them both out a moment later. Enwen's going to want to drink as much as Kearan to relieve the headache he'll have when he wakes. I honestly feel bad, but I don't have the time to wait for them to fall asleep. That could be a while, and I need to take advantage of a nearly empty ship.

Once I'm up top, I observe everything carefully. The two pirates who were guarding the deck have gone, and Theris is nowhere to be seen. They were probably permitted to go ashore now that Riden is on board. Shame, that. Best to avoid him. Probably in his quarters now. I pass by them silently and walk over to the railing, where I ended my search the previous night. I run my hands over it, thumping with my feet as lightly as possible on the wooden planks below, checking for dead spots.

"Hello, Alosa."

I sigh and look heavenward before turning around.

"Hello, Riden."

"Been waiting for you to come up. You don't disappoint." Riden steps out of the shadows cast by the stairs leading up to the second level. Ah, no wonder I didn't see him.

"You knew I would try to escape again?"

"There are only three pirates left on this vessel, assuming you left Enwen and Belor alive. We're close to land. And I couldn't find whatever it was you used to escape your cell last time. So, yes. I assumed you would try to escape again."

"So you're no longer convinced I'm up to more nefarious deeds?"

"I would have continued to have my doubts had you not gone straight for the edge of the ship."

Thank the stars I went there first. Who knows what would have happened if Riden had seen me searching the ship?

"Now, Riden. There's no reason why you can't let me go. You can tell your dear captain I got away due to your own stupidity. Shouldn't be too hard for him to believe."

"I'm afraid not, Alosa."

"Please don't put me back in that cell. I hate it down there. The smell is awful."

"Perhaps we should find you different accommodations, then."

I don't like the sound of this. "How do you mean?"

"Here, allow me to escort you, princess." He picks me up and throws me over his shoulder.

"What do you think you're doing? Put me down right now!" I push myself up and get a hold of his head. His hair is tied back as usual, nice and long.

Perfect for pulling.

"Ow!"

He gets a door open. I'm too focused on him to realize where we are, but a moment later he throws me onto a bed. Then he grabs my wrist in a death grip, forcing me to release my hold on his hair.

I don't know why, but it's *very* difficult to play the beaten prisoner. I can't stand giving up too easily, no matter how many times I remind myself to make my stay on this ship look unintentional.

Which is why I don't lie passively on the bed. Riden stands over me, his hand still holding my wrist captive. My knee connects with his stomach, which causes him to hunch down farther. I grab his other wrist with my own and pull him over the top of me before shoving him down onto the bed. I roll off and stand so I have the higher ground.

But he shoots up a moment later. I don't expect him to recover so quickly, so he's able to grab my waist and pin me to the bed. The last position I would ever want to be in.

"You're stronger than you should be," he says.

"What is that supposed to mean?"

"Just that you're not a large woman, yet you were able to lift me off the ground."

And those words are the only reason why I don't shove his sorry arse off me. I have to remember to hold back. But it's so *damn* hard! When this is over, I'm going to kill him out of spite.

"I have my father's rigorous heavy lifting training to thank for that."

"No doubt."

"Get off me."

He looks down at me, trailing his gaze from my eyes to my mouth. So very slowly. "Are you sure you want that?"

"I'm quite sure," I say, but the words don't come out as forcefully as I intend them to.

He leans down farther, placing his nose next to mine. "How about now?" he whispers.

He's too cocky for his own good, but I admit he's pretty. And he makes my blood boil, but mostly out of anger. He's a decent sort of fellow inside. But he chooses not to be on the outside. What does that make him?

I'm about to tell him to shove off, but then I feel his lips at my cheek. He's not kissing me exactly, just touching my cheek with his lips. They drift downward to my jawline.

I have to make a serious effort to keep my breathing calm. Even. Not at all excited. Now is not the time to get all tingly. I have a job to do.

But his lips. I can picture them perfectly when I close my eyes. They're a dark pink. Full and unmarred. And right now they're being impossibly soft for a pirate.

When he does finally kiss me, it's right below my ear in that sensitive spot.

Then he moves lower, trailing his lips down my neck at the side, then back up in the middle. He kisses the corner of my chin and then hovers expectantly over my mouth.

He wants me to kiss him, for me to be the one to actually lean forward and do something.

Of course he does. Men like Riden live off the thrill of victory.

Unfortunately for him, I do, too.

He's loosened his hold, so it's effortless for me to flip him over and hover above him. His hands grip my upper arms tightly. He's worried I mean to strike him or choke him in some way. I probably should.

Instead I move my lips to his ear. My teeth graze his ear lobe, and his hands tighten in a different way. They move to my back, pressing there and trying to get me closer.

When I move to his neck, his hands reach for my hair, gliding through the strands.

"You are so beautiful," he says. "Like a goddess born out of the sea."

That is what finally snaps me out of it, his obviously exaggerated exclamation. He wants answers from me. He'll say and do anything to get them. I'm just some pretty face to him. And that is all he is to me. I don't have time for meaningless fun. I have a part to play. This will only make my job more difficult. Besides, how can I forget how I found Riden when I peered through the window of the tavern? He told me himself that he's spent months at sea, and I interrupted his one night on land. Now he expects me to make up for it.

Stupid pirate. I do not get swayed by men looking to add to their list of female conquests. I'd imagine I'd be a fine one, being the daughter of the most notorious pirate of all time.

I stand and move away from the bed. "I want to go to my cell now."

Riden looks confused for a moment. He shakes himself out of it. "You're not staying in your cell anymore. Your continued attempts at escape leave me no choice but to move you."

"To where?"

"My room." And with that, he leaves, shutting the doors behind him. I hear the wiggling of a key and the click of a lock.

I note that he's still on the other side of the doors. I can see his silhouette from the space underneath. I press my cheek against the door, hold my breath, and wait.

He sighs. "What are you doing?" He's talking to himself.

Then he's gone.

Interesting.

I turn to survey the room. I hadn't had a chance to earlier because—well, my mind was on other things. But now I wish I could have gotten a look at it sooner. If for no other reason than I could have been using it to mock Riden.

Because the room is clean. *Spotlessly* clean. Now, as I look at the bed, I can tell it had been made. His desk is neatly arranged with an even stack of parchment. Quills lie next to it, spread apart at even intervals. He has a case of books, and—yes, they're in alphabetical order. The rugs on the floor are free of dust and dirt, likely beaten regularly. His boots are all polished and stacked by twos. His clothes lie flat so as not to gain any wrinkles.

It would be difficult indeed to toss this room without Riden noticing. But toss it, I must. It's clear Draxen trusts Riden more than he does anyone else, so why not give the map to Riden for safekeeping? If the map wasn't in Draxen's room, then Riden's room would be the next choice. Since I know how light of a sleeper Riden is, it's been difficult to find an opportunity to search his room at night. But now I can make the most of being stuck in here. Short of breaking the door down, I don't have a way to get out of here. I put my lockpicks back in the table leg after incapacitating Enwen and Belor.

I get to work, opening drawers and checking pockets. It's difficult to tell what I've already searched through because I have to put everything neatly back in its place as soon as I'm done. I try to start at one point in the room and move in a circle.

More than an hour must pass, and I've found nothing.

Where did you hide it, Jeskor? Who did you give it to if neither of your sons has it?

It simply must be somewhere else on the ship.

Why should I have thought that Riden had it at all? He's certainly portrayed himself as the least favorite of Lord Jeskor's sons. Not sure I can say which is my least favorite of Jeskor's sons at the moment.

Riden's a bloody half-wit. Locking me in here, trying to toy with me, using me to kill a pirate he couldn't kill himself. Sometimes I think him a coward. But not a coward by fear. A coward by choice. Which is worse?

I'd purposely kept my mind focused on the search, but now that it's over, my mind is free to wander. And it shifts straight to what I'd been doing with Riden an hour ago.

Sometimes I'm an idiot. I clench my hand into a fist before giving the table a good slam.

I feel the pressure in my hand, then hear the rumble of the desk and the shattering of glass.

Stars!

Among maps, compasses, and other navigational tools, Riden has an hourglass on the table.

Had an hourglass on the table.

Now it's broken at my feet.

I hope that didn't have any sentimental value.

Actually, no. I hope it *did* have sentimental value. Lots and lots. Serves him right. In fact, why stop with his hourglass?

Riden wants to keep me locked up in his room. Well, he'd better be prepared to deal with the consequences. I rearrange his boots so each left foot goes with the wrong right one. I throw his clothing onto the floor in heaps. That's not good enough, though. I can't help but jump up and down on them. I hope there's plenty of grime on the bottom of my boots.

I rearrange his bookcase. I crumple his papers. I knock everything over that stands upright.

I'm going to be the biggest pain in the arse Riden has ever dealt with. That'll serve him right.

When the door opens a while later, I'm sitting at Riden's desk, drawing pictures of sea creatures all over his maps, using a quill dipped in ink.

"What the bloody hell!"

"I got bored," I say, not bothering to look at him.

"What did you do?"

"Well, I made you something. Look here. I gave this squid your face."

There is silence, and then, "Alosa, I'm going to kill you."

"It'll be awfully hard to collect a ransom from my father if I'm dead."

"Are you sure the man doesn't want to be rid of you? We haven't heard from him yet. I'm beginning to think we did him a huge favor. His loss was our bloody demise."

I set the quill down and look up. "I'm out of parchment. Is there any more on the ship?"

Riden clenches his fists. I think his eyes might pop out at any moment. His face is as red as a crab.

"You don't look well," I note.

"I'll have you know it takes every ounce of self-control I have not to pummel you right now."

"Can't imagine what it takes to break you, then. Tell me, Riden, does your skin itch to see your room so filthy?"

"I'm going to bed. In the morning, you're going to wish you hadn't done this."

"Mmm. I'd be careful in the bed. I think I saw some glass shards in there earlier. You really should watch what you do in there."

Riden rips off the sheets and shakes out his blankets. Glass does indeed fall to the floor. He takes the time to sweep it all up before dumping it over the side of the ship. At least I assume that's what he does. Can't be sure, since I'm confined to the room while he leaves.

When he gets back, I ask, "Where will I be sleeping?"

For the first time in a while, he grins. "I'll be sleeping in my bed. Feel free to join me, but something tells me you'd prefer the floor. 'Tis a shame there's not much room for you now that it's covered with all my things."

Riden locks the door on the inside. Then he pockets the key. He removes his boots and his shirt before climbing into bed.

"You're seriously going to sleep while I'm in here alone with you? Aren't you afraid I'll kill you?"

"I've already made sure there are no weapons in this room. Besides, I'm a *very* light sleeper. You won't be able to take one step without waking me."

"Is that so?" I ask cheerily.

Riden's face falls at my tone. He knows it can't be good.

This night is already one of the best I've had in a while. First I destroyed Riden's room and saw him blow up over it. Now I get to drive him mad when he tries to sleep.

His eyes droop closed. I wait a few minutes. Then I stomp on the floor. Riden's eyes shoot open. He sits up, ascertains I'm not up to anything. Then he falls back asleep.

I repeat this process three more times, when Riden finally gets out of bed. He strides right up to me and gets in my face. "Do that again, and I will knock you unconscious."

I stop my knocking and instead start humming.

It doesn't seem to bother Riden, though. His eyes stay closed. If anything, he looks like he huddles down farther in his bed. My humming turns to singing. I'm not really saying any words, just testing out different notes. It's a random tune that comes to me.

In moments Riden snores softly.

I'd hoped that by keeping him up later, he would sleep more deeply.

I take a hesitant step forward. Riden doesn't budge. At the bed, I put my hands in his pockets, trying to find the key. Still he doesn't stir. I find it quickly. Then I'm at the doors, stepping outside, closing them behind me.

Tonight is the first night I can scour the ship uninterrupted. All the men are ashore, save three. And I've rendered those unconscious. I abandon my orderly search in favor of tearing through the deck. Normally there are lookouts wandering about, and tonight might be my only chance to get free rein of the deck. I search deep into the night until I hear splashing water and laughing men. Some have returned to finally sleep off their celebrating.

Though my eyes strain with the effort it takes to keep them open, I'm disappointed I won't find the map tonight.

I'm getting close, though. And that's enough for now.

Chapter 9

I TRY TO SLEEP on the floor when I return, I really do. But after so many nights spent on the cold, wooden floor of my cell, Riden's bed is too inviting. Even with him in it.

Besides, he's asleep. He stayed out of it the entire time I searched the deck. He won't wake if I just sidle up there on the end.

I barely fit in the space. I can feel the heat pouring into me from Riden's back. He's awfully warm. I don't think he needs that blanket.

So I snatch it and return the key to his breeches before drifting off.

My first thought when I wake is that I'm so *warm*. I'm wrapped in it, like I've been trapped inside a large, heated cocoon. It feels so good, I lie there with my eyes closed. I don't care where I am or what I'm doing. This is too pleasant to ruin by doing something as rigorous as moving.

I feel lips on my forehead. Now someone's nuzzling my neck.

"You stole my blanket, Alosa," a voice whispers in my ear.

I should know that voice, but I'm still addled by sleep.

"That's all right. I don't mind sharing. You kept me plenty warm last night."

"Mmm" is all I say in response.

"This is fun, but we have to get up. You've got work to do today."

"Stop talking."

He laughs softly. A hand brushes my hair back from my face. "I love this hair. Fiery red. Just like your spirit."

My eyes snap open at last. Riden's rolled halfway onto me, his head propped up in his left hand. His right one is still playing with my hair.

I roll off the bed and land hard on the floor. "Ow." I'm standing a moment later. "What are you doing?"

"Well, *I* was sleeping in *my* bed. Don't know what you were doing. However did you manage to climb into the bed without waking me?"

"Must've walked in my sleep."

"I'm sure."

I rub at my eyes and straighten my clothes.

"No need for that," he says. "I'm sure no one will get the wrong impression when you walk out of here."

"Indeed," I say, clenching my teeth. But as I look around the room, my mood brightens. "Should we show them what I've done with the place?"

Riden sits up, winces. "About that. I've decided we've been wasting your potential, what with the way we've been keeping you locked up in that cell all the time. You've got too much energy for escaping and wreaking havoc in my room. I think it's time we put your skills to use."

"What does that mean?"

"You'll see. I'll be back in a moment." He dons a shirt and boots before leaving. A cold burst of air enters the room as the door opens. That's enough to wake me all the way.

I do some stretches, pull my boots back on, and try not to be discouraged by the fact that the map still hasn't turned up. I've yet to check the aftercastle and the crow's nest. Then there are still plenty of places belowdecks that need searching. I don't think Draxen would hide it where his crew could stumble onto it—but as I remember the hidden panels in the smuggling ship, I have to acknowledge that there could be plenty of good hiding places belowdecks.

Riden interrupts my thoughts by coming back into the

room only a few moments later. He doesn't return empty-handed. He has a set of manacles in his hand.

"You're going to clap me in irons, is that it?" I ask. "What for?"

"Numerous escape attempts, causing bodily injury to the first mate as well as several members of the crew, the death of a pirate—and for your own humiliation."

"That reminds me, I wonder how interested Draxen would be to hear that you let me kill a member of his crew."

"Lass, do you honestly think he'd believe you over me?"

"That depends on how much of a coward Draxen already suspects you really are."

Riden's face hardens. "That's enough of that." He clamps on the manacles. I can tell he enjoys it far too much. He's right: The humiliation of it all will be awful. I do not want to go out there and face the rest of the crew.

I turn toward him fully. "When I get out of this, I'm going to grab my crew and hunt you all down. I will not stop until every pirate on this ship is dead."

"We're all trembling with fear."

"You should be. I've some of the best trackers in the world aboard my vessel." My heart warms with pride to think of Zimah.

"Are they fiery redheads as well?"

"No."

"Shame. Now, let's go. You don't want to be late."

"Late for what?"

Riden leads me outside. Naula is now far in the distance, a mere speck on the horizon. I wonder what our next destination could be.

The men are everywhere, scrubbing and mopping at the deck. Moving cargo around. Seeing to the sails. Draxen stands near the helm, overseeing the navigation. He has his hands at his belt, feet spread apart, ever-present sneer on his face. He looks down.

"Ah, *princess*, how are you enjoying your stay?"

I'm tempted to spit on the deck, but I don't spit. That's disgusting. "Just fine, Captain. But I'm more excited about what will come after my stay."

"Yes, I'm sure we'll hear plenty more death threats from you today. For now, get to your duties."

"Duties?" I ask, looking between him and Riden.

"You'll be assisting the crew with swabbing the deck," Riden explains.

"Ha. I think not."

"You've proven you can't be left alone. For various reasons." I can tell his mind drifts to his ransacked room. "And I'll not have you being a nuisance, following me about. You'll make yourself useful."

"And just how do you intend to make me?"

"Liomen?"

"Aye, Master Riden?" a voice calls from a ways off.

"Bring me a rope and hook."

"Yes, sir," the voice answers with merriment.

I know exactly what that means, but the prospect doesn't trouble me. Such hooks can be hung down from many places on the ship's masts, and they attach nicely to the chains stringing together manacles.

After a while, a hook is lowered from up above. Riden places it through one of the middle chains on the shackles I wear.

He hesitates a moment, as if he's waiting for me to give in. To agree to the work so he can take the hook away.

But I say nothing. I even glance away from him, as though I couldn't be bothered to look at him.

"Hoist her away," Riden finally says, a note of eagerness in his voice. All his hesitation seems to have vanished.

I can't tell which is the show: Is it the hesitation for me or the eagerness for Draxen? Maybe both. Maybe neither. I can't tell with him. He seems to go back and forth frequently, as though he isn't sure what he wants himself. Is he trying to prove himself to his brother in some way? But why should he need to? Especially if his brother loves him unconditionally, as Riden claims.

Perhaps Riden can't admit the truth even to himself.

I grip the chains on either side, just above the cuffs around my wrists. If I let the full weight of my body pull on my wrists, the metal would bite into my skin, and it would hurt. A lot. It's best to take the weight on my tightened fists.

Riden isn't blinking. Draxen watches the spectacle with interest. The pirates are all eager. They want some sort of show? I'll give them one.

Instead of allowing this Liomen to get me up into the air, I give the rope a good tug before my feet get even close to being off the ground.

Liomen, either not expecting it or unable to stop it, falls from the mainmast. A few pirates duck out of the way just before Liomen hits the deck, cutting off his scream.

There's moaning. He probably broke one or both of his arms. Maybe a leg. Hard to say when someone's falling so quickly.

Some pirates laugh. Others, who must be his friends, surround him.

His moans quickly turn to cursing as a stream of obscenities are directed at me.

I don't blame the lad. I would curse, too, if I were in his position.

Draxen descends from the upper deck, getting level with me. He looks at me closely before calling out the names of three more pirates. "Get the lot of you to the mast. I want her off the ground. Now!"

They climb quickly, hurrying to follow orders. I wait, bored. If there's a fault with these pirates, it's surely their simplemindedness.

The three men get to the top. They're very careful, wrapping the rope around their wrists several times before tugging me up. I don't bother to try to yank them down. It would involve more theatrics on my part.

Not that I'm opposed to theatrics. I just have something better in mind.

They stop when I'm five feet off the ground. Then they tie off the rope while I hang, clinging to my chains. A spectacle for all the pirates. They stole me. I am a prize to them, clearly strung for all to see.

But I'm also stronger than they're used to seeing.

Draxen gets close enough to see my face clearly. "You killed one of my finest men yesterday. I should let Ulgin have you. But it won't do to have the pirate king's daughter unidentifiable once we swap you for the ransom. This will have to do."

I ignore him, focus only on the three pirates descending to the ground. I wait for them to mold back into the crowd to ensure they can't beat me to the top.

I needn't have worried. Everyone's too stunned to do anything once I start climbing.

"Oi, she can't do that," one pirate exclaims.

I don't bother to look down at them; I focus on the movements of my arms. One hand over the other, relax, pull. Other hand, relax, pull. The chain length doesn't allow me to gain much rope with each pull, but it is enough. I can still climb.

And I do, all the way to the top. I hitch a leg over the rounded wooden beam that rests below the sail. Then I sit, straddling the wood. I'm not even breathing hard. If only I could think of a brilliant plan for getting the chains off. But I've got nothing to work with from up here.

"Bring her down," Draxen calls, face red—not that I can see it clearly, but it's fun to imagine it all red and puffy, fuming with anger.

More and more men start to climb up the mast. But I've no intention of letting any pirate touch me. So I start to climb back down.

I stop when I'm halfway down the rope. The pirates hesitate at the top, no one seems to want to climb down and join me.

Riden steps up to Draxen, puts a reassuring hand on his shoulder. "Alosa!" Riden shouts. "Come all the way down, or I'll order the rope cut."

I sigh and roll my eyes. Riden, Riden. It's sad, really, that they all have to try so hard to make me behave.

I do as he says, though. I've no intention of gaining breaks or bruises.

I just really don't want to clean the deck.

Hanging at the end of the rope, I wait. It's the only trick I have left. It's moments such as these when I'm truly grateful for my father's blasted endurance tests. They made me strong. They made me aware of how much I can handle.

And no one has ever been able to outlast me at holding up their own body weight.

Minutes pass and still I hang. Everyone watches, waiting for me to sag from exhaustion. Curious to see how long I'll be at this.

Riden coughs. "Captain, perhaps the men should get back to work while the princess suffers her punishment."

"Aye," Draxen says.

"You heard the captain. Back to your positions. Get on with it. Who knows? She might still be conscious when you're done."

The men laugh as they scatter to different areas of the ship. The muscles in my arms and stomach start to sting.

At least I don't have so much of an audience now. It's mostly Riden and Draxen. Draxen looks on with satisfaction. And Riden—Riden looks . . . I cannot tell. He just looks.

The sun moves in the sky. The wind changes direction. My body begins to tremble. It's hard to breathe.

And then I can't take it anymore. I drop myself. The iron pinches at my skin, digs into my bones. It hurts like hell, but I'll not utter a word of complaint. Even if I agreed to clean, the captain would only keep me up here now. He wants me to suffer for what happened to Sheck. I can see it in his eyes. There will be no relief for quite some time.

Eventually Riden and the captain move on. They have duties to perform as well. I think they're consulting in the captain's quarters now. It's difficult to tell. Turning my head involves too much effort.

"Miss Alosa," a voice whispers.

"Yes, Enwen? Can I help you with something?"

He smiles, knowing very well I can't do anything for him in my present condition. "It would take a hurricane to dampen your spirits, lass. I have something for you."

"What is it?"

"The siren bracelet. I bought it from Belor after we woke up from the conk to the head you gave us."

"I'm really sorry about that."

"You already apologized, miss. Remember? No harm in trying to fight for your freedom. 'Tis a noble cause. I can't fault you. Would've done the same thing. Now, here."

He ties the leather string to my ankle.

"That's a bootlace, Enwen."

"Maybe so. Maybe not so. Important thing is that you have it anyway."

"Why would you give me something you bought for yourself?"

"I stole some of your hair. And I had to be your prison guard. Kidnapping and mistreating women is not why I became a pirate. I'm a proper thief and good with a knife. Nothing more. It don't sit right with me what we're doing to Your Highness. Besides, I'll steal the coins back from Belor tonight."

He steps closer and whispers so softly now that I can barely hear him. "And between you and me, the men were laughing at me something fierce. The only thing that bracelet brought me was mockery."

"Hmm. Then I think its powers were working on me before you tied it on me."

"No, no, Miss Alosa. I already thought of that. This token is a bracelet. Bracelets are for women. It'll bring you protection from the sea but not me."

I laugh softly. "Thanks, then, Enwen."

"'Tis a pleasure, miss. Be seeing you around."

Blood starts to slide down my arms. Bah, now my clothes are stained.

Every once in a while, I'll start to regain my strength enough to pull the pressure off my wrists for a brief moment. But always I end up back where I am, dangling above a ship full of barbarians. Except for Enwen.

Maybe Kearan, too. He hoists a flask up in the air, a question in the gesture. My returning look must be something like, *How exactly would I drink that from up here?*

He shrugs and downs the rum himself. I suppose it is the thought that counts.

At one point, I spot Theris through the mass of working pirates. He glances up at me a couple of times. It's not sympathy or worry on his face, but curiosity. Like all the other pirates, he's probably wondering what insane thing I'll do next.

All I can wonder is when the pain will go away.

The truly agonizing thing is that I could free myself. If I didn't have to hide what I can do, I could get out of this in no time. But I need to stay on this ship longer. I can't give myself away.

After a while, it becomes hard to think. Hard to see. Hard to swallow. Everything goes hazy. People become blurry shapes. I try to look beyond the ship, straining into the distance. Just as there is a destination far beyond this one, there will be a time far beyond this one when there won't be any pain, just the memory of it. As I try to hold that in my mind, I think I see a black blur on the horizon. A ship. But once I blink, it's gone.

It isn't until it's time for everyone to retire to their beds that I am finally released.

"Cut the rope," Draxen commands.

After a day without food or water or solid ground, my whole body is too weak. Even my legs. I cannot catch myself. So I fall onto my back.

"Upon your next mistake, princess, I will have you dangling by your feet. We shall see how long it takes for the blood to make your head explode. Get her out of my sight, Riden."

"Aye, Captain."

"Try not to have too much fun with her while she's staying in your room. Can't have her in a bad condition when we meet the pirate king."

"She'll be safe with me."

"Off with you, then."

Riden scoops me up in one smooth movement. Somehow

he manages not to make anything hurt more than it already does. He's very gentle with me, holding me close to his chest. I think I'd rather have my head dragged on the ground, but I haven't the power to move.

He carries me into his room, shuts the door, and lays me on the bed. An instant later the manacles are off, and I gasp at the pain the removal causes.

"Shh," Riden says soothingly. "I know, Alosa. Just a moment. I'll put something on that. Stay here for now."

Where would I go? I can't move.

He's drifting around the room, looking for something. "This would be easier if you hadn't moved and broken everything."

I open my mouth, but I think something similar to a croak rather than words comes out.

"What was that?" Riden asks.

I cough and try again. "I think I remember kicking something under the bed."

He sighs before dropping down to his knees.

"Here's something, I think," he says.

The bed dips as he sits on it. He puts his hands under my arms and hauls me up.

I hiss through my teeth.

"Sorry. Almost there."

I'm sitting in his lap, my back pressed against his chest. His head cranes around my neck to see my hands while he puts some sort of salve on them.

"Oh." I sigh in contentment.

"Bet that feels better."

He lets the salve stay on my wrists for a few minutes before applying some more. Then he wraps bandages over my raw, ripped skin.

I try to think only about breathing. Not the pain or ache. Just breathe. Riden's done. Yet he continues to sit here, holding me. It's quiet for some time.

"I'm sorry. I had no idea he'd let you hang for so long."

"If I remember correctly, you're the one who suggested hoisting me up there."

"It was a means of persuading you to do as the captain wanted. I expected you to agree to the chores before the rope was even hung. You weren't supposed to be stubborn."

"You should have known better," I say.

"Yes, I should have. I'm truly sorry."

For some reason his apology frustrates me. Levelly, I say, "If you're sorry, that means you want forgiveness. Is that what you're asking for?"

He's silent. I speak again before he can answer. "If you want forgiveness, that means you want to make things right. And if you want to make things right, that means that you don't intend to put me in harm's way again. So, if you are saying you're sorry, I don't think you understand what that entails."

"I didn't have a choice," he says.

"Of course you had a choice, Riden. You just had a hard one. And you chose the easy option, which was to do nothing."

"Easy? Do you think it was easy for me to watch you? Seeing you up there, knowing the pain you must be in, it . . . it made me feel—it would have hurt less if I had been the one hanging. I hated myself for what happened. And the only way I could punish myself was to force myself to watch you in pain. That was my punishment."

Riden starts stroking my hair. I'm tempted to let the conversation drop, to sink farther into his embrace and sleep. But despite how he's taking care of me now, I'm still furious with him.

"What a nice sentiment," I say. "But words only mean something when backed up with actions. Even if all you say is true, you're too cowardly to ever do what you want to do. And it seems to me that until you break away from your brother, you won't be able to do anything at all."

The hand at my hair stills. "That's rich coming from you. You're serving a tyrant, a man who basically has control over the entire world. We're pirates. Not politicians. Our sort weren't meant to rule. There needs to be order so we can disrupt it. If there's no order in the first place, then where does that leave us? The world has changed in recent years. And you've chosen to help it change. Not for the better. Our choices are to die out or join the pirate king. Why do you serve Kalligan? So that Papa will love you?"

"You don't know anything about me or my father. You should stop pretending otherwise. Now, let me go." I try to pull away, but he holds me more securely.

"No."

"Let me go. I don't want you touching me. You disgust me."

"Lass, you're too weak to force me. Let me take care of you for now. It's all I can do for you, so let me do it. You may think you have me all figured out, but you don't. I've got my own reasons for wanting Draxen to succeed. We need you. It's for the best. Letting you dangle over the deck never should have happened. I will do what I can to ensure your safety, if you can promise to stop being so damn stubborn."

I don't want to talk to him anymore, so I pretend to be asleep.

He huffs quietly. "Might as well tell a fish not to swim."

Chapter 10

FOR THE SECOND TIME I awake in Riden's arms.

He's still asleep, and I like that I'm allowed to stare at his face for as long as I want. Full lips, straight nose, a scar that recedes into his hairline on the left side of his face. That must have been quite the hit to the head. I wonder if his father did it. Riden never seems to want to talk about his father. Might be because of how his father treated him, or it might be because Riden killed him. Maybe both.

He stirs then. I quickly look down at my wrists so as not to be caught staring. Suddenly, I'm overcome with the urge to rip the bandages off.

Riden's hand shoots out, grasping right below the injury on

my right wrist. "Not yet. Keep those bandages on. You need to keep your wounds clean for a while."

"It itches something fierce."

"I know, and it will only get worse, but you mustn't scratch."

"And I suppose you've had to wear manacles before?"

"Everyone on the ship has."

"At the same time?" I clarify. His response is a little unusual, full of bitterness and regret.

"Yes."

"What happened?"

Riden's hand is still on my arm. He's taken to stroking my skin with his fingertips. I don't stop him because it makes the itching subside.

"I'll tell you what, Alosa. I'll offer you a story in exchange for a story."

"What do you want to know?"

"Tell me about your scars."

"That's many stories."

"But I'm sure you can give me something."

"I suppose I could, but you first."

Riden thinks for a moment. He props his head up with his free hand, the other still tracing my skin. "All right. I trust you. I'll go first."

He trusts me? What exactly is that supposed to mean? Is he a fool? I've given him *no* reason to trust me. It's more likely he feels obligated to go first, what with yesterday's events and all.

There are many kinds of pirates, but Riden is the first I've met who feels remorse for his pirating. Perhaps that's why I find him so interesting. He treats me better than any other pirate would a prisoner, I'm sure.

"About a year prior," Riden starts, "my father, Lord Jeskor, was still in command of this ship. Draxen and I had been living on the *Night Farer* practically our whole lives. I'm sure you can relate. Pirate lords need sons to pass their legacy on to. Or, in your case, a daughter. Peculiar, that one. You'll have to explain to me someday how that all started out."

"No, I don't," I say.

He smiles. "I suppose you don't, but I'd be curious to know."

"Your story?"

"Right. Well, many of us on the ship are the sons of the original crewmen. Others are young thieves and murderers who we picked up along the way. We put together a crew after the ship was ours."

"And how did the ship become yours? Where do the irons come in?"

He puts a finger to my lips. "Shh. I'm getting to that part. You can be downright impatient sometimes."

I frown under the pressure of his finger. He removes it and sets it on the bed.

"My father had become careless. He and his men spent far too much time on land and less time on the sea, pirating. They were lazy, drunk, loud—all the time. We, their sons and fellow crew members, were all but forgotten. So we decided to try to take the ship from them."

I raise a brow in disbelief. "You expect me to believe your father, a pirate lord, became lazy, and that motivated you all to take the ship?"

"You know what it's like to be raised by pirates—I've seen your scars. Ours are less visible. They barely fed us. They gave us the more dangerous jobs during our robbing and plundering. We were beaten whenever they got bored, which was quite regularly. Finally, we'd had enough. And we tried to take the ship."

"And you failed."

"Yes, we failed. They put us in chains, locked us in the brig, then decided to kill us all one by one for mutiny."

"They obviously didn't succeed."

Riden shakes his head. "No, but they came close. My father wanted to start with me. I was . . . a disappointment to him. I hadn't turned out the way he wanted me to. Didn't look enough like him. Didn't talk, walk, drink like him. I think my father chalked it up to the fact that we have different mothers—but whatever the reason, Draxen was always more like him. Do you have any brothers or sisters, Alosa?"

"I'm sure by now there's near a hundred of them. My father has quite the . . . appetite. But I'm the only one he's claimed. If there are others, I do not know of them."

"I see. I was raised with Draxen. We did everything together. Played and fought. He always looked out for me, being my older brother. When my father yelled and hit me, Draxen would come to my defense. He was my protector in our younger years, during the time when he was bigger than I. Then we grew, and I could start looking out for him in return."

Normally, here is where I would throw out some amount of snark. Riden's story is very sappy. But strangely, I feel the need to be still. To listen.

"We have a strong bond. It's the strongest thing I have in my life. And I would never do anything to break it because my whole life has been built around it. So without it, I don't know what I would be. Nothing good."

I wonder what it would be like to have something like that. Someone whom you could trust and call your friend since childhood. I have many good women aboard my crew whom I trust and call friends. But they are all recent finds. Within the last five years or so. I don't have anything I've held on to since I was little.

Except my father, of course.

"My father was about to kill me for what he assumed would be my last disappointing act. But then Draxen was there. He'd broken free of the men holding him and come to my rescue. Yet again. That act saved my life. When it most counted, Draxen chose me over our father. I owe him my life and my allegiance. He is the best thing I have, and I would never do anything to hurt or betray him.

"Draxen then pitched his skill with the sword against our father. But Father was an excellent swordsman, drunk and lazy or not. He disarmed Draxen and was about to kill him. But I picked up my brother's fallen sword. And I killed him."

"And what happened after that?" I ask.

"Killing our father had a strange effect on Draxen and me. We felt freer with him gone, stronger. We fought our way to the brig. We released everyone. And we took the ship."

"Just like that?"

"Well, I left out all the fighting bits, but I'm sure you know what a fight looks and sounds like."

And smells and feels and tastes like.

"Now tell me about your scars," Riden says.

A deal's a deal. So I tell him. But I don't want him to feel sorry for me. So I state everything like it's fact. No feeling. No remorse. I tell him about my endurance tests. My rigorous fighting practices. The regular trials my father gave me. I don't go into too much detail. He just needs a sense of life with my father in order to be satisfied that I didn't lie to him by saying I would share if he did.

At the end, Riden asks, "And are all your father's men trained in the same way?"

"Well, I'm the only one he's trained personally, but—" I cut off quickly.

"What?"

"Why do you want to know about their training? Is this another blasted interrogation?" I jump out of the bed in an instant, shoving half of Riden's weight off me in the process.

"I can't believe you. What the hell is this, Riden? You show me kindness and then expect me to open up to you, is that it?"

Riden shrugs. "You're a woman and the pirate king's daughter at that. Something tells me you wouldn't budge under torture. We needed to approach you in a different way."

"Damn you. And your blasted crew. Is any of this real?"

Riden sits up and regards me seriously. "Is any of what real?"

"Your story? This?" I gesture about the room. "All the niceties? Are they just a way to get me to open up?"

He stands and puts his hands on my shoulders. "Most of it is real, Alosa, even though it shouldn't be."

I shove him back and wince at yesterday's wounds. "What is that supposed to mean? You're playing a part. The conflicted first mate. You're a lie."

"So are you. Why don't you tell me what you're really doing on this ship?"

"I'm not doing anything!" I scream. "Just let me go. I want to go now!"

It's hard keeping up appearances when I'm so furious. But it needs to be done.

"Can't do that. Not unless you want to tell me where your father's hideaway is? Then we'll take you right to him."

I can feel my whole body tense. I'm going to explode if I don't hit something.

"Ah," Riden says. "I've come to understand that look. I'll leave you alone for a while."

He leaves right before my foot connects with the door.

∞

I try to tell myself that it doesn't matter. What do I care if Riden's been trying to gather information from me? I already knew he was doing it. I just hadn't expected him to try using a sentimental approach.

Nothing's changed. I'm still trying to get the map. And as long as I keep the location of my father's keep a secret, I can continue searching for it. So what if Riden gets a little clever now and then? He can't touch me.

I'm sitting on the edge of Riden's bed, waiting out the day, when the door opens. Was it too much to hope it wouldn't be Riden?

He grabs my upper arm. "Captain wants to see you."

I try to punch him in the stomach, but he's expecting it. He catches my fist. "Come on, Alosa. Let's see what he wants."

"I don't want to see what he wants. Every time I see Draxen, something terrible happens. I want to be left alone. I'm done with you, and I'm done with being on this ship."

"Come on." He drags me toward the door. "Something terrible won't happen."

I give him a look.

"Something terrible *probably* won't happen. Just give Draxen whatever he wants."

"How about if I give Draxen what he deserves?"

He laughs as he drags me the rest of the way. Up the companionway. Into Draxen's quarters.

"Ah, here she is," Draxen says. He has a couple of men already in here with him: Kearan and Ulgin. I suppress a shudder. "I think it best that the princess be kept in irons when she's not locked up." He nods toward Ulgin, who pulls a set of manacles from his belt.

"She's still weak from yesterday, Captain," Riden says, jerking his head toward my wrists. "I don't think that's necessary."

"If you say so, Riden. Alosa, have a seat."

"I think I'd rather stand."

"I wasn't asking."

Riden moves me in front of a chair and puts pressure on my shoulders. Reluctantly, I sit. If I don't like what happens next, I can always get back up.

"We received word from your father yesterday."

"How's that? I was told no one knew our location."

"We've been using yano birds."

I don't expect to hear that. Yano birds are used for carrying messages out to sea. They're very fast and excellent navigators. They're also perfect for silent communication, because the birds don't utter a note of song. But they're extremely rare. My father himself has only five of them.

"How did you come by one?" I ask.

"I've a crew of men who are very good at getting things done. Your concern should be what happens to you within the next five minutes. I want to know where your father's keep is."

"He didn't tell you in his letter? Shocker, that."

Draxen scowls at my tone.

I ask, "What exactly did his note say?"

"He's willing to negotiate a ransom. I just have to name an amount and location."

"So do it, then."

Draxen smiles his evil smile, baring his gold tooth. It's a calculating, malicious grin matched with cold eyes. So different from the way Riden smiles when he thinks he has the upper hand on me. Riden's is victorious, even cocky, sure, but harmless somehow. But Draxen—his is laced with poison.

"See now," Draxen says, "I have this feeling I would show up and be surrounded by ten of your father's ships. I think it would be far better to surprise him and negotiate when he is unprepared, don't you?"

"My father's promise of peace isn't enough to sway you?"

"Riden's informed me that you are special to your father. It seems to me that when it comes to you, we can't count on promises. We need something more to work with. I told you what would happen if you continued to be uncooperative with Riden. I've grown impatient. I need your father's location now."

"I'm not giving it to you."

Draxen clenches his teeth and jerks his head violently to the side. "I was going to let Ulgin have you if you weren't cooperative, but I find I've got far too much of a desire to handle this interrogation myself."

This is not going to be pleasant.

Draxen gets behind me and yanks my head backward by my hair. I grimace at the pain. He strikes the side of my face with a closed fist.

"Where is Kalligan's keep, girl?"

I don't answer. He hits me again.

"Draxen." It's Riden.

"What?"

"This doesn't sit right with me."

"Then leave. It needs to be done and you know it." I receive another blow to the head. My nose starts to bleed.

You can't fight back, I tell myself. You can kill Draxen yourself when this is all over, but right now you can't fight back. It's my father's voice in my head.

"Draxen, please," Riden tries again.

"I said 'leave,' Riden." Draxen hits me with his other hand. This one bites more deeply. I think it's his ring hand, where he bears the seal of the Allemos line. It cuts my cheek.

"Brother," Riden tries again. This time more forcefully. It's the most backbone I've seen from him.

Draxen's eyes must be alight with blood lust. But he halts at that one word. He sighs as if to clear his head. "Fine, Riden. If you insist. Are you ready to talk yet, princess?"

I remain silent.

"What do you think, Riden?" Draxen asks, and I don't like the new tone his voice takes. "The pirate king doesn't need a daughter with hair, does he?"

I hear a knife slide out of a sheath.

Riden doesn't protest at this. Why would he? It doesn't hurt to have one's hair cut, but he seems not to understand the value a woman's hair has to her.

And I've no intention of losing mine. "Stop!" Drops of blood spray outward as I speak. The blood from my nose has run into my mouth.

Kearan tilts his head to the side and speaks for the first time. "That's what it took? Her bloody hair?"

"To interrogate a woman, you have to think like a woman," Draxen says.

"Which is strangely effortless for you," I say.

Despite Riden's earlier protests, Draxen hits me again. But I don't care. That one was worth it. The other pirates in the room have the sense not to laugh.

"The location, Alosa," Draxen demands.

"Lycon's Peak. Do you know it?" I ask.

"Aye." Kearan's the one who answers. Naturally. Enwen told me that Kearan was once a traveler and adventurer.

"The keep is two weeks' sail northeast of there."

"Is that possible?" Draxen asks. "Is there anything above that?"

Kearan says, "There could easily be a few small islands there."

Draxen releases my hair and stands in front of me. "If you're lying, girl, I will take both your hair and a hand."

"Do you truly think you'll be successful sneaking into my father's keep? Once you get there, my father will hang you all."

"We'll take our chances. Riden, take the prisoner back to her quarters. Bring me back a map. Kearan, meet us at the helm to set our course."

A few moments later, I'm back in Riden's room, holding a towel to my nose while Riden digs through the pile of maps in his room.

He can't see my huge smile under the towel. It's not just because I've all but destroyed all of his maps. I also didn't have to give away the location to my father's keep. No, the location I gave them is one my father and I discussed before I set out on this mission. My father and many of his men will be waiting there for me to return with the map. We knew Draxen would try to discover where my father's keep is. We had a location already in mind to give him should things turn sour.

The only problem now is that I have a deadline for finding that map. I have to have it before we reach my father. Or he will *not* be pleased.

Bad things happen when he's not pleased.

Chapter 11

RIDEN LEAVES ME ALONE for several hours that day. Though my face doesn't hurt anymore (I've always been a fast healer), my stomach aches something fierce from the want of food. It's been a day and a half since I've eaten.

I try to imagine I'm home at the keep, attending one of Father's grand feasts. He'll have every kind of meat imaginable, from pork to beef to fowl. My mouth waters at the imagined taste of steamed vegetables and sweetened fruits. Pies and wine. Bread and cheese. If they don't feed me today, I'll have to risk sneaking down to the kitchens tonight.

But I needn't have worried.

I can smell something hot and delicious from the other side of the door.

As soon as Riden enters, I pluck one of the bowls out of his hand.

"Careful," he says, "it's still hot."

I don't care. I burn a spot on my tongue as I take a few gulps of the soup. I hardly even taste it as the liquid burns all the way down to my stomach. When my bowl is drained, I grab the other one in Riden's hand and start on it.

"I'm sorry. I hadn't realized how long it'd been since you'd eaten. You should've said something."

I don't look his way while I eat. I've enough food in me now to patiently use the spoon and blow on the soup. My teeth eagerly bite into the vegetables and potatoes in the mix.

When I've finished the second bowl, I drop it to the ground and retreat to the bed. I still feel weaker than usual. It might be midday, but something tells me I could drift off now and sleep all the way until morning. Too many nights with too little sleep.

My eyes are closed, but I can hear Riden moving around the room. "What are you doing?"

"Trying to clean up your mess."

"Could you do it more quietly? I'm trying to sleep. I've had a rough couple of days, you know."

He snorts, but the rustling sound of cleaning still continues.

"Good idea, you cleaning the room and all," I say. "I'll need something to do tomorrow."

There's a loud slam as he throws down whatever he'd been holding. My eyes fly open as Riden hauls me up by my arms.

"What are you doing?" I demand. "You cannot keep touching me as though I'm a small child you can pick up and move whenever you want to."

"If you insist on continually acting like a child, then there is no reason why I shouldn't treat you as one."

"What on Maneria are you talking about?"

"My room!" He huffs. "Look at it. It's *filthy*. Half of my things are ruined, thanks to your damned drawings. I ought to toss you overboard!"

"You locked me up in here! What did you think would happen? You should toss yourself over for being a complete idiot. And if you wanted me punished, then you should have let the captain continue on with me instead of asking him to stop!"

"Are you complaining because I helped you?"

"I had things under control."

"Just yesterday you were making a fuss because I didn't stick up for you. You can't have it both ways! So pick one!"

"What do you care what I want? Why don't you have the balls to do what you want?"

Riden sighs and looks heavenward. "Stop doing that."

"Doing what?"

"You're a woman. Act like it. You shouldn't be saying such foul—"

"I'll say whatever I please. I'm not a lady, I'm a pirate!"

"Well, you shouldn't be!"

"And why's that? I'm plenty good at it."

"Because pirates aren't supposed to look like you look and talk like you talk and do what you do. You're confusing, and it's messing with my head."

"How is that my fault? I'm sure your head was plenty messed up before I came along."

I can feel Riden's breath in my face. He's so close and so angry, I almost want to laugh.

"No, it wasn't," he insists.

Then he's kissing me.

What the—I misread where that was going. I wanted to irritate him. To get under his skin. To mess with him because he's working for the enemy. I hadn't exactly expected him to get all mushy as a result.

But then again, I can't exactly describe this as mushy.

It's pure irritation expressed as a physical need. Interesting.

I've kissed many men, pirates and land dwellers alike. Normally it happens right before I'm about to steal something from them. Or because I'm bored.

Right now I'm not sure I have an excuse. In fact, I'm sure there are several reasons why I shouldn't be kissing him. I just can't think of them at the moment.

Perhaps it's because Riden's lips taste even better than I'd imagined. Or because his hands make my skin tingle where they hold the sides of my face. Maybe it's the thrill of doing something my father wouldn't approve of. I mean, he's not exactly the overprotective type. He couldn't care less about my dalliances. But he would most definitely be upset if he knew I was kissing the enemy, especially when I've nothing to gain from it. No, wait, that's not true. It could definitely benefit me to have the first mate wrapped around my finger.

When Riden's lips move down to my neck, I forget all about my father. There's nothing except heat and chills all at once. He reaches the hollow at the base of my neck, and I let out a soft moan.

He returns to my lips with a new intensity. The burned spot on my tongue tingles when he traces it with his own. I rip out the band that holds together his hair and run my fingers through it.

The moment is perfect.

But the thought hits me like a hammer: *This shouldn't be perfect.* In fact, it isn't. I've gone too long without proper sleep and food. It's making me act like a silly tavern wench. I can't do this. I have thieving to do.

It is with great effort, not the physical kind, that I push Riden away.

His chest is heaving up and down. I'm sure mine is, too.

"That's enough of that," I say.

"You're bleeding again," Riden says, touching a spot on my cheek.

I hadn't felt the cut reopen. "Probably your fault."

"As I'm sure you believe most things are."

"Of course."

He smiles and starts to lean down again, and I'm so very tempted to let him close the distance. Wouldn't be so hard if he wasn't so good at this. Instead, I say, "I said that's enough."

He steps away from me quickly, as though he doesn't trust himself to be near me.

"I have duties to perform," he says, turning around.

"I'm sure."

∞

I wish I didn't have to wait until nightfall to continue searching the ship. All I have to do when I'm left alone is think. And thinking is the last thing I want to do right now.

I'd rather be punching something.

Enwen comes in later to bring me another meal. I smile once he retreats. Riden's a coward. He doesn't want to face me right now. Perhaps that kiss was a good idea. It'll certainly be worth watching him squirm later.

I get in a quick nap so I'll be ready by nightfall. It was tempting to go right back to sleep once I awoke, but I have no time to waste now that Draxen and his crew are heading for my father.

It's late when Riden enters the room again. He looks surprised to see me. "Oh, I thought you'd be asleep."

"You mean you were hoping," I say with a smile.

"And miss out on whatever snappy comment you have ready for me? Not a chance."

"I don't have a snappy comment prepared."

"That's a shame. I was rather hoping for a repeat of what happened after the last one."

"I'm sure. Unfortunately for you, I'm a bit tired."

"Then why aren't you asleep?"

"I was getting there."

"Looks more like you were waiting for me."

Oh please. Maybe I should knock him out for the night. I can't do that, though. He'd remember in the morning. I'd be all out of explanations if I knocked him out but stayed on the ship. I can't leave until I have that blasted ever-elusive map!

"Just go to sleep, Riden. Here." I get off the bed and sit in the chair instead.

"You're going to sleep there?"

"Yes."

"Why?"

"Because I want to, all right? What's with all the questions?"

"I'm your interrogator, remember?"

"Right now you're off duty, so go to sleep."

"Why do you so desperately want me to drift off? Hoping to climb in bed after I'm out?"

"Actually, I want the silence that comes after."

Riden looks about the room. "You know, it's really difficult for me to sleep knowing how filthy my room is. Maybe I'll stay up until you conk out."

I don't have time for this. And I can't risk pretending to fall asleep until he does. I might actually drift off, and that would be a whole night wasted.

I'm irritated. And perhaps if I weren't so irritated, I wouldn't have jumped so quickly to this solution. But I'm impatient after sitting around all day. I had my face pummeled. I'm still cranky for the want of sleep, and, honestly, I'm still hungry.

So I begin to sing. The melody is deep and soothing. I can feel my whole body humming with energy as it drifts out of me. I can feel every place in the room. The way the sound bounces off the wood, seeps into the blankets, enters Riden's ears.

He steps closer, trying to hear the tune better. I indulge him by removing the distance for him. I take his hand and lead him to the bed. He follows, captured by my spell. I know what Riden wants in life. Love and acceptance. I weave those into the song and command him to sleep and forget that he ever heard me sing.

He has no choice but to obey.

Chapter 12

I FEEL THE EXPECTED longing of the ocean. I always feel it after I use my song. My chest aches. It burns, yearning to go under the water where it can be soothed and nourished. I don't need the strength of the ocean to survive, though, only to replenish my song—to strengthen the part of me that I try to keep hidden. But replenishing my abilities has its own consequence. That other part of me tries to take over, something I can't risk until after I've completed my mission.

I am mostly human. But when I allow myself to use the gifts my mother gave me, I become something else. And it kills me a little inside each time I have to fight it back off.

I slip back into Riden's room right before the sun starts to rise. I've got to put the key to the door back into his pocket.

But Riden groans as he sits up in bed. I quickly move away from the door and jump into the chair at his desk.

"What happened?" he asks, putting his hand to his head.

"Do you have a headache?" I ask. "You were groaning something fierce in your sleep."

"No, it doesn't hurt. It feels . . ."

I've sung to many men in the past. Those whom I've allowed to keep their memory of the experience have tried to explain to me what it feels like. I've heard it's euphoric. That it's pleasure and happiness all rolled into one. When I make them sleep, they dream about me all during the night. While I was growing up, there weren't many men who let me practice my songs on them. But I practiced anyway. It wasn't as though my mother was around to teach me. Father was eventually able to keep my abilities known to only a select group. He didn't want his rivals to know just how powerful I am. The fighting skills he taught me alone make me dangerous. And being half siren—well, that makes me deadly.

"It feels what?" I ask.

"Nothing," he says quickly. He's retreated into his mind, searching through memories or dreams. Waking is usually disorienting for my victims.

While it's amusing to watch him fumbling with his thoughts, I need to get this key back on Riden before he notices it's gone. "Did you sleep well?" I ask. "Good dreams?" I know he dreamed about me, but that doesn't mean I know what I was doing in his dream.

Of course, I don't expect Riden to be honest.

He looks dazed for a moment more. Then he seems to compose himself. "Yes. What happened yesterday? I can't . . ."

I look at him sternly. "Were you drinking?"

He sits up, puts his bare feet on the floor. "I don't drink that often. Never enough to get drunk. Especially not when I'm watching you."

"But you don't remember our night together?" I'm thinking fast here. I need to get rid of this key. I have to find an excuse to get close to him.

"Our night together?" Riden looks beyond confused.

I move to sit on his lap, making myself comfortable as I wrap my arms around his neck. Riden freezes in place.

"You really don't remember?" I whisper seductively into his ear. My hands are at his shoulders. I move one down his chest. He's solid as a rock, but his skin is smooth and warm. When I reach his waist, I drop the key into the pocket of his breeches.

It's really just thieving, only backward.

Riden exhales and puts his hands on my hips. "Why don't you remind me?"

I slide my hands down his arms until I can entwine our fingers. "There was some of this."

"Mmm hmm."

"And this." I press my lips to his and kiss him gently. He returns in kind.

"Then what happened?" he whispers when I break away and trace my lips along the edge of his ear.

"Then—" I pause and lean farther into him. "You promised to help me get off the ship."

He leans me back as if to lay me on the bed. Then he drops me. I hit the sheets with a soft *plump*.

"I think I would remember that," he says, shoving my legs onto the bed as well.

"Don't worry," I say. "I'm sure everything will come back to you soon enough."

"In the meantime, Draxen will be expecting me." He walks over to the closet and rummages through the clothes I've left in heaps on the floor, grunting in displeasure as he searches.

Once he finds what he's looking for—a pair of breeches—he starts sliding off the pair he has on, watching my reaction as he does so.

"Stop that," I say, turning around quickly.

He laughs softly.

I should have kept calm, and I shouldn't have turned around. If I had simply shrugged as though it didn't bother me at all, Riden wouldn't have been so amused. He would have taken his clothes elsewhere, I'm sure of it. But it all started so suddenly that I was unprepared with a response. There's nothing to do about it now.

"When you're confined to this room," he says, "how do you expect me to be able to change into clean clothes?"

"Go get dressed in Draxen's room!" I snap.

"Where's the fun in that?"

I exhale angrily as I wait for him to finish. I listen to the rustling of cloth, the cinching of a belt, the thud of newly adorned boots smacking the floor—and I wait for it all to stop.

I'm listening so hard that I don't even register that the boots are moving toward me until I feel a hand at my lower back.

His lips are at my ear. "It's safe to look now, Alosa." He brushes his lips across the side of my head before leaving.

I don't realize how tense I am until my whole body relaxes.

I suppose I should be bored out of my mind during the next few days, but I'm not. Riden comes into his room often to check on me. We talk until he tries to morph the conversation into an interrogation. He wants to know things, like the layout of my father's keep, how often supply ships deliver shipments, how many men guard the keep, and so on and so forth. I tell him none of these things. I will die before I give that information up. Well, actually *they'd* die, since I wouldn't allow them to kill me.

I've noticed that Riden's been keeping me at a distance. Still, he can't help it when I bait him during the conversation. It's fun watching him struggle, trying to find a balance with me. Toying with Riden is certainly more entertaining than scouring the ship. I become a little more anxious each night that goes by without the map turning up. I check our heading frequently, gauging how much time is left before I have to present the map to my father. We pass Lycon's Peak and start sailing northeast.

It won't be long now.

I wake early, even though I made it to bed late. I'm too worried to sleep anymore, so I stare at the ceiling, thinking it all over in my head. I go over every spot I checked, searching for anything that may have been overlooked. My two weeks are almost up. The checkpoint could show up on the horizon at any moment.

"You're up early," Riden says from where he lies next to me.

"Couldn't sleep," I say.

"Are you worried about something?"

"Actually, it was your snoring that kept me awake."

He smiles. "I do not snore."

"My ears beg to differ."

He rolls onto his back, staring upward with me. "Tell me what's worrying you."

"Aside from the fact that I'm being held hostage by enemy pirates?"

"Yes," he says simply, "aside from that."

Well, I can't very well tell him that either Draxen or his father hid a map somewhere and I can't find it. Instead, I ask him, "What's the most reckless thing you've ever done to try to impress your father?"

He's quiet.

"Does it pain you to talk about him?" I ask.

He shakes his head. "No, that's not it. I try not to think about him because I hated him so much."

"I understand." I wait to see if he'll still answer my question.

He sighs. "It's difficult to say. I did many reckless things."

"Tell me one of them."

"All right," he says pensively. "Once, when we were sailing far out at sea, we pillaged a ship before burning it down. My father dropped a chest of jewels into the ocean while trying to haul it over to the ship. I dove in after it."

"I think perhaps we should go over the meaning of *reckless*."

"There were acura eels in the water, finishing off the sailors that survived the initial attack on their ship."

I turn my head in his direction. "Now that *was* reckless." Acura eels are more feared than sharks. They're faster and more sensitive to human blood. In some cases, they're even bigger and toothier. Most of the time, they stay near the ocean floor, but if they sense a disturbance at the surface, they'll come to investigate.

"Were you able to get the chest back for him?" I ask.

"No. An eel headed for me. Draxen saw it and lowered me a rope. He hoisted me out of the water just in time."

"What did your father do?"

"He tried to toss me back over to get the chest, but Draxen was able to talk him out of it."

"Sounds to me that if you hadn't killed him, someone else would have eventually. He sounds awful."

"He was." Riden turns to look at me. "I'm guessing that question wasn't random. Are you doing something reckless to impress your own father?"

"I do reckless things for the fun of it."

"I have no trouble believing that."

"Do you feel like you knew your father well?"

He shrugs. "Well enough. Why?"

I have to be careful. I need to make the conversation seem harmless. He needs to think it's all about me. "My father trusts me more than he does anyone else in the world, yet I can't help but feel like he keeps secrets from me."

"Everybody has their secrets. We would all feel too exposed if we weren't able to keep things to ourselves."

"What are—" No, I can't ask Riden about his own secrets. I need to keep the conversation focused. "But this feels different.

Couldn't you tell when your father was keeping things from you? Big things?"

"Yes, usually."

"My father had a hiding place on his ship, a loose floorboard in his rooms. He would keep important things there. When I felt like he wasn't telling me everything, I could usually find his plans and secrets there." I'm making this all up quickly. I hope Riden can't tell.

In truth, my father has a room he alone enters at the keep. His private getaway. I've been tempted many times to sneak in. I even made an attempt once. When Father found me outside fiddling with the lock, he said if I was so interested in his locked doors, he'd put me behind one.

And he did. In a cell deep down. For a month.

"But then one day," I continue, "the space below the floor-board was empty. And nothing has been kept there ever since."

"He found you out."

"Or suspected what I was up to and didn't want to take any chances."

Though he seems natural, relaxed—Riden has to be holding on to my every word. There's no chance he isn't hoping I'll tell him some of my father's secrets. But that's not the purpose of this conversation. I'm trying to learn Lord Jeskor's secrets.

"What about *your* father?" I ask. "Did he have a place where

169

he kept secrets? Did you ever learn something you weren't sup-posed to?" *Do you know where he hid his section of the map?*

"Honestly, I was never curious enough to care. When we were younger, Draxen would coax me into helping him find secret panels belowdecks. It never turned out to be profitable, though."

I can relate. I've already been through all of those panels.

I can't deny I enjoy talking with Riden, but I was really hoping for something useful to come out of the conversation. Something that would make me realize exactly where the map is.

I should have known better.

"Besides, if there was anything so important to my father, he probably wouldn't have let it out of his sight. He likely would have kept it on him at all times. And Draxen and I were never foolish enough to try stealing something off him."

Oh.

Chapter 13

RIDEN LEAVES TO FIND me some breakfast. Meanwhile, I ponder on my own stupidity.

Of course you would keep something so valuable *on your person* at all times.

After Jeskor died, his sons would have searched his body. They would have found the map. Draxen is one of the greediest men I've ever met. If he didn't already know what the map was, he would have done everything he could to find out. And once he did—

Draxen's despicable and abusive and manipulative. He's the last thing I'd ever want to touch on this ship.

Perhaps that's why I never thought to check if he *carries*

the map on him. Of course he would. Where else would you keep something you don't want anyone else to find? I'll bet that's the real reason why Riden and Draxen rebelled against their father, tried to take the ship, and ended up slaughtering the original crew. How could it be over anything less than the map that leads to the treasure of a thousand ages?

To think, I might've been so close to it so very many times.

But it could be anywhere on him. Any pocket on his coat, shirt, breeches. Even tucked into his underthings. Oh, I truly hope it's not there.

Unfortunately for me, there's only one way to find out.

I've no choice but to seduce the captain.

I *hate* doing that. But how else am I to get him alone? I could wait until tonight when he's asleep, but I don't want to waste what little is left of my song to *keep* him asleep. Draxen may be a deeper sleeper than Riden, but how could anyone stay asleep while someone is stripping them of all their clothing?

No, I need to act now. As soon as Riden returns.

I cannot risk getting to the checkpoint without already having the map to present to my father.

Time to use more of what Mother gave me.

Riden comes back with breakfast: more eggs. I eat quickly, then I tell him, "I want to go outside today."

"Why?" he asks suspiciously.

"Because I've been cooped up in here like some child's pet, and I want out."

"If you're out on the deck, the captain will expect you to work."

"Fine."

Riden fumbles with the empty dish in his hand but catches it before it connects with the ground. "What did you say?"

"I said fine. Is there something wrong with your ears?"

"I was under the impression you didn't do anything that involved getting your clothes dirty."

"I learned as a little girl that pirating means being filthy from time to time. You just have to be rich enough to afford regular bathing and several changes of clothes. Speaking of which, I want a new outfit."

"But you're going to get dirty."

"I know that, but I've already been in this one for too many days." Enwen's been bringing me new clothes since I was moved to Riden's room. It's very thoughtful of him, but I don't have the time to wait around for him to decide to bring me more. I need to be clean and fresh when I seduce Draxen.

"All right, I'll go grab you something," Riden says.

"No, I want you to bring all my things."

He snorts. "Not a chance. Who knows what else you're hiding in there? You'll get one outfit and one outfit alone."

Enwen didn't grant that request, either, but it was worth a try.

"Fine," I say, "bring me the green one."

"The green one?"

"Yes, you'll know it when you see it. And I want a fresh blouse and leggings."

"Anything else? Some undergarments, perhaps?"

"I wouldn't dream of giving you the satisfaction."

He laughs. "You can't exactly stop me, now, can you?"

He leaves much too quickly for me to believe he's simply doing a lady a favor. Too eager, he was. Perhaps he didn't want to listen to my arguments. Or it's the thrill of going through my underthings.

"What is this?" Riden demands some time later. He doesn't even bother to shut the door behind him when reentering.

"My clothing," I respond. "Honestly, Riden, have you forgotten the names of—"

"No," he says, cutting off my rather witty remark. "This is not clothing. This wouldn't cover a child."

"It stretches, you dolt."

"Stretches!" he exclaims. "No. You will *not* wear this." He tosses me instead a wad of purple fabric that he'd been holding in his other hand. It's a corset, but this one is an over bust instead of an under bust. It's complete with a hood and short attachable sleeves.

"Whatever did my green top do to offend you?" I ask.

"You're not daft, Alosa. Do you think a single member of the crew would be able to focus on their duties if you wore that?"

That is exactly why I chose it. I need to get Draxen's attention. He's never looked at me as anything more than an inconvenience. Today that has to change, and I have to do it without wasting what's left of my song.

He's the captain, and I'm his prisoner. But I need him to look at me as more than that. He needs to be unable to see me as anything other than a woman. In that green assortment, it's *impossible* to mistake the fact.

"That's hardly my problem," I say. "I want the green one."

"Well, you can't have it. I'm tossing it over the edge of the railing."

"Come now, Riden. That's hardly fair."

"You're a prisoner. Nothing's supposed to be fair for you."

Fine, I will have to make do with the purple corset, but I can't help but tease Riden a bit first. "Are you sure there's not something more at work here, Riden?"

"What do you mean?"

"I think you're acting like a jealous husband."

"A what?"

"You know, men that women shackle themselves onto."

"Yes, I know what a husband is." He clenches his fists and glares at me. He's awfully handsome when he's angry. "There is nothing to be jealous of."

"So you're saying that if I were to wear that top, it would in no way affect you personally?"

"Not at all."

"Then there's no problem with me wearing it, is there? Give it to me."

He clenches his teeth. "No."

I suppose I will have to rely more on body language, but I think it can be done. With some men, I can catch their attention in a potato sack.

Draxen seems smart. Smart enough to realize if I'm trying too hard. This will have to be done very carefully.

"Fine. Leave so I can change. Or will you be unable to handle knowing I'll be naked in your room?"

I'm baiting him, and he knows it. I'm impressed he manages another glare before slamming the door.

With expert fingers, I lace on the top and attach the sleeves. They curve out into points above my shoulders. I put on the hood as well. If I end up doing anything too embarrassing, it might be nice to have something to hide my face behind.

Riden did indeed bring me underthings. I try not to think about the fact that he touched them while I slip on the rest of my clean clothes. It's amazing what a new outfit can do for my spirits.

I emerge from Riden's room a new woman—free of snark, attitude, and morals. Everything I assume Draxen is attracted to.

Time to play.

I've spent so much time around pirates that I've adopted

my own sort of swagger, but that is not my natural inclination when I walk. Sirens are creatures of grace and beauty. They're more driven by instinct than learning and habits. I tap into that side of me, that place that I usually hide.

I suppose I don't really need the green top.

In this form, I can sense exactly what men want. And I can be that for them in order to get what *I* want. They can't hide their emotions from me. Each one swirls around them in a haze of color.

Each step on the deck is soft and graceful. My movements are fragile and angelic. My face is devoid of the intelligence lurking in my mind or the thieving force that drives me. I can feel each fragment of the wind as it slides along my skin. I can feel the salt in the air. I can feel each strand of hair on my head, sense the movements of those around me.

Sirens are creatures whose sole existence depends on enchanting men. I can switch over to that nature effortlessly, but I loathe it. I don't feel like myself.

I live on the cusp of two worlds, trying desperately to fit into one.

Heads turn as I exit Riden's quarters. I pretend not to notice. "Where would you like me?" I ask Riden. My voice has softened, taking on an almost musical tone. But I'm not enchanting anyone with my voice. I can't control more than three at a time. It wouldn't do me any good on a ship with so many men, even if I had enough song in me. Probably shouldn't have put so much into Riden the other night, but I couldn't resist once I'd started.

Riden's mouth drops open after I speak. He looks at me as though he's never seen me before. In a way, I suppose he hasn't. My appearance hasn't changed at all, only the way I hold myself. The way I act, speak, move. I've taken on my siren nature, and while I look the same, the men can still tell something is different, and it piques their interest.

"What's going on? Why has everyone stopped—" Draxen now looks my way. For a moment he is caught like everyone else. I lock eyes with him. Showing my interest in the subtlest of ways. He shakes his head as though catching himself out of some sort of daze. "Get back to work or there will be lashings for everyone. Riden, what is she doing on my deck?"

Riden, too, shakes himself out of the momentary stupor. "She's opted to work on the deck rather than rot in my quarters. I think she's getting a bit restless, Captain."

Draxen eyes me carefully. I give him a gentle smile that makes him swallow before speaking. "Did the chains make you change your mind, then, *princess*?"

"Yes, Captain." No sarcasm. Just sincerity. And innocence. Submissiveness. I try not to cringe as the word enters my mind. Horrid word, that one. But it is what I must be if this is to work. For my father, I'm willing to become everything that I hate.

Riden and Draxen both pause as though they're waiting for me to say more. Ah, they're waiting for the smart comment that is sure to follow. Let them wait. Siren Alosa is the promise of a man's fantasy. Right now I'm tuned into Draxen, trying to become his.

Riden turns to Draxen as though he will have some sort of answer for my behavior. If I weren't so in tune with my role, I would laugh.

Draxen is seeing me anew. He sees my weakness as his strength. I am something to be dominated. Something to be controlled. Draxen likes corrupting innocence. I'm hardly innocent. I've killed far too many men to ever be thought of as that, but it's all about perception.

A light red of interest hangs over the captain's shoulders. It's battling with the orange of indifference. Good.

And Riden—I turn toward him, reading his desires. He is not nearly as captivated by this form. Riden likes a challenge. He likes games. I'm not nearly as compelling for him like this. Interesting. Might make the deception more difficult, though. Currently, he's surrounded by blue. Blue is confusion.

I've spent years trying to understand the meanings of the colors I see. I've had to ask pirates what they're feeling when I'm like this, so I can associate words with what I see. It's difficult, because people are less inclined to talk when they're deep in emotion. But I've managed to fill in the gaps.

I wait silently. The embodiment of patience and tolerance.

Riden looks as though he's about to fall over: He's craning his neck so far, trying to make sense of what's in front of him.

Draxen's the captain, though. He has to set an example for the others, has to force himself to come to his senses more quickly. The man has a reputation to make, being the new and young captain that he is. Draxen is definitely the hardest mark on the ship.

Were we alone, he'd probably be on me within five minutes. It's amazing the things people will do in secret, when others can't see their actions. That'll be the trick: getting him alone. And especially away from ever-perceptive little brother, Riden.

"For stars' sake, someone hand her a mop," Draxen says.

There are five men already at the deck, swabbing it with mops. The nearest pirate eagerly jumps forward and hands over his.

"Thank you," I say as I delicately touch the wooden handle with my fingertips.

Every seaman finds himself swabbing the deck at some point. The task is one that must be done frequently to keep salt and excess water from building up. Never did care for it myself, but I can't let that show now.

I start my task, moving the mop in smooth movements. I bend over farther at particularly tricky spots. Everything I do has a purpose. I'm aware of each movement I make and Draxen's reaction to it. When fancy strikes, a man gets this notion in his mind that everything a woman does is for him. Right now this is true for Draxen. Though he tries to hide it, I know he watches me. He can't make sense of the change, but he doesn't think me that intelligent to begin with. And now his desire is growing, burning redder and redder.

"What are you doing?"

I'm pulled from Draxen's emotions as Riden speaks. "Swabbing the deck."

"No, not that. You're being different."

"Different how? Could you move over please? I need to get that spot."

"See, now, that is exactly how you're being different. Since when do you say 'please'? And why are you moving like that? You look ridiculous."

"You're free to think as you like," I say delicately, like it's a compliment.

"Stop," he says, dragging out the word.

"You don't wish me to mop anymore?"

"I'm talking about your behavior. Cut it out. It's . . . it's . . . wrong."

"I'm not sure I understand what you mean."

"You're attracting the wrong kind of attention on this ship, lass. It's going to get you into trouble."

"And what would be the right kind of attention? Yours, per-haps?" I can't help but egg him on when he's like this. Besides, I can still sense Draxen from behind me. I take a quick peek and see that a little green is weaving into his colors. Good. Draxen doesn't like me talking to Riden.

"I didn't mean—" Riden begins.

"Didn't you, though?" I home in on him now. Focusing on his wants and needs. I can see into the deepest desires of his heart. "You long for happiness, Riden, but you don't have the courage to go find it. You are strong and courageous in many ways, but when it comes to taking care of yourself, you're weak."

"Alosa," Riden says, lowering his voice. His expression has turned to one of earnestness, and I can feel that he means whatever he's about to say. "I'm sorry for what happened between us before—if that upset you. You don't need to retaliate by doing this."

"You think this is all for your benefit, Riden? How wrongfully conceited you are. It's exhausting to fight all the time. I'm done with it."

"Alosa, please. Can't you see what you're—"

"Riden!" It's Draxen calling out.

Riden exhales slowly. Perhaps he can read his brother without any special abilities. "Aye, Captain?"

"Bring the girl up here."

Riden doesn't answer. He's looking at me. I'm still focused on him. His colors are split. He's torn between the loyalty he has toward his brother and what he feels for me. Two entirely different swirls of red—the hardest color to decipher. With most pirates, I can safely assume it's lust. But it's not the right shade for what Riden feels toward his brother. Or me.

Frustration is probably what it is.

"Riden!" the captain calls again.

"Coming, Drax." To me, he says, "Here we go. Leave those behind." He points to the mop and bucket.

I oblige. Riden holds out an arm, indicating that he wants me to go first. At least he's not going to perform that dreadful upper-arm grasping bit that he is so fond of.

As we pass through the throng of working men, I spot Enwen, who is shaking his head and smiling. He's *impressed*. Just as I admired his thieving abilities, he is admiring my own skills. Though I cannot read his mind, I can easily tell that he sees right through me. He may not know exactly what I'm doing, but he knows a fellow actor when he sees one.

It's a quick walk along the starboard side of the ship and up the companionway. We stop at the aftercastle, near the helm.

"That'll be all, Riden."

"Are you sure, Captain?"

"Yes."

"But she might—"

"I'm quite capable of handling myself."

"Of course." Riden descends the stairs again. He takes position at the other end of the ship, on the forecastle, where he can survey all the men and keep them in line. I note that he also has a clear view of us up here. Even from this distance I can read his colors. He's black with a little green. Black is fear. Why should Riden be afraid?

"You are relieved, Kearan," Draxen says. "Go fill yourself with drink."

"Don't need to tell me twice. Just keep her due northeast, Captain."

Draxen takes the helm while Kearan leaves, giving me a bored nod as he swaggers on by. That leaves us alone on the upper deck. Of course we're in view of most of the pirates. But they're not able to hear anything that might be said. And I can tell that Draxen wishes to talk. Peculiar, that.

"Have you directed a ship before?" he asks.

"No," I lie. It's the answer he wants to hear. He's a fool for believing it. I'm the pirate king's daughter. Of course I've directed a ship.

But Draxen isn't exactly thinking at his best right now.

He grabs my hand and leads me in front of him. I grasp two random knobs on the helm.

"No," he says. "Put one hand here." He moves my hand for me. "And the other here. There, doesn't that feel better?" His voice is as commanding and firm as ever. He enjoys telling others what to do. It's a good trait in a captain.

I can't help but glance over at the other end of the ship. Riden hasn't moved from his spot, and I can't see his face to tell if it's changed. But I can sense what he feels.

And he does *not* like Draxen touching me.

That makes two of us.

"Keep the bow of the ship heading northeast. The sun is close to setting, so see that it remains behind you on your left. Once it sets, we use the stars to guide us."

It takes some effort not to roll my eyes. "Really?" It is an innocent question. Not sarcastic.

"Yes, we should all worship the stars. They are as useful as they are beautiful. Some never change position. They are constants in the sky. Without them, we would be lost."

"Fascinating."

He continues to prattle on. He prefers that I stay silent. I can feel it. This change in his attitude is not really a change. It is more of a performance. Everyone changes when they want something. And right now, Draxen wants me. How can he not? I'm giving him exactly what he wants. He can't help but be pulled nearer and nearer. That darker, pirate nature is momentarily cast aside. He is trying to enchant me in the way I'm enchanting him. It's a usual response. But it never works, of course.

I am always the one in control.

Chapter 14

IT'S FINALLY NIGHTTIME. I can soon be done with this charade.

Unfortunately, being able to see the stars only prompts Draxen to talk more.

"You see this constellation here?" He points north. "And this one here?" He points toward the south.

"Yes."

"They weren't always stars."

"What were they?" It's incredibly sappy of him to use this story.

"They were lovers. Filirrion"—he points to the one in the south—"and Emphitria." He indicates the one in the north.

"Theirs is said to be the greatest love story ever told. Sadly, it does not end well."

"What happened?" I ask, hoping he'll move it along more quickly.

"There was another in love with Emphitria: Xiomen—a sorcerer of the blackest arts. He loved her dearly, but Emphitria had eyes only for Filirrion. Enraged by his jealousy, Xiomen cursed them both. He changed their forms and placed them both in the sky, on opposite ends of the world so they could never be together."

"How tragic," I say.

Draxen nods. "While all the other stars in the sky move, there are three constellations that never change. Filirrion and Emphitria are two of them."

"Who is the third?"

Draxen points upward again. "Xiomen. It wasn't enough to separate them. So he cursed himself as well. There he remains, equidistant from the two lovers, blocking their view of each other. See how he's pointed toward Emphitria and she toward him?"

"Yes."

"Emphitria tries to see her Filirrion, but no matter how hard she looks, she can never see past Xiomen's form."

If this story ever persuaded a woman to climb into bed with Draxen, I'd slice my arm off.

A soft silence follows his story. Every once in a while, I lead us off course, forcing Draxen to grab my hands and redirect me. He doesn't think I'm trying to steer us away. He only thinks me incompetent. I'm giving him encouragement to touch me, to want more. To take me into his quarters so I can search him for the map.

The night sailor comes up top. "Shall I take over, Captain?"

"Yes, I think I'll retire now."

"Very good, then."

"Come over here, girl," Draxen demands. I follow him over to the door leading to his quarters. "Shall we continue our discussion of the constellations for a while more?"

"Oh yes." As if we could still see the constellations while in his room. Blundering idiot. I don't know how much longer I can stand this.

Draxen lights a few candles once we're alone in his quarters.

"Tell me more about the two lovers," I say.

"I've a better idea," he says.

Here it comes. He just wanted me alone so his crew wouldn't see him. Or see me struggle. Though I don't see how he can conceal what we're doing when every man still on deck saw me enter his room.

"And what might that be?" I ask.

"Lie on the bed."

"What for?"

He loves my questions. He wants to answer them. He wants to show me. He's too caught up in the moment to realize this is all a ploy. He should know better. But when I focus on one man, they never can tell. They're too caught up in, well, me.

"I'm going to show you something more magical than the stars."

Oh yuck. Yuck. Yuck. Yuck. I can't do this. I can't stand to hear him talk anymore. He needs to shut his mouth.

I step forward, get right into his face. "How about if I show you?" When I lift my head up to his, he greedily meets me for a kiss.

He's not a bad kisser—though I doubt Draxen has had as much practice as Riden.

But I get no enjoyment out of this. Because I'm not bored and looking for fun. I'm trying to get something done. And I know exactly the kind of foul man Draxen is. It's impossible to ignore when I'm so focused on the desires of his heart and mind.

I remove his coat and toss it to the floor with the intent to search it soon. Draxen takes it for an invitation. He goes right for my breeches, fumbling with the clasp.

Ugh. That's enough of that.

I shove Draxen down onto the bed and climb on top of him. From there I make it look as though I'm hurrying to undo the belt on his pants. I can feel the lust burning in him. It's disgusting and wretched, and I want to stamp it out.

When I get his belt buckle undone, I slide off his sword, sheath and all.

I use the end to knock him out, square on the head.

"Oof," he says before lying down, motionless.

I'm not sure what's worse: what I just did or what I still have to do.

Don't look at him, I tell myself. *Focus on the clothes. Not what lies beneath.*

I undress him. Every last article of clothing. I leave him lying naked on the bed while I search through every pocket, check for hidden linings, a fake sole in his boots.

But it's . . .

Not here.

My stomach sinks. *How can it not be here?* I was so sure. I was desperately counting on it. Now what am I to do once he wakes? He'll know I conked him. He'll know I used him for something. And he will not be happy.

And then we'll soon reach my father. And he'll—

No, I have to stop that line of thinking at once. It'll do me no good. I must keep my mind firmly in the present. How can I fix this?

Singing Draxen into forgetfulness isn't an option. I haven't enough song left to erase his memories. Fiddling with memories takes more than putting men to sleep.

I've made a fine mess of things. Seduce Draxen? That has to be my worst idea yet.

I have to cover my mouth to keep from grunting out in frustration.

Suddenly, there's banging at the door.

"Draxen!" It's Riden. "Open up now or I'm coming in."

I hear the handle unlatching, so I race to the door. As it opens, I climb out and shut it behind me before Riden can see inside.

"What is going on?" he asks.

"Your brother was telling me about the constellations," I say.

Riden's eyes widen. This must be a usual play for Draxen. "He didn't . . ."

"Didn't what?" I ask.

"You didn't let him . . ." He can't get it out.

"Riden, we were hardly in there for two minutes."

He shakes his head. "Of course. But what's he doing now, then?" His eyes widen. "Tell me you didn't kill him!"

While I'm flattered he knows I'm easily capable of killing Draxen, I still roll my eyes. "I didn't kill him."

"Then why isn't he yelling and swearing?"

Fair point, that. I'll have to throw in a bit of honesty if I'm to get out of this one. "He was getting too handsy, so I knocked him out."

Riden relaxes a bit. I find it humorous that he isn't offended or worried I knocked out his brother. He eyes the door.

He absolutely cannot go in there. I can't explain why Draxen's naked if I didn't bed him, and, well, I don't want Riden thinking I bedded him.

"What is going on, Alosa? Why did you go in there in the first place?"

We need to get away from here. Right now. I don't know how much time I have before Draxen wakes.

"Can we talk somewhere else?" I ask. "Back in your room, maybe? I'll answer all your questions. It's cold out here."

He still eyes me suspiciously, but he finally consents, weaving the way back toward his room. There's extra force in his strides. Riden leaps onto the main deck, not bothering with the stairs. The night watchmen turn their heads to see the cause of the racket. When Riden wrenches open the door to his room, I can't help but smile. He's in a mood.

But my amusement vanishes almost instantly. I have a big problem. It's taking everything I have not to panic. Maybe I should go back and kill Draxen. When he wakes up, everything will go to hell anyway. And Draxen deserves to die.

I'm just not sure I could do that to Riden. For reasons I can't explain, he loves his brother. I think he would be devastated at his death. Maybe even broken.

But what other choice do I have? Where else could the map possibly be? If it's not on the ship and Draxen doesn't carry it on his person—

I'm staring at Riden's back when it hits.

What if Riden has it?

After I searched Draxen's room on the first night of my capture, my next thought was that he might've given the map to Riden to hide. But what if Riden hides it on his person? How could I be so slow? I've had ample opportunities to check Riden for it. On the night I sang him to sleep, not even a hurricane could have woken him.

Now I suppose I'll have to knock him out like I did Draxen. I can't really do any more harm now, can I? I've already sabotaged the mission. Or perhaps not. Maybe when Draxen wakes, he'll do no more than put me back in my cell. But I doubt it.

When we're alone, Riden stands expectantly, arms crossed. As soon as I knocked Draxen out, I released the siren part of me. It takes its toll on my mind after a while. It's hard to explain, but I lose myself in others if I'm focused on their feelings and desires for too long. They start to become my own, and I forget who I am. It's terrifying. Father would push me, help me understand how long I can endure being consumed in others before I start to become like them. I've never allowed myself to pass my breaking point since then.

If that weren't enough, I have to deal with the short-term side effects as well, the feelings of otherworldliness. I hate the desires and emotions that are as clear to me as paint on a canvas. They're not mine, and I don't like feeling them, sensing them. Besides, I don't need to read Riden. I just have to be careful because he's already suspicious and confused. If I'm to get the drop on him, I'll first need to get him to relax, to talk. I'll need to give him lies mixed with truths.

"I'm worried, Riden," I start. "My father—he may seem as if he cares for me, as if he's eager to have me back in exchange for a ransom, but he'll be furious with me."

"Why?" he asks.

"For getting caught in the first place. He'll think me careless and stupid. And he'll rage about the money he lost as a result. I—I don't know what he'll do to me once he gets me back."

Riden glances down at my legs, no doubt remembering the scars he once saw there. "I can believe that, but what was with all of that?" He jerks his thumb in the direction of the deck. His face hardens.

"I was trying to get Draxen's attention. I needed to speak with him about it. I thought maybe we could work something out. Find a way for him to get his money and for me to be set free."

"And?"

"Draxen wasn't interested in talking."

Riden winces at that. He puts his hand up to his face, scratches the back of his head. "I'll speak to him."

I don't have to fake my confusion. "About what?"

"I'm sure there's a way we can get our money and then let you walk free. You'll have to divulge all the information you've been holding back, but you don't have to return to your father."

I laugh, a short, doubtful sound. "Where else would I go?"

"Anywhere."

"He'll find me no matter where I go."

"Then don't leave. Stay." Riden's mouth widens at his own exclamation.

"Stay? Why ever would I do that?"

"I don't know why I said that. Forget it."

He looks very uncomfortable, possibly ready to bolt. I need to act quickly. How am I to get a clear shot to his head? And what am I supposed to knock him out with? Riden's removed all weapons from the room. And he's definitely still suspicious after everything that happened with Draxen.

This doesn't leave me with many options. It's hard to think clearly when everything's falling apart. For now, I need to keep him talking. Something will come to me eventually.

"You said it because you were thinking it," I say.

"No, I wasn't."

"Really? Your mouth came up with it all on its own?"

"It's very talented."

"Yes, I'm well aware." I could slap myself for saying that, but I need to keep him talking. I need to think.

He smiles, knowingly. "We probably should talk about that."

"About what?" I ask, too innocently to be believable.

"You know what."

It's been a couple of weeks. Why should he want to talk about it now? Actually, he's a pirate—why should he want to talk about it at all?

"What exactly do you have to say?" I ask, curious as ever.

Riden says nothing. I can see him searching for the words, but nothing will come to him.

"Here is all that needs to be said," I say. "I'm a prisoner on this ship. I'm also the only woman on the ship. You got a little lonely, and I got a little crazy. That's it. It was stupid, but it's over, so let's move on."

Should I ram him into the wall? He'll be knocked unconscious like Draxen, but if he sees me do that, he'll be *very* suspicious when he wakes. How many women have the strength to do something like that? Riden already knows something is off about me. What if he guesses?

Paranoia must be setting in. I need more sleep.

"I don't think so."

"What?" I ask, coming back to the conversation.

Riden knows I heard him, so he doesn't bother repeating himself.

Has he gotten so used to arguing with me that it's all he can do? Even when I speak the truth? Why is he so adamantly pressing the matter?

I decide to cheat. Right now my curiosity is more powerful than my revulsion, and I have plenty of time before I lose myself.

I home in on Riden. On his mind and his heart. I can feel his frustration. Both with himself and with me. I just don't know why. I can sense feelings and desires. But I can't read minds, helpful as that would be. I never know the whys behind people's intentions.

All I know is Riden wants to kiss me again. Right now it is his greatest desire, and he can't hide it from me. I feel it as though it were my own emotion. And though I'm sure it's merely because he hasn't had some alone time with a woman in a while, this is most definitely something I can use to my advantage.

Forget knocking him out. I need Riden's greatest desire to become sleep. Once he's asleep, I can keep him that way with my song. There's enough in me for that.

But there's only one way to change what he wants most. I have to give him the first one, so he will be satisfied and think of something else.

I swallow. For some reason, the thought excites me. Must be the thrill of the game.

So how to start?

"You don't think so?" I ask. "What do you think happened, then?"

A deep, stormy gray surrounds him. He feels guilty. That'll be the betrayal to his brother, no doubt. He wants to be assuaged from that guilt. He wants to get what he wants without the consequences that'll come with it.

Typical pirate.

No responsibility. Just selfish desire.

"I think," Riden finally says, "there is more here than either of us is willing to admit."

"More of what?"

His frustration flares, as does the desire. Interesting how

they're tied together. But I can't hold on to this anymore. Time to let the siren go again.

"What did you do?" he asks.

I quirk an eyebrow. "What do you mean?"

"You . . . you just changed. You looked off for a moment, but I thought I'd imagined it. Now you look yourself again."

Nobody has ever been able to tell when I'm using my abilities before. Riden couldn't have actually noticed the difference, could he?

"Well, Riden, if this conversation has been any indication, you are clearly not at your best. Perhaps you should get some rest."

"Sleep is the last thing on my mind."

I know that. I need to get him onto the bed. "You need to relax. Here. Come, sit." I sit on the bed and pat a spot next to me.

He looks conflicted, pained. Maybe I shouldn't have put the siren away so soon. But I will not be reduced to pulling her out again tonight. I'd have to be *truly* desperate indeed.

"Don't worry. I'm not going to hurt you," I say.

He scoffs. "As if you could."

I point to his side, where I cut him when we were on the island.

"I allowed you to do that."

"Right. Because you're so bold and brave. Come, sit. Even conflicted pirates need a break."

He finally yields. But he won't look at me, and he's ensuring there's a good foot between us on the bed. Interesting, since I already know what he really wants. He must be trying to stay away from temptation. If so, he shouldn't have relented the bed. That's all the invitation I need.

"I imagine being the first mate is stressful for you," I say.

"Why's that?"

"Because you're not the captain. I couldn't stand being the first mate. I always have to have my way."

He laughs.

"I like the freedom it gives me," I continue. "You seem like you want more freedom."

"Am I so easy to read?"

I didn't have to use my powers to learn that. Riden is easier for me to read than others. "At times. There's more going on in here than you say." I tap my finger once to his head.

He finally turns toward me at the contact. "How do you know so much? How are you . . . you?"

"I am me because I choose to be me. I am what I want. Some people say you have to find yourself. Not I. I believe we create ourselves to be what we want. Any aspect of ourselves that we do not like can be altered if we make an effort."

That might have been a bit much, but Riden eats it up. His eyes burn. They really are a beautiful brown.

I reach out and grasp his hand with mine.

"What are you doing?" he asks.

"Nothing. I wanted to touch you, so I did."

"Simple as that?"

"Simple as that."

"I want to kiss you again."

"So then why don't you?"

"Because I can't help you. All I can do is take but give nothing in return."

I'm struck speechless by his honesty. Maybe not the honesty, but the sincerity and selflessness in what he said. I've never heard a pirate say such a thing. It's wrong. Uncomfortable. Almost makes me feel guilty for how I'm playing him.

Almost.

I slide closer to him, move my hand up to his face, and whisper, "But you are giving. You're distracting me from the fate that awaits me. That's more than I could have hoped for."

I lean forward and press my lips to his. Rather than kiss me back, he puts his hand in my hair and says my name softly, with a touch of hopelessness.

I know he wants this; I just have to make him give in to it.

I lift up my legs and slide them over his lap, drawing him nearer to me at the same time.

Though I'd die of embarrassment if anyone on my crew knew I said this, I add, "Please, Riden. I want this. Don't you want this?"

That does the trick. I finally feel movement under my own lips. It's soft, unsure. Curious to be coming from Riden, who has always seemed so sure of himself. Perhaps he needs some more encouragement.

I trace his upper lip with the tip of my tongue.

The change is instant. Before I know it, he's got his hand at the back of my head, the other on the side of my thigh. I move my lips down to his neck, teasing him in just the right places to get his heart pumping even faster.

But he's done with letting me have all the fun. With a hand at my chin, he brings my lips back up to his. He takes control of the kiss, setting his own rhythm and pace. I let him, give him a sense of control. I have a feeling he'll need it, if I'm to get him right where I want him.

Riden removes his coat. Obviously, things are getting warm for him in here.

Good, one less thing I'll have to remove for myself.

For a moment, I allow myself to get caught up in the kiss. It's all for a greater purpose, but I can't deny how different it is to kiss Riden than it was to kiss Draxen. Draxen felt wrong. Draxen is a selfish lover. That much was obvious.

And Riden—

Riden is not.

Riden knows where to stroke my skin to make me feel more alive. He has me practically panting under the pressure of his lips. I gasp when his teeth nip at the skin above my throat.

Riden lowers me back onto the bed. I reach for the base of

his shirt and pull it up. He helps me get it over his head before discarding it to the floor. But I take careful note of exactly where it lands. Hidden pockets can be sewn anywhere.

The plan was to give Riden a little of what he wanted. To make him less frustrated. So he'd want to sleep. I can see now how this might not have been the best plan. Maybe it wasn't even a real plan, just my way of justifying kissing him again.

At least I'll have fewer articles of clothing to remove once he's out. Men are heavy.

But what am I to do about what's happening now?

Riden fingers the string that laces the side of my corset. While he's not undoing it, the action is driving me mad. Does he realize this? He can't be doing it offhandedly. He's far too devious for that.

My stomach burns with excitement. My mind battles against it.

Draxen's knocked out. You don't have much time.

But Riden's hands are so soft and warm. I don't want him to stop touching me.

You need to find the map now. Think of what Father'll do to you if you fail.

But the thought of Riden's lips makes me salivate. I could stay in his arms forever.

Alosa, have you forgotten your desire to become the queen of pirates? There's an island filled with treasure out there. Get the map and everything will fall into place.

Right. Blast it.

This'll be the most reckless thing I've done since coming to this ship. But I need to act before Draxen wakes and before I get lost in the moment.

There's so very little left, but it'll have to do.

I let out a song. One single note. It's all I have.

But luckily for me, Riden is already so very much in tune with me. He topples over onto the bed. Out in an instant. There's no way that'll last long. There was hardly anything in it.

My breath is still traveling faster than the wind. That was very stupid. While I had enough song to put Riden to sleep, there was none left to make him forget. He'll remember me singing to him.

But once I have the map, I can be off this ship, and it won't matter. Father will take possession of the *Night Farer* and kill everyone on board. There will be no one left to tell.

A wooden plank creaks. My eyes dart toward the door, but I shake my head and quickly look away. The ship is old. Wood creaks.

Though I'm pressed for time, I have to take a few seconds to breathe. My heart pounds at an impossible pace.

Eventually, I check his coat and shirt, running my fingers over the material several times. I can't tell if I'm disappointed or not when I know for sure it's not in either of them.

Because that leaves his boots, leggings.

And breeches.

It's not like Riden wasn't hoping he'd get these off anyway.

I hurry with the rest of it, but unlike with Draxen, I don't take so many pains to avert my eyes. I've been stuck on this ship for quite a while. It's the least I deserve.

The novelty wears off quickly once the unavoidable conclusion sinks in.

The map's not here.

Wrong again.

Blast, where else could it be? I've checked just about everything. Draxen wouldn't have hidden it somewhere on land. There's too great a chance of losing it or forgetting where he's placed it. No one makes a map to find a map.

I try to take deep breaths, but I have to turn away from Riden's naked form in order to do that successfully.

Now then, Father can hardly fault me if the map simply isn't here to begin with?

But I know better than that. He'll blame whoever he can get his hands on. Which'll be me, once I deliver him the news. Who knows what it'll be this time. Locked in a cell for a month. Flogged daily in the strip. No meals for a week.

It's not my fault. The map is nowhere on this ship.

Nowhere on this ship.

On it.

My mind turns and tosses. Yes, I've checked everywhere on the ship.

But what about on the outside of the ship?

Chapter 15

HOW MANY REALIZATIONS CAN a person have before one actually proves to be right?

I close my eyes as I try to remember what the *Night Farer* looks like from the outside.

Sixty feet long. Made with a combination of oak and cedar wood. Three sails. Rounded stern. But these are not what interest me.

The bowsprit extends twenty feet in front of the ship. Below it, carved out of the same mixture of wood, is the figure of a larger-than-life-sized woman. She's beautiful, with long flowing hair and big glassy eyes—probably made from actual glass. But it's the dress that leads me to believe that the girl is supposed to be a siren.

She's wearing a long dress that's made to look as though it's rippling underwater. She appears weightless, too, by the way her legs are unattached to the boat, hanging above the water. She is connected only by her back.

I feel as though the entire future rests in my hands as I hurry from Riden's room. I scurry about the ship, finding myself a long sturdy rope. Using a bowline knot, I attach it to the railing at the bow of the ship.

Effortlessly, I lower myself down and hang right in front of the siren's large face. My wrists are mostly healed from hanging in front of the pirates for an entire day. They trouble me little now. Besides, I'm more concerned with finding this map and doing it quickly. A little pain now will be nothing compared to what could happen should I fail.

I move my hands over the wood that makes up her skin, looking for any hidden slots, trick buttons, or anything else that might be concealed in the wood. I feel an indent at the top of her hairline, but that turns out to be just a groove in the wood. But my heart raced at the possibility of it. Then it crashes as that proves to be useless as well.

Was Jeskor's line careless? Did they lose their map over the centuries? Riden did say his father grew to be sloppy. Maybe he gambled the map away. That would make it nearly impossible to find.

I can hear light footsteps up on deck, but that is likely just the watch. I had to slip past them on my way down here.

How can all this have been for nothing? I've been kid-napped, questioned, tortured, and reduced to playing horribly demeaning roles to get what I want.

I'm so furious, the rope I cling to starts swaying. My body is tight, occasionally rocking as I lurch with frustration.

What was that?

I swear I caught a glint of something in her eye. Leaning forward, I cause the rope to swing again.

There it is again. Her left eye. It looks darker than the right from this angle.

I can feel my blood pounding under my skin. My heart beating in my head. I reach down to grab a lower end of the rope. I wrap it around my foot several times and then hold the end under my chin. I'll need both hands for this.

My dagger is still in my boot. Riden has not once asked me for it. He must have forgotten about it.

I wedge the blade in between the glass and the wood and apply pressure at an angle. The glass pops off, and I barely catch it before it topples into the water.

From the back, I can clearly see that a piece of parchment has been encased within. How can it be anything else than what I seek?

"Finally," I say breathlessly.

I cock my head sideways at the one-eyed siren. "Sorry about that. But I need to take this."

The eye is about the size of a large apple, but I still manage to fit it into one of my pockets so I can climb the rope. I'm smiling as I haul myself over the edge and drop onto the deck.

But then I look up.

I'm not alone. Not even close.

It appears that the entire crew is on deck. That'll be including a clothed Riden and Draxen.

Oh, stars.

"Well, look who it is," Draxen drawls out. It's hard to tell his mood. On the one hand, he looks pleased to have caught me. On the other, he is very unpleased to see me. I did, after all, leave him knocked unconscious and naked in his room. "Our little prisoner. Or would *thief* be a better term here?"

"Thief?" I say with a mixture of confusion and anger.

"Well, you're either a thief or a whore, princess. Those are the only words that would explain the situation you left the two of us in."

"I believe the only thing I've stolen from the likes of you is your dignity. Perhaps your reputation."

Draxen lowers his eyelids. If I thought he hated me when I first came onto the ship, it's nothing compared to what he thinks of me now. He takes a step forward.

"Turn out your pockets," Riden says. I turn my attention over to him. He's trying so very hard to keep a mask over his face. But something keeps peeking through. Disappointment? Anger? Maybe even a tinge of sadness?

Am I the reason for that?

Draxen draws his sword. "Turn out her pockets? Why don't we have the princess take off her clothes so we can inspect her properly?"

A few men whistle. But I'm not worried. I'd jump overboard before I let that happen.

Riden tries to solve things on his own. "Hand it over, Alosa."

"What am I handing over?"

"Oh, don't be daft, lass. We know you've found the map."

"I just managed to dig out a few holes near the bottom of the ship. I've a mind to set you all to sinking."

Draxen tries to advance on me again, but Riden beats him to it.

He whispers, "I don't know why I'm still trying to protect you. But know my brother is in a foul mood that even I might not be able to assuage. You must give it over now."

"I don't have—"

But he must see the bulge in my clothing. He reaches it before I'm able to stop him.

No, no, no.

Riden removes the eye from my pocket. He studies it carefully. I can see the precise moment when he's convinced the map is inside. He nods in satisfaction and steps back, handing the glass to his brother.

The map is enough to calm Draxen down ever so slightly. "At last," he says.

"Wait," I say, realizing something given Draxen's reaction. "You knew about the map. You just didn't know where it was?"

"Hadn't a clue," he says cheerily, rubbing the details into my face. "We stole you away to get the drop on the pirate king in order to get our hands on his part of the map. You finding our own map for us turned out to be quite serendipitous."

I stare back, openmouthed. "But how did you know I was looking for it?"

"Riden started to suspect long ago. Did you really think you were being so careful? Your nightly raids of the ship. Your pathetic fake escapes. The fearless way you've carried on about the ship. Only a woman who wanted to be here wouldn't show an ounce of fear in front of enemy pirates."

That's not true at all. They don't know me or what I would or wouldn't do in any given situation. But Draxen's low regard of me is not what hurts the most.

It's Riden selling me out.

I know he was playing a part. Pretending to be my protector at times. I know deep down this is always the role he was meant to perform. But it still hurts. Can I even call it a betrayal? How can I be betrayed by someone who was never on my side to begin with?

My mission was to procure the map *without anyone noticing*. Then I was supposed to lead the ship to the checkpoint.

I've utterly failed the first part, even if I'm on track with the second.

"Take her to my room, gents," Draxen says. "It's about time someone had some proper fun with her."

I frown before realizing this works out well for me. Fighting off Draxen alone while the men calm down is much easier than trying to take them on all at once.

I'm hauled forward by three men. One at each arm and one at my legs. I make forced attempts at ripping free from their grasp. I don't scream, though. A promise is a promise, and I told Draxen he would never hear me scream.

Riden's there, too. Draxen gives the map back to him for safekeeping. He tucks the glass into his pocket. Then he's helping the men escort me. I'll bet he's loving this. Giving his brother what he wants is Riden's specialty. First the map and now me. Draxen is done pretending he's holding me for a ransom. There's no need to play nice now.

They throw me, very ungracefully and ungently, into the room. Riden stands by the door, apparently wanting a few moments alone with me before his brother arrives.

But I don't want that.

"Get out," I say. "You've done enough."

His expression remains calm, focused. "Do you still have that knife in your boot?"

I exhale a laugh of incredulity. "Of course not."

"Good. Keep it close. But please, only use it if you have to. He's still my brother. Don't kill him."

"So used to my lies now, are you? You can tell truth from

fiction? What are you doing, Riden? What is your play? I'm sick of trying to figure you out. Just when I think I've got it, you do something else to irritate me. Who are you putting on a show for?"

"No time, Alosa. Get free and get out of here if you can. That's the best I can do. The map for my brother, and freedom for you. Please. Again I'll ask you, don't kill him."

"That's a big gamble you're taking, Riden. What happens if Draxen overpowers me? How will you feel about that?"

"Oh please. We both know you are hiding more than your intentions to get the map. You are skilled, Alosa. More skilled than any human girl could possibly be. No one man could get the better of you. I don't know what you are. I just know you've somehow gotten into my head. And you managed to enchant the whole crew the other day. I'm still trying to figure out why you haven't killed us all already."

The door wrenches free, and Draxen strides in. "Leave us," he commands. Swiftly and forcefully at the same time.

Riden obeys, then sends one more pleading look in my direction. *Don't kill him.*

I'm still stuck on Riden's words. *Human girl.* He knows. I know he remembers me singing him to sleep, but was it too much to hope he would explain it away as coincidental?

But then, why wouldn't he tell Draxen? Or, well, why wouldn't he *warn* Draxen? It probably shouldn't matter. But it does. I don't know how I feel about Riden knowing my secret. Or at least guessing part of it.

I'm still puzzling this all out when Draxen slams me against the wall in his room.

"I'm going to enjoy this. If you had gone along with everything last time, you would've had it good. But not now. Now I'm going to make you scream."

"Actually, Draxen," I say, struggling against his weight, "you're really not."

He laughs as he tries to force me toward his bed. "I've thought about doing this for a long time."

"Me too."

Draxen braces my back against the wall. His arms are at my shoulders. I manage to lift both legs, plant them on his stomach, and kick, using the wall to steady me. That sends him reeling backward several feet.

I land painfully on the ground. My mind quickly travels back in time to when Draxen questioned me in this room. Some of my blood is still dried onto this floor. Draxen hit me again and again, trying to get me to give him the location to my father's hideaway.

I've always lived with the eye-for-an-eye mentality.

I send my right fist into the side of his face. I don't have to hold back now, and I don't. I put everything I have into it. I know I've hit sure and sound when I can feel the resulting stinging pain in my knuckles. After being cooped up and holding back for so long, this is bliss. A painful bliss.

Draxen grunts from the impact. He's still unsure of what's happening when I send a second strike with my left fist.

"How does that feel, Draxen?" I hiss. "Don't worry—we're not done yet."

He growls as he tries to see me in front of him. He advances, trying to pummel me with his own fists. But a quick duck and two strikes later, I land him onto the floor.

He utters a few exhausted curses.

I'm still not done with him.

"You threatened to cut my hair. What manner of foul scum does that? How about if I cut off something you value, Draxen?"

He takes in a large gulp of air. Of course that threat would make him scream for help, but I can't have that. One quick kick to the face and he's out.

I get my knife out of my boot. What should I take from him? An ear? A finger? Something from down low?

I cringe at that thought. Too gross. Perhaps I should stick this in his heart and be done with it.

But Riden's voice comes circulating in my ears again. *Please don't kill him.*

I've never had a brother. I don't know how I would feel toward him. Especially if he behaved like Draxen. I think I'd still kill him.

What do I care what Riden thinks? He's the only one who gets hurt as a result. Draxen won't feel a thing. The pirates under him can always find a new vessel to crew for. Most of them seem more loyal to Riden than they do their captain anyway. Lord

Jeskor isn't around to claim vengeance. But Riden might. I suppose he might even rally up the crew to join him.

I'm not afraid.

I get on my knees and find myself staring at the dagger.

It's the dagger that Riden let me keep. He knows I have it. He's known I've had it for a while. But he's trusted me not to abuse it. It was a gift of protection from him. He took everything else I owned away from me, but he let me keep this one token out of good faith.

And he trusted me enough not to kill his brother?

What a fool.

I hover over Draxen's chest, visualize the knife sinking in, imagine the resistance of the skin and innards, hear the sound of the knife sliding between the ribs.

But no matter how many ways I think about it, I can't seem to make my hand advance downward.

As much as I try to be unaffected by Riden, for all I'm worth, I can't seem to do the one simple act of killing his cruel brother.

I've killed hundreds of men. Why not this one?

Blasted Riden.

I try to make myself feel better by thinking it's not worth the time to make the kill. Of course, I've wasted more than a minute, sitting here, thinking about it. But never mind that.

I need to get that map.

I need to find Riden.

Chapter 16

I CAUTIOUSLY PEEK MY head outside of Draxen's quarters.

I can't see anyone from where I stand, but it's getting dark, so it's hard to tell for sure. No one is needed for steering because we're not moving at the moment. Draxen is biding his time, probably formulating some sort of plan for infiltrating my father's keep if he hasn't already. No matter what he has planned, he will not get far. My father will have scouts everywhere. They might have even spotted the ship already.

Over the last few days, we've passed by several small, empty islands. This area is dotted with them. My father has chosen one of the larger ones as the meeting point. We can't be more than a few hours' sail from it.

I reach the main deck and take another look around. There's movement by the port side. A few more steps and it turns out to be Riden, preparing a boat.

"Did you kill him?" is the first thing he asks me.

"Surprisingly, no. You're welcome."

"Thank you. That means more to me than I can say."

I shrug. "Is that supposed to be for me?" I ask, pointing to the boat he's lowering into the water.

"Yes. I've ordered the crew to go belowdecks. You should have enough time to get to your father's keep. The only thing more I ask is that you give us a head start before sending the pirate king after us."

"If I were to send my father after you, it wouldn't matter how much of a head start you had. The only reason you're not all dead now is because he was never looking for you."

Riden looks up from the rope in his hands. "What do you mean? Are you saying that—"

"My capture was all a ruse."

The look he gives me is priceless. "But I thought you decided to make the most of your kidnapping by searching the ship once you'd arrived."

"Afraid not. I planned to get kidnapped from the start. My father ordered it."

Riden's face is open confusion. "Why would the pirate king send out his only heir on such a dangerous mission?"

"Because I'm the only one he trusted to be successful. I have certain abilities that others do not."

Riden releases his hold on the rope. The boat must have reached the water. "Are you using them now? Is that why I'm doing this? Helping you?"

"If I were, you would've given me the map already. Since you're trying so hard to conceal it from me, you can rest assured you still have control over your mind."

"Your eyes have changed," he says, seemingly randomly.

"What?"

"They were blue when you first got here. Now they're green."

He's awfully perceptive. My eyes are blue when I have the strength of the sea with me. Once it's all gone, they shift back to green.

"My eyes are blue-green," I say.

"No. They've definitely changed." He leans against the railing, looking surprisingly unafraid. "What are you?"

"As if I'd tell you."

"Are you a siren?"

I cringe at the word. It's so strange to hear it coming from Riden's lips. "Not exactly."

"Your mother is a siren. That story. The rumor that your father is the only one to have bedded a siren and lived—it's true."

Is there any point in denying it? My father will be hunting down this ship shortly anyway. "Yes."

"But why are you the way you are? Sirens depend on human

men for their survival, but they produce more sirens. What makes you more human than sea creature?"

"That is an excellent question. You're right: I'm not fully a siren, more half siren–half human. And there is something special surrounding my birth. I'll tell you what it is if you tell me where you hid the map."

"Tempting as that is, I can't tell you that. Why don't you get it over with and make me tell you?"

"It doesn't work like that."

"Then how does it work?"

"I'll tell you. Just please hand over the map, Riden."

"Sorry, Alosa."

"Fine. I'll get it out of you. But I'll have you know I loathe doing this." I reach down to that unnatural part of me. Suddenly, I'm uncomfortable in my own skin. Goose bumps rise on my arms and legs. My hair seems to stand on edge. Mentally, it's exhausting to be so aware of everything around me.

"You're doing that thing again," he says. "You've changed."

I've never had anyone be able to detect the change in me before. Not even my own father can tell, so how can Riden?

"I'm tapping into the part of me that comes from my mother. I hate using it. Feels awful and unnatural."

"Does it give you the ability to read my mind?"

"No, I can only tell what you're feeling."

This seems to give him great alarm. His emotions turn from a glowing, vibrant red to light gray almost instantly.

Gray is an interesting color. When it's the dark gray of storm clouds, the emotion is tied to guilt. In a lighter hue, the emotion is grief.

A deep sadness has come over Riden. But the change is so immediate, it causes me to believe he's thinking about something extremely sad to him on purpose so I can't get anything else out of him.

"Are you thinking sad thoughts on purpose?" I ask.

"It's terrifying that you know what I'm thinking."

"Not thinking. I don't know why you're sad. Only that you're thinking about something that causes you grief."

Now I need to play on his fear. His fear of me finding the map. He won't have hidden it on his person. He had to have known I would search him for it. He'll have hidden it somewhere on the ship. I'll have to gauge his fear if I'm to find it.

I start moving about the ship, but I keep him talking as I do. "How did you figure out that I'm . . . different?" I ask as I walk to the starboard side of the ship. I'm near the entrance that leads belowdecks. The men laugh and talk loudly. They'd have to be for me to hear it from up here. Probably grateful for some downtime.

"That time I woke up and couldn't remember what happened before I passed out. At first I assumed you knocked me out, but I couldn't remember any sort of a struggle. In fact, I remember something quite the opposite."

I smile to myself. Yes, that was a fun night.

Riden's still trying to mask something with his deep sense of grief. If I were to guess, I'd say he's thinking about his father's death. But there are flares of red that shine through as he talks to me. Particularly when he mentioned that night.

"But then there was that day when you changed. It was like you were someone completely different. You weren't putting up a fight. You weren't talking like you usually do. It was ... unnerving. I swear, you looked different, too. If I squinted, I could see a faint haze of light around you."

That, he imagined. There is no physical difference when I alter my actions and words—when I call up the siren.

"I've known about my father's map since I was a little boy," he continues. "I know about sirens, even if I don't understand them completely. I put my limited knowledge together with what I knew of you and your father. It wasn't a hard connection to make. I had my suspicions long before tonight—before you sang to me."

I'm only getting flickers of heat amidst his sadness. No fear. The map can't be over here. I start toward the upper deck.

Riden follows at a safe distance. "Why can't you make me tell you where it is? You made me sleep, didn't you?"

"Yes, I put you to sleep. Twice. But I exhausted my"—I don't want to call them powers; that sounds strange—"abilities. That's why I couldn't put you to sleep deeply the second time. I'm all out."

"And how do you get them back?"

"The sea. She gives me strength. The closer I am to her, the stronger I am."

The map's not up here. I stride back down the companionway and head for the bow of the ship.

"What else can you do? Besides put people to sleep?" Riden steps back, almost like he's afraid to touch me, when I pass him on my way to the other end of the ship.

I can make men see things that are not there. I can put thoughts in their heads. I can make them promises they'll believe. I can get them to do anything I want. All I have to do is sing. I'm not sure I should tell him any of this, though. Even if I do believe my father will capture this ship soon.

"If I choose to, I can feel what men want. I know their every desire. And I use that to get what I want. It's something I can turn off and on at will." And lose myself in, if I go too far.

Riden freezes at that. Wait, no. There's a flash of black. Of fear. I stop where I am and look around. I passed the center of the ship, where the mainmast extends into the air.

"Is that why you act the way you do?" he asks. I think he's trying to distract me.

I take a few steps toward Riden, back toward the mainmast. "What do you mean?"

"The whole time you've been on this ship. Everything you've said and done. Have you been reading me? Giving me what I want? Is that why I feel the need to protect you? Or did you get in my head? Force me to feel things I've never felt before?"

That stops me short. "Riden, the only thing I've ever made you do is sleep. I have not played with your mind or acted a certain way to toy with you. I only used that on Draxen once to try to find the map. Whatever it is you think and feel—it comes from you. I didn't do anything."

The light around him turns blue.

"You're confused," I say. "Why?"

He narrows his eyes. "Because I don't understand you. And I don't know what to believe."

"You can choose to believe what you wish, but I speak the truth. Now, if you'll excuse me, I have a map to find." I look upward. "The crow's nest, eh?" I ask. That must be where Riden's hidden it.

Riden cocks his head at something behind me. "What are you doing up here?"

I was so focused on Riden's reaction to my moving about the ship, I didn't realize someone was coming up behind me. I'm about to turn when I feel a sharp pain at the back of my head and fall into darkness.

Everything is hazy. I can make out a couple of forms, but mostly I feel the rocking—the rocking of a boat on the sea.

"She's waking," someone says.

"She heals faster than I thought. Hit her again."

Blackness greets me once more.

Cold.

Everything is cold. I feel it at my cheek. Clinging to my fingers. Seeping in through my clothes.

My eyelids are heavy, but I manage to open them. They're met with bars. Am I back in my cell?

No.

Beyond the bars is not the interior of a ship, but sand and trees. I hear the rolling of waves not far off, though I can't see the shore.

I am alone.

The trees rustle in the wind. I shiver through the cold. Creatures slither and crawl on the ground, making their way through the undergrowth. The sounds of the night do not frighten me.

No, it is the cage that frightens me. I am without song. Without my lockpicks. Without any company at all.

For the first time in a long time, I am truly afraid.

It is morning before anyone approaches me.

I do not recognize the man. He's tall, though not as tall as my father. Bald on top of his head, a brown beard on his chin. Five gold hoops hang from his left ear. His clothes are fine, yet roguish. He has a sword and pistol at his hips. Though I can't imagine he has to use them often. He looks as though he's built out of solid muscle, but I bet I could take him were I not locked up.

He pulls something out of his pocket, an orb of some sort. Ah, it's the map. He tosses it up in the air and catches it lazily. A show for my benefit.

"Do you know who I am?" he asks. His voice sounds exactly as I would expect—deep and demanding.

"Am I supposed to care?" I ask indifferently, as though I'm not trapped. I'm proud of myself for my tone. It masks completely the coiling of nerves in my stomach.

"My name is Vordan Serad."

I hide my surprise. I have been kidnapped by the third pirate lord, and this time my capture is not planned.

At least not by me.

I try for faked confidence. "Do you know who *I* am?" I ask in return, matching Vordan's air of authority.

"You are Alosa Kalligan, daughter of Byrronic Kalligan, the pirate king."

"Excellent. Then you already know how foolish you're being for keeping me like this."

"Foolish? Not at all. Your father thinks that young Allemos captain has you, so he will not be coming after me. I have it on good authority that you have been depleted of the power the sea gives you, so you cannot save yourself. I would say it is *you* who are being foolish by not being afraid."

My stomach sinks through the ground as my mouth dries. "And whose authority would that be?"

"Mine," says a voice from behind me. Several men break through the trees. Riden is among them, but he is not the one who spoke. No, Riden has two pistols pointed at him. They're forcing him to walk in my direction. Why isn't he locked up like I am? Running low on enormous cages, are we?

My mind empties as soon as I lay eyes on who spoke, the fourth man who enters the clearing.

It's Theris.

He slouches against one of the trees and pulls out his coin, turning it over his fingers.

I shake my head at him. "Betraying my father? That will be the last mistake you ever make. Do you know what happened to the last man who fed information to his enemies? My father tied him up by his ankles and sawed him down the middle."

Theris is unaffected by my words. "Fortunately for me, I'm not betraying him."

He doesn't need for me to say so to know I'm confused.

"I was never your father's man," he continues.

It takes me longer than it should to interpret his words. But the symbol—he knew my father's mark. He clearly identified himself as serving the Kalligan line.

"My reach is deep." Vordan explains this time, returning the glass-encased map to his pocket. "Kalligan is foolish. He thinks himself untouchable. He doesn't realize that those closest to him are so ready to give him up. And, more importantly, give you up."

I turn on Theris. "You weren't on the ship to help me."

"No," he answers. "I was sent to watch you."

"Then who is my father's man aboard the *Night Farer*?" I say more to myself.

Theris answers. "That was poor Gastol. I'm afraid you slit his throat when Draxen took control over your ship."

What were the odds that one of the two men I killed was my father's man? The guilt hits me, even though I know it's not entirely my fault. My father should have had the foresight to tell me who his informant was aboard the *Night Farer* before I faked my capture. Then Gastol wouldn't have died, and Theris wouldn't have been able to fool me. Father doesn't take these minor details into consideration. What does he care if one of his men dies by accident? There is always someone to take his place. But in this instance his folly might cost him Draxen's map.

And maybe me.

Then again, maybe I should have realized that Father never would have asked his informant to help me. He knows I do not need to be looked after. I should have known Theris was faking from the beginning. Furious with myself, I return back to the conversation at hand.

"Why did you have Theris watching me?" I ask Vordan. "What could you possibly want with me?"

"You don't realize your own value," Vordan says. "Do you think Kalligan keeps you around because you're his daughter? No, Alosa. It is because of the powers you possess. He uses you for his own gain. You are nothing more than a tool to him. I've heard all about Kalligan's punishments, his training, his testing. I know all the horrible things he's put you through. And I am here to liberate you."

For a moment I wonder how he could possibly know so much about me. Then I realize that if he has someone high up in my father's ranks working for him, he would know . . . well, just about everything.

I say, "Putting me in a cage was probably not the best way to show how much you want to *liberate* me."

"Apologies. This is merely a safety precaution for me and my men while I explain things."

"You've explained. Now let me out."

Vordan shakes his bald head. "I have not finished."

And I don't want him to. I want out of this cage. Now. But I stay silent so I don't risk angering him. I may not have my song to enchant him, but I can read him.

As if I weren't already uncomfortable being locked in a cage with no hope of escape—now I have to call upon the siren. Again. There is a nasty taste in the back of my throat. Goose bumps rise on my skin, and it has nothing to do with the cold.

His color is red—the most complex of all. It can mean

so very many things: love, lust, hatred, passion. Really any overwhelmingly strong emotion looks red to me. Using my best guess, I would say Vordan is feeling the bright red of passion, but passion for what?

Vordan is most eager to succeed, I decide. He wants something from me. If only I can be patient enough to hear what it is.

"Continue, then," I manage to say.

"I'm here to offer you a place on my crew. I want to give you the freedom to do as you wish after you help me get to the Isla de Canta."

"I am the captain of my own ship and crew. I have the freedom to sail where I wish. Why would I find your offer even remotely tempting?" I do not ask in anger. My tone is only objective. I'm trying to reason with him. To remain calm.

"Because ultimately you are under your father's rule. When this is all over, Alosa, when you and your father have all three pieces of the map, when you've sailed to the Isla de Canta and claimed the wealth of ages—what then? I'll tell you. Then your father will not only still have complete control over the seas of Maneria, he will also have all the wealth he needs to maintain that control. And you will always have to serve him. You will never be truly free of him."

"But I will be if I join you?" I ask skeptically.

"Yes. Help me obtain what your father wants. Help me reach the Isla de Canta. Help me to usurp Kalligan's rule, and I shall free you. When we are successful, you will be free to go as you please, do as you wish, have whatever you want. I shall not bother you or call on you again."

Vordan Serad is a fool. Does he think I could ever trust him to keep his word? Does he really think I would turn so easily on my father? Does he think it a burden for me to serve Kalligan? He's my father. It is the love of family that drives my actions. I do not long for freedom, for I already have it. I have my own ship and crew that are mine to do with as I see fit. Now and again I assist my father when he needs me. He is, after all, the king. And I shall become queen when my father's reign has ended. Vordan expects me to give that up for him? Not a chance.

I dare not say any of this, though. I'm still sensing Vordan's feelings and desires. He's hopeful. Very hopeful for . . . something.

Agreeing is the only way I'll get out of this cage and have a chance of escape.

"You're right," I say in an attempt to tell Vordan exactly what he wants to hear. "I have been too afraid to break free of my father. I long to be rid of him. I want nothing to do with the Isla de Canta or Kalligan, but if you swear to me that you will grant me my freedom in exchange for my services, I will help you obtain what you seek."

Vordan looks behind me. I turn. Theris shakes his head. "She's lying."

"I am not," I say through gritted teeth. I was so focused on Vordan, I didn't bother feeling for what Theris wanted to hear.

I didn't realize it was he and not Vordan who I needed to convince.

Theris smiles. "She's using the same trick she used on Draxen. I witnessed exactly how Alosa can manipulate others by telling them what they want to hear."

"I may have used my abilities on Draxen, but that doesn't mean I'm using them now," I say, though I know it's pointless. I know now what it was I needed to say, and it's too late to change my response.

"You didn't put up enough of a fight, Alosa," Theris says. "I watched you for a month on that ship. I listened to your conversations and . . . interactions." At this he looks pointedly at Riden.

Riden has not said anything yet. He's watching our captors closely, though, trying to understand the situation so we can get out of it. At Theris's last words, he looks at me.

Just how much did Theris see? I think with disgust.

"I know exactly how stubborn you are," Theris continues. "And I know how you feel about your father. You did not defend him as you usually do."

I want to kick him, but he's too far away for me to reach, and I couldn't fit my leg through the bars if I wanted to. An arm, yes, but not a leg.

"Fine," I say as I try to think of a new plan. "What now?"

"In the likely event that you did not prove accommodating," Vordan says, "we are prepared to use you in a different way."

I do not like the sound of this. I've put away the siren. I have no way to even prepare myself for what Vordan might be thinking now.

"Bring the supplies," he orders to the two men who still have pistols pointed at Riden. Instantly they turn around and leave the clearing.

I can see Riden's mind turning. Even though I can't sense what he's thinking, it's not hard to guess. He's trying to decide how to make the most out of not being so heavily guarded.

But before he can take a step, Theris has his gun out and cocked back.

"Don't even think about it."

"Why is he even here?" I ask. "You have me. Why would you take a second prisoner? Now Draxen will be out looking for him."

"In time all will be revealed," Vordan says.

He's enjoying himself too much, and he's eager for what is to come. I guess it didn't matter whether I agreed to join him or not.

I wonder if I should change myself. Should I become Vordan's perfect woman so he will wish to free me? It's the only weapon I have left, but will it do any good? As I glance back over at Theris and his coin, I realize it won't work. If I try something on Vordan, Theris will know, and he'll put a stop to it.

I'm helpless. No weapon. No power. At this point, I can only hope someone will venture too close to the cage or that Riden somehow frees himself and then me. Since Riden isn't too pleased with me at the moment, I doubt he'd want to help even if he did free himself.

When Riden's guards return, they are not empty-handed. Each holds a bucket filled with water in one hand and something that looks a lot like a stick in the other. I can't tell what they are at first.

"Alosa," Vordan says, "you are here so I can learn all the skills you possess. For if I can't use you to help me reach the Isla de Canta, then I will use you to learn all about sirens so I can be adequately protected once I'm there."

An ice-cold dread freezes me.

I'm to be his experiment.

Chapter 17

"WHAT?" I SAY BECAUSE I can't think of anything else *to* say.

"I can't very well expect you to be honest about your abilities, so I'll have to determine them for myself," Vordan says. "Together, Alosa, we will identify all the powers sirens possess."

He doesn't realize how terrifying I find the prospect. How could he know how much I loathe, and sometimes fear, using my abilities? I hate the way I feel inside and out. I hate the emotional toll they take on me. And then there's the way I change when I have to replenish my abilities. Vordan will have me demonstrate everything over and over. The thought causes bile to rise in my throat. I swallow it back down.

"I am only partially a siren," I say in desperation. "What I can and can't do will not apply to the creatures you will find at the Isla de Canta. I am of no use to you."

Vordan pulls at the hair on his chin. "That is not true. Even if you are not as powerful as a true siren, your abilities will give me the information I need to prepare for such a venture."

During our quick exchange, Vordan's men have been moving. They place their buckets about five feet away from the cage, far out of my reach. They put what looks like a long, hollow, tube-like branch into each bucket.

"To start," Vordan says, "you will sing for me."

"Like hell I will."

Vordan smiles. "And that is why the young first mate is here. Theris, show Alosa what will happen each time she refuses me."

Theris pulls out his cutlass and rakes it across Riden's upper arm, cutting through his shirt and sending blood streaming downward.

Riden winces, but other than that he shows no sign of pain. Instead, he laughs, applying pressure to the fresh wound. "You're all fools if you think the princess cares whether I live or die."

Theris snorts. "You're wrong, Riden. Alosa lives by her own rules. She has a strong tendency toward vengeance. She can't stand to see those who have wronged her walk away unscathed. Draxen kidnapped her, he beat her, he humiliated her, he tried to take her body. She loathes him. Yet he's alive. Do you know why?"

Riden looks at me. I quickly turn my gaze downward.

"If she didn't care about your pain, she would have killed him. Slowly and agonizingly. The fact that he lives proves there is at least one thing she cares about more than her own justice. You."

That's not true. I . . . I owed Riden. He let me keep my dagger when he should have taken it from me. I settle my debts. He helped me stay safe, so I didn't kill his brother. It was no more than that.

I'm certain of it. . . .

Wait—my dagger!

From my seated position, I wrap my arms around my ankles, as though I'm trying to comfort myself. I pat my boot.

Except for my foot, it is empty.

"Looking for this?" asks Theris, pulling the weapon from his belt, where I hadn't noticed it before.

I try to appear as though this doesn't trouble me at all. In reality, I'm outraged. Not only did Theris take away my only hope of escape, but I'm rather attached to that dagger.

"Here's how this is going to work," Vordan says, pulling my attention away from Theris. "I will tell you what to do, and you will do it. If there is any hesitation or deviance from my words, Riden will sustain another injury. Attempt to use your abilities to escape, and we'll kill him and bring you someone else to enchant. Is that understood?"

I send Vordan a murderous glare. "When I get out of this cage, the first thing I'm going to do is kill you."

Without even waiting for a signal from Vordan, Theris stabs Riden in his forearm.

My eyes widen as I hold in a gasp.

"I said, 'Is that understood?'"

Though it's against my nature—whether that be my human or siren one—I swallow my pride. "Yes."

"Good. Niffon, Cromis—the wax."

Vordan's men hand him and Theris two wads of yellow-orange wax. Then they each pull out a pair for themselves. Each man inserts the substance into his ears.

So clever, Vordan. You think yourself invincible. I *will* find a way out of this. I always do. It's only a matter of time. But I wish the fear penetrating through every limb in my body had the same confidence.

I'm not even attempting to hide the fury on my face when Vordan points to the buckets. His underlings each grab one of the thin branches and stick it into their bucket.

"Hold out your hands, Alosa," Vordan says a little too loudly.

No. I won't do it. I can't. I won't be subjected to this. Not again. My mind flashes back to being in my father's dungeon.

Manacles clamp around my wrists, chaining me to the wall. My ankles, likewise, are immobilized, clinking as chains prevent me from stepping more than a foot away from the stone wall.

"Relax," Father says before splashing a bucket of water into my face.

I choke and sputter as the water drips around me.

"Take it in, Alosa. Now, let's see how we can make you even more powerful...."

I'm brought back to the present by a loud grunt. Riden has his right hand clutched around his arm. Blood squeezes its way out of a new cut, past his tense fingers.

"Hold out your hands!" Vordan demands, this time shouting.

Your memories are just memories, I tell myself. *Father made you strong. He helped you learn everything you can do. If you survived the pirate king's pressure and scrutiny, you can certainly take it from any other pathetic, mindless, slimy eel of a man.*

My self-encouragement passes through me in less than a second. So before Theris can damage Riden further, I do as Vordan says. I won't look at Riden. What does my obedience mean for me? What does it mean to Riden?

Niffon and Cromis kneel side by side in front of their buckets. Niffon plugs the end of his hollow branch, lifts it out of the bucket, and hoists it high into the air in front of me.

Vordan has thought of everything, it seems.

If only Niffon would lower the branch an extra foot, I could reach it. A simple underestimation on their part would be extremely helpful to me right now. But no. Theris has seen what

I can do with limited resources. He won't even allow me to get my hands on a stick.

I'm caught with anticipation and dread as I wait for what will happen next. Niffon removes his thumb from his end of the branch. The ocean water caught inside now falls into my waiting hands.

I let the water slip through my fingers and fall to the ground, but I hope it looks like I absorbed some of it. It's my hope that I can fake my way through this. I can't actually replenish my abilities. Not like this.

But Vordan will have none of that. He shakes his head in displeasure. Theris drags his sword against Riden's skin again. This time near his calf.

"Do not let the water build up on the ground," Vordan says. "Take it all in."

He's worried I'll preserve the water until there's enough for me to do something truly dangerous with it. So long as Vordan and his cronies have wax in their ears, it doesn't matter how much water I have at my disposal.

But I don't point this out. I haven't any time to waste if I'm to avoid causing Riden any more pain. So when Niffon allows more water to drop, I catch it all and absorb it instantly. Nothing escapes me, and my hands dry immediately.

The change is instant. The soothing water becomes part of me. It fills the emptiness that I've felt for the last couple of weeks, replenishing my song, strengthening my confidence, easing my fear. I want to feel that comfort everywhere at once. I want to jump into the ocean and swim for the deepest, blackest space so the comfort will never leave me.

For a moment, all I can think about is the ocean. I have no cares except to return to her. Nothing else matters.

"Alosa." It's Riden's voice cutting through my longing thoughts. I try to rein in the desires of the siren. This is why I cannot replenish my song unless I can take the time to get my bearings. For using the ocean to nourish me opens me to a siren's instinct. And a siren's instinct is not to care about anything except herself, her sisters, and the ocean.

This man is nothing to me. What do I care if they kill him? He does not matter. I matter.

"Alosa," Riden repeats.

I narrow my gaze in his direction, attempting to focus my thoughts. *Don't become some soulless creature.* You are a woman. Think of your crew, your friends, your family. Remember the time you stole a ship and made it yours. Remember how it feels to be a captain, to have earned the respect and gratitude of your crew. Think of the pride in your father's eyes when you please him.

Think of Riden. Remember when you had fun fighting him, sword against sword? Remember the taunts and jabs. Remember the dagger. Remember his kisses. Think of Riden, who doesn't deserve to die all because you can't control yourself!

That does it. I return my gaze to Vordan, awaiting instructions.

"Sing to him, Alosa. Impress me."

Vordan no doubt wants to see Riden dance and perform other ridiculous stunts. Under other circumstances, I think it would be funny to make Riden humiliate himself. But not now. Not to satisfy a man who has put me in a cage. Riden is no monkey, and I am no slave.

I look at Riden. He doesn't look afraid exactly, just uneasy. "Go ahead," he finally says. Since Riden faces me and the men have wax in their ears, they can't tell he's speaking to me. "We'll get out of this eventually. Do what you need to in the meantime."

Vordan watches me carefully, so I don't risk nodding at Riden. Instead, I begin. I start with something simple and undetectable. My lips open ever so slightly as I sing a soothing, slow melody. The notes do not matter. It is the intention behind them that gives the song power. It's what makes Riden do what I want. And what I want right now is to take away his pain.

Instantly, his tense arm and leg relax, no longer feeling the cruel slices or the deep gash near his wrist. Then I tear a strip of cloth from the bottom of my blouse and throw it at Riden.

Vordan's men stand, prepared to intervene should I be attempting to make Riden flee or free me. I should be flattered that they think I can manage something with naught but a strip of cloth.

But it is for Riden's arm. I weave a few more notes into the song, making Riden tie up his severest wound to stanch the bleeding. I wish I could heal it for him, but my abilities are limited. I can only alter the mind, where I've discovered pain truly comes from. I can ease Riden's suffering temporarily, but nothing more.

I have only a few notes left, so I try to give Vordan what he wants. Riden stands up straight. His eyes don't glaze over or anything. He looks perfectly normal, as though his actions are his own. But they're not. He does nothing more or less than what I tell him through song. Riden moves through a couple of combat moves. I make him kick and punch at invisible foes. He jumps through the air, dodging and striking his opponents. Finally, he sheathes an imaginary sword.

I release him from my spell once my powers are drained. Then I sit on the floor of the cage.

Riden blinks. He looks around in confusion until he sees me and everything comes back to him. I did not take away his memories of the song, so he knows exactly what I made him do. He inhales a quick breath. The pain from his injuries comes back to him. I cannot keep the pain away once I stop singing. It was only a temporary relief, but I gave him what I could. It's my fault he's here in the first place.

Well, actually it's Theris's, but I can't expect Riden to see it that way.

Vordan steps closer to the cage, peering at me intently. "Your

242

eyes truly are the window to your soul, Alosa," he says loudly in an attempt to compensate for the wax in his ears. "In less than a minute, they've turned from green to blue to green again. Such a handy tool to tell when you have the power of your song and when you do not."

Damn.

I hoped they wouldn't be able to tell when I was out. They're observing me too closely. I won't have any secrets left by the end of this.

"But back to the task at hand. I think you can do better than that, Alosa," Vordan says in an encouraging voice that makes me even sicker to my stomach. "Try again." He points a finger at the other pirate in front of me.

This time Cromis stoppers his branch with his thumb before raising it over my arms, which hang limply outside the cage.

This is an act. I want them to think that using my powers weakens me momentarily. Might help me get the drop on them later.

I pull the water into myself as it falls. I feel it running through me, rushing into all my limbs. Doubt becomes certainty. Weaknesses become strengths. Fear becomes resolve. These men don't know who they're dealing with. I am power and strength. I am death and destruction. I am not someone to be trifled with. They are beneath my notice. I shall—

"Alosa." Riden's voice cuts through my alarming thoughts. Does he notice how the siren tries to take me? Or is he merely urging me along because he's scared of what Theris will do if I don't immediately obey?

Whatever the case, I'm grateful he seems to have the ability to bring me back to myself. And quickly.

"Alosa, you don't have to do this," he continues. Again, he's turned away from Vordan and his men, so they can't possibly tell that Riden is speaking to me. "It's all right. Ignore them. Focus on getting yourself out of this. You're good at escaping. So do it."

I smile at him despite the situation.

"Each time I escaped, it was because I planned ahead. I didn't plan this capture." I hope Vordan will assume my moving mouth is the beginning of my song. To keep the illusion, I blur the last word into a note and start a new song.

To me, the melody sounds fast-paced, exciting, thrilling. It always seems to match my intention. For this time, I run Riden through an impressive display of flexibility and dexterity. I make him do somersaults in the air. He runs up trees and flips off of them backward. I make him run faster than should be possible with his injuries. He performs stunts I'm sure he can't do on his own, for as long as *I* know how to do them, he will be able to as well.

When I drain myself of notes, I sink to the bottom of the cage once more.

Vordan takes the wax out of his ears. His men, taking his lead, do the same.

"Much better, Alosa." Vordan now has a piece of parchment

and a stick of charcoal in his hands. It doesn't matter that the wax is gone now; my abilities are gone, too.

"Let's start breaking down the extent of your abilities." Vordan begins writing with his charcoal. "If I'm not mistaken, you essentially have three abilities. The first is your song. You can enchant men to do essentially anything, so long as it doesn't defy the laws of nature. For instance, you cannot make Riden fly. How many men can you enchant at a time, Alosa?"

I hesitate. Should I lie or tell the truth?

Riden gasps in front of me. Theris pulls back a bloody sword.

"Three!" I shout. "For stars' sake, let me think a moment, would you?"

"There's nothing to think about. Answer, and no harm will come to Riden. Now, you replenish your song with water from the ocean. And the ocean water only goes so far. You couldn't make Riden do very much with the amount Cromis gave you. I'm sure the complexity of the instruction will determine how much water is necessary."

And each man's mind is different. That affects the amount, too, but I'm not going to bother mentioning that. Riden's mind is much more steadfast and firm than I'm used to seeing. Enchanting him takes more out of me than most men would normally.

After a moment's pause, Vordan looks over his notes.

"Splendid. Now, the power of your song affects the mind. But to what extent? Theris has seen you make men forget. When you enchanted poor Riden here the first time, he didn't remember the experience. Theris has also seen you put Riden to sleep. I'm sure you could easily make a man kill himself. But could you give him a different reality?"

"Yes," I say quickly, not wanting to risk any hesitation.

"Show me." He puts the wax back in his ears. His men follow suit, and a fresh flow of water is lowered down to me.

I look to Riden as I take it in. For some reason, looking at him allows me to keep a clear head as I feel the water's strength flow into me, something I've never experienced before when replenishing my abilities.

"I hate playing the puppet," I say. "Do you have any ideas?"

"If anyone's the puppet, it's me," he says agitatedly. "You're the puppeteer."

I look at him in annoyance.

"I'm working on one," he says to answer my question. "Keep taking orders until I can get it all sorted out."

I don't allow myself to hope as I start singing, closing my eyes and picturing what I want Riden to see. I imagine a magical world full of new colors and sounds. Butterflies with brightly lit wings flutter around me. Shooting stars pelt across the purple sky overhead in rapid succession. A nearby body of water sends sprays of droplets flying into the air at impossible heights. Birds larger than whales soar overhead, featuring feathers in reds and blues. I put together the first random elements that come to me, adding more and more details until I'm satisfied. Then I open my eyes.

Riden bears a look of sheer wonder and astonishment. He reaches out in front of himself as if to touch the invisible creatures I've placed in front of him.

"Beautiful," he says.

"Alosa," Vordan says. "Project that image onto Theris as well."

I see now that Theris has handed his pistol to Vordan. He removes the wax from his ears and places it into his pocket. I quickly expand the song to encompass him also, relieved now that Theris is unable to hurt Riden. He, too, is soon amazed by everything around him. He spins, trying to see every bit of the magical world I'm showing him.

My mind reels as I try to think of something I could do now that I have one of Vordan's men under my influence. With Riden and Theris, the fight would be two against three. But I haven't enough song left after my projected world to make Riden and Theris do anything substantial. Vordan is so very careful not to give me any scrap of power over him.

But I wonder why he'd bother having me enchant one of his men at all. If he's so curious about my abilities, then why not offer himself up?

"Excellent," Vordan says, scratching his charcoal quickly over the parchment. "Now release Theris."

I do. Theris instantly looks all around him, adjusting to reality, then replaces the wax in his ears. Vordan returns his pistol to him.

"Now show me something really impressive," Vordan says.

I look from Theris to Vordan, raising an eyebrow in confusion.

"Make Riden see something horrible. Make him feel pain that isn't really there. Show me how men are at your mercy."

Cromis releases another rush of water, and I barely catch it in time.

I feel as though icy needles puncture my stomach. He can't expect me to . . .

I stop singing as the water seeps into my skin. Riden is released from the fake reality I've given him. I feel my mind drifting away from me.

These men are all dead. Once I get my full strength, I will reduce them to shreds of flesh. I imagine the way my body will change. The strength I will have. I see myself pulling all five of them down to the ocean's floor, watching their eyes as the life drifts out. Feeling their bodies squirm until they're caught into oblivion. . . .

"Alosa!"

It's as if I've woken from a deep sleep, though my eyes have been open the whole time. I've drifted off to my own alternate reality. My alternate self.

"It's okay, Alosa. Come back to me," Riden says.

I turn my gaze to him.

"Whatever it is they've told you to do, do it." He won't have heard the order, not when he was caught up in another world. "We'll get through this. Just keep going."

I can't. What does it matter if I let them cut Riden because I hesitate? Either way, he'll be hurting.

But the pain won't be real if you sing to him, I try to tell myself. *He'll hurt for a moment and then it will be over. You can't falter, or he will truly be hurting from another sword injury. Just do it quickly.*

"I'm so sorry," I tell him.

Instantly, Riden screams. He writhes on the ground in pain as imaginary hot pokers drive into his skin.

I hate myself. I hate my abilities. This is not how my powers were meant to be used. I am despicable, lowly, unforgivable.

I end Riden's suffering as soon as I dare, hoping it was long enough for Vordan. I relinquish the leftover song into the air, disposing of it quickly. I don't want it anymore. I don't want anything to do with it. Get it away from me.

The sick bastard laughs. "Well done." Vordan writes some more on his parchment. I wish I could drive real pokers into *his* flesh.

"I'm satisfied with your singing abilities for today," Vordan says, freeing his ears from the wax. "Let's talk about your second set of abilities. If Theris overheard you correctly, you can read a person's emotions, but this ability does not require nourishment from the sea. It is something you innately possess."

Riden gasps on the ground, trying to recover from the imaginary pain. I watch him rub his hands over his skin, convincing himself it wasn't real.

"Alosa," Vordan snaps, pulling my attention from Riden. Theris steps forward and kicks Riden in the face. Blood trickles out of his nose, staining the sand red. In a way, I'm relieved that Theris kicked him so hard. Riden is now unconscious and can't feel any pain.

"Yes," I answer. "I can know what people are feeling, if I choose to."

"And you don't have to sing?"

"No."

"Excellent." More scratching on the parchment. "Tell me what each of my men is feeling."

I've used this one plenty of times today already. I can't risk using it much more, or I'll lose myself. The last thing I need is to forget who I am when I'm in such a life-threatening situation. The exposure to the sea's power almost claimed me several times already. And Riden's not awake to pull me back again.

I'll try to rush it. Then shut it off.

I admire the complexities of emotions. They're paintings for me to see. I just have to suffer through the otherworldliness in order to see them. As the sickly sensation rushes over my skin, I look quickly at each of Vordan's men. "That one is hungry," I say pointing to Niffon. "That one is bored." That's Cromis. "He is excited—no, happy about something." That's Theris. "And you are…" Vordan's is a bit more complicated. "Content," I finish.

Vordan looks to each of his men in turn, who nod, showing I'm right.

"Bored, are you, Cromis?" Theris asks. "Perhaps we should reassign you to kitchen duty."

Cromis looks determinedly at me, his mission. "I am fine, C— Theris."

Theris purses his lips for a moment, but his face returns to normal quickly thereafter.

Interesting falter, though I shouldn't be surprised that Theris gave me a false name. Frankly, I don't care what his real name is. His name will cease to matter once I am free and he is dead.

"Shut up," Vordan hisses at his men. His eyes are on his parchment until he looks up at me. "We'll toy around with that one some more tomorrow. Let's hurry on to your third and last ability, Alosa. Tell me, what would you call this power? I've had a hard time coming up with a concise name for it."

I think for a moment.

"Riden may be unconscious, but I can still have Theris hurt him. So speak up."

I glare at Vordan's despicable form. "I can become any man's idea of a perfect woman."

"Essentially you're a seductress. Can't expect anything less from a woman, can we?"

If I hadn't already marked him for death, he would definitely have a black mark on him now. Through clenched teeth, I say, "I can become whatever I need to be to get a man to do what I want him to."

"You're a manipulator. I imagine this ability goes well with the emotion reading. Couple those two with your song, and you truly are a formidable creature—a master over all men. Now, I'm assuming this ability only works on one man at a time?"

"Depends. Many men are attracted to the same things. I can only discern one man's perfect woman at a time, but if those characteristics are liked by many in the vicinity—"

"Then you could affect them all."

"Yes."

"Give me a demonstration. I want you to use this on each of my men."

Of all my abilities, this is the one my father found least useful. He didn't test it out like he did the other two. I had to experiment with it on my own. I haven't yet found any consequences for using it. Aside from feeling like a complete strumpet when I'm done. But I'm not above using it to get what I want. Though I usually prefer to have some song left to erase the memory from my victims afterward.

But by the end of today, it seems I will have lost my sense of safety, my secrecy, and my dignity.

Chapter 18

VORDAN HAS ME CHANGE myself for each of his men. In turn I play the parts of a whore (for Niffon likes a woman who knows what she's doing), an innocent country girl (Cromis likes corrupting innocence without consequence), and a married woman (because Theris likes the danger and secrecy of an illicit affair).

I'm kept in the cage. Thankfully, the men aren't allowed to touch me, but I want to punch myself for the foul, coy, and suggestive comments I'm forced to utter. The entire time I'm performing my act, Vordan stands there with his infernal paper and charcoal, making notes as I go.

I vow to shred that parchment so none can read the things I'm reduced to say and do.

"You may stop," Vordan says after what must have been fifteen minutes of talking to Theris. "Don't bother reading me. I have seen enough."

Theris looks questioningly at Vordan. I must be giving him a similar look. If there's anything that would have made me *want* to continue using my—as Vordan so elegantly put it—seductive powers, it was telling me not to read him.

I can read Vordan's desires as though they're written on a board above his head.

"Oh," I say, "I can see you wouldn't find me appealing no matter how I acted."

Previous to this moment, Vordan has regarded me with nothing more than a pleasant interest, but now he looks at me as though I'm some vile creature he's found sticking to the outside of his ship. He draws his sword and advances toward me.

"What are you doing?" Theris asks. "Captain?"

Vordan, called to his senses, sheathes his weapon and returns to his parchment.

I'm still worried. I've never had to use my abilities on men who only like the company of other men, and knowing Vordan is immune to that particular talent of mine makes the cage around me seem more solid somehow.

"That's enough for today," Vordan says. "Grab the boy and supplies."

Niffon and Cromis start to move while Theris looks disapprovingly at his captain.

"I said to grab the boy, Theris!" Vordan repeats.

Theris hurries to comply while Vordan sizes me up one last time. "We'll be back tomorrow. I suggest you prepare yourself for another rough day ahead of you."

At my scathing look, he adds, "Don't worry. We have weeks of fun ahead of us, you and I."

Once again I feel my last meal climbing up my throat, but I manage to keep it down as I watch all the men retreat, carrying Riden's limp form away with them.

Weeks?

Weeks?

Vordan didn't leave me much time to think of a way out of this while he put me through test after test, but now desperation sinks in.

I have to find a way out.

I can't reach any of the surrounding trees. On the ground, there's nothing but tall grass and sand. A rock here or there. Nothing helpful for getting out of a cage.

I have nothing else except the clothes on my back. Useless, all of it.

They can't keep me in this cage forever, can they? Eventually they have to let me out to—to what? Eat? They'll feed me through the bars, no doubt. Relieve myself? Not a chance. Vordan has already been extra careful thus far. He'll no doubt expect me to go in a corner of the cage.

It's a strange thing realizing all you need is to eat and drink and you will go on living. You don't need to interact with others. You don't need to move, run, walk. You really don't even need to sleep. I can be trapped forever and go on living.

There were some days, shackled deep beneath my father's keep, when I thought that might be my life. I would live as an eternal prisoner. I refused to use my powers back then. I pretended they didn't exist. It was only when I was faced with being trapped forever or using them to escape that my father could coerce me into using them.

In the present—though I'm still hesitant to use them—I will use my abilities to survive, but they're not even an option now.

And what else do I have? Nothing at all.

Wait. No.

I have Riden. But what good is he, being injured and isolated at the moment?

I think on this as hard as I can. My mind is working so tremendously, I don't even realize when my thoughts turn into dreams. I see myself looking through the bars, watching Theris take blood from Riden as he attacks him again and again. First with his fists. Then with his sword. Finally, he pulls his pistol from his belt, puts it flush against Riden's head, and fires.

The shot rings through the air, shaking my whole body. When my eyes fly open, I realize it's not the sound of a gunshot I hear, but someone banging against my cage with a sword.

Cromis steps away from me quickly once he sees my eyes opening.

"Alosa," Vordan says, "are you ready to start another day?"

Riden is alive, though bloodied from yesterday's injuries, lying before me on the ground. He looks up at me and smiles.

Why is that idiot smiling? There is nothing to be cheerful about.

Call it what you will: confidence or conceit. But if I haven't thought of a way out of this, there's no way he has.

"Couldn't sleep, I was so excited," I say, deadpan.

"Glad to hear it," Vordan says, unfazed by my sarcasm.

The setup is as it was yesterday. Niffon and Cromis have their buckets back. Theris leans against a tree lazily, one hand on a pistol pointed at Riden, the other rotating a coin around his fingers. Vordan stands straight and sure, muscled arms grasping his parchment and charcoal. A bulge in his pocket reveals he has the map on him again, no doubt so I can be smacked in the face with his victory. I'm proved correct when he catches me staring at it and smiles.

Exhausted and aching from sleeping in a cramped cage, I look downward as I rub my eyes. A piece of fruit and slice of bread sit next to a wooden cup filled with water. Cromis must have dropped them in before waking me.

"Did you get anything to eat?" I ask Riden.

Vordan answers for him. "The boy is to be kept weak. You, however, need your strength. I expect a full day of theatrics, so eat up."

I poke at the food in front of me distastefully. What if he's drugged it?

"You have exactly one minute to eat that before I order Theris to shoot Riden."

"Do take your time," Theris adds. "It's been a while since I've shot something."

I sniff the bread. Doesn't smell funny, but if the alternative to eating it is watching Riden get shot, do I have much of a choice? I make a face as I bite into the fruit. It's not quite ripe. I swallow large mouthfuls in an attempt to avoid tasting too much. When I'm done, I rub my tongue against the bread as I chew, trying to scrape the taste off.

Riden watches me eat, smiling all the while. He had better have a plan and not simply be enjoying the fact that I'm stuffing my face for him. Otherwise, I'll have to let Theris shoot him.

When I've swallowed the last morsel, I wash the scanty meal down with the water. Since it's freshwater, it does nothing to restore my song, but I need to drink just as much as regular humans do to survive.

Vordan and Theris start discussing their plans for today, momentarily taking their attention away from me and Riden.

Riden makes a flicking motion with his hands, catching my attention.

He's moving his lips.

I glance over to the men in front of the buckets. They're watching Riden, but their heads are inclined toward Theris and Vordan's conversation. They can't be paying much attention to us.

"What?" I ask Riden, barely a whisper.

He repeats the motion. This time I have no trouble reading it. *Get ready.*

For what? I mouth back. What could he possibly do?

This time he chances a whisper. "Remember our sword fight?"

I nod. He was a cocky idiot, allowing himself to get hurt so he could win. What does that have to do with anything?

Now, he mouths.

I tense, though I don't know what I'm waiting for.

And Riden, who is unrestrained, yet injured, leaps forward toward Niffon's bucket. He cups his hands in the water as a shot goes off.

Smoke billows out of Theris's pistol. Riden collapses to the ground, holding his hands above him, trying to preserve the water cupped so carefully.

But Niffon finally jumps to action, slapping Riden's hands to force the water to the ground. He wipes Riden's hands on his own pants before tossing him back toward me, away from the water.

"Idiot," Theris says calmly. He begins reloading his pistol, applying more powder to the weapon and lodging in another iron ball.

"You idiot," I repeat, not caring if the others hear me. "This whole time I've been making sure you *don't* get shot. Shouldn't have bothered."

Riden's grasping his leg, just above his knee. His voice is heavy. "I've never been shot before. It sort of hurts . . . a lot."

I know exactly how it feels to be shot. It feels as you would expect it to. Like iron is splitting your flesh at lightning speed and wedging up against your bones.

"Try that again," Theris says, "and you'll feel it twice as strongly."

"At least they didn't kill me," Riden says, ignoring Theris.

"Except now you can't walk."

Once Theris has his weapon reloaded, he turns back to Vordan as though there was no interruption. Niffon and Cromis are much more alert, hardly taking the time to blink as they watch Riden and me.

"That was your brilliant plan?" I ask. No one seems to care that we're talking now. Riden's injured past the point of usefulness, and I'm locked up. We're hardly a threat.

"Yes," he says, swallowing a moan. "But it needs some refining."

Before I can ask what he means by that, he's crawling back toward the buckets, dragging his injured leg behind him.

Everyone halts what they're doing and stares at him.

"Look at that," Cromis says.

"Doesn't give up," Niffon adds.

"Riden, stop!" I finally find my voice, but he seems to have lost his senses entirely. Doesn't he realize they'll kill him? At the very least he's going to get shot again.

He ignores me, pulling himself onward. He's almost reached the buckets.

I hear the pistol cock back. Theris takes aim and fires.

Riden gasps before his body collapses, his head falling right into the bucket.

Niffon hauls him out and tosses him back toward me.

Riden's eyes are closed. He's not breathing. I search all along his body, trying to find where the shot struck him. Finally, I see another blood-soaked hole. Theris got him in the same leg, this time below the knee. It looks like the second shot missed the bone, streaking clean through the muscle on the side of his calf.

"Boy's got a death wish," Theris says.

"Should we kill him, Captain?" Cromis asks.

"Yes, kill him."

Niffon and Cromis stand. I fight furiously against the bars, willing them to bend. I don't want to watch Riden die. I don't want—

Riden lifts his head. I try to touch him, but he's just out of my arm's reach.

He smiles.

Cocky, little— Wait. Something's off. His face. His cheeks are too round. He looks like he might heave.

But when he opens his mouth, it is not vomit that comes spewing out. No, it's seawater. He shoots it out into my waiting hand.

"No!" Theris shouts, but it's too late. He can't reach for his wax faster than I can sing.

I pull Theris, Cromis, and Niffon under immediately. *Where is the key?* I demand of them. Theris instantly pulls the large bit of twisted metal from his pocket.

I give him an illusion. It's completely dark. He can't see a thing except for the lit match in his hands. He needs to light the candle if he wants to erase the darkness, if he wants to feel safe and calm. I am the candle, and the key to my cage is the match.

I wince as Theris knocks over the second bucket of seawater in his haste to reach me. Had I paid closer attention, I could have swerved him around it, but right now I'm going for speed rather than accuracy. The water soaks quickly into the ground. It will be long gone by the time I make it out of here. I've only got what Riden managed to get to me. I'd better make it count.

As Theris approaches, I send Cromis and Niffon to keep Vordan busy. I can only enchant three at a time. Vordan quickly stuffs the wax back in his ears before fighting for his life, one against two.

Riden's breaths are short and quick from where he lies on the ground. I wrench the key from Theris and send him to fight Vordan as well while I unlock the cage.

Vordan, deciding he can't possibly best three men at a time, turns around and runs for it.

I demand a pistol from Cromis, who is the nearest with a loaded gun. He rushes over, pulls the weapon from his side, and offers it to me. As I hold the pistol out in front of me, I slow my breathing and take aim at Vordan's back. Right where the heart rests under his skin. It's difficult because I now have to make the ball dodge Theris and Niffon.

Get out of the way! I order the two of them. As soon as they both leap aside, I fire.

The shot rings out and Vordan falls.

Riden coughs. "That was impressive, but you were wrong. I'm still the better shot."

I toss the gun aside and turn to him. I'm unable to say a word to him because I have to keep the other three occupied with my voice, but I still shake my head at his ridiculous claim.

He asks, "Can we go now? I'm sort of bleeding over here."

I shake my head once again, this time with determination. Oh no. I'm not finished with these three yet.

I quickly reach Vordan's body. Once I do, I pluck the paper detailing out my abilities from his greedy paws and tear it to shreds. Then I wrestle the map encased in glass from his pocket and place it within my own.

With that done, I take the sword from his side and turn toward the remaining three men. I have no qualms about slaughtering them while they're helpless. They were prepared to do the same thing to me.

But then another thought strikes me. *What about* Vordan's *map?*

I turn back toward his body and search him thoroughly.

The power of my voice is running out, but the map has to be right in front of me. I can't stop now. If I gave *both* maps to my father at the same time . . . I can only imagine how pleased he'd be.

I pull off Vordan's breeches and shake them out, praying to the stars that a slip of paper will fall out of them.

"What are you doing?" Riden asks weakly from far behind me.

My guess is he knows what I'm doing but is startled by the manner in which I'm doing it. I haven't the time to search Vordan carefully, and I don't see why anyone would feel the need to. I hope wild animals feast on his rotting flesh.

When I don't find the map on him, I kick his limp body.

Bastard must have it on his ship.

That's when the last of my song leaves me.

With Vordan's sword in my hand, I turn toward the three men who have regained their wits.

"This should be fun," I say.

Chapter 19

THREE SWORDS SLIDE FROM their sheaths. I pounce onto the closest man, Niffon. He deflects the blow as Cromis tries to get behind me. I jump to the side so I have both of them clearly in my sights.

"Keep her busy," Theris says. "I'm going for the rest of the crew. *Don't* let her get away."

"Stay," I tell him. I thrust at Niffon while sliding under a slash from Cromis. "I'll have all three of you face-first in the sand in no time."

He doesn't delay, rushing off along the shore in the direction Vordan's ship must be anchored.

Fine, then. I'll deal with him next time we meet.

The two pirates in front of me are good at keeping me on my toes. They strike simultaneously, hoping that one of them will be able to hit their target. The movements I have to make to dodge them are dizzying, but I don't slow down. I lash out with my sword and legs, but successfully striking one of them would require taking a hit from the other if I'm not careful. I have to wait for an opening.

It comes when they make the mistake of stepping back from me at the same time. One, to regain his footing from my last strike, the other, to get more force behind a timed blow. I fling my sword at Niffon, who was preparing to strike. I have just enough time to see my sword catch him in the neck before I turn to Cromis, who is still off balance. My closed fist pummels into his stomach. When he doubles over in pain, I take his own sword from him and use it to help him take his last breath.

When both men lie dead at my feet, I try to get my sights on Theris, but he is long gone. I don't know how much time I have, but I do know Theris will bring reinforcements. I won't be able to fight a whole crew of men.

With an angry exhale, I rush back over to Riden's side.

"Don't mind me," he says through quickened breaths. "I'm only bleeding to death."

"You're fine," I tell him. "Unless we don't get off this island right away."

Riden is not too heavy for me to hold up, but his injuries

make the journey to the water impossibly slow. We're racing against Theris and the rest of Vordan's crew. I can't make out footfalls over the wind, but that doesn't mean they're not there.

When at last we break through the trees and see the shoreline, I hurry our pace, despite Riden's grunts of pain. We're so close now.

But of course there's no boat or other means of keeping us afloat in sight.

"We'll have to swim for it," Riden says.

"We can't," I say, anxiety creeping into my voice. I use the sleeve on my free arm to wipe the sweat from my brow. All the singing and fighting have taken their toll. "I can't be submerged in the water. It's too much. I won't be able to help taking it in."

"It's our only option. Theris will be back any instant."

I hesitate still.

"I can't swim by myself, Alosa," Riden says.

I look at him. For some reason, he was enough to keep me sane during my interrogation with Vordan. I hope he's enough for this, too.

"You won't need to. I'll do all the work. I just hope I still remember you while I do it." I survey his cuts. "This is going to sting."

Riden and I plunge into the waves, wading out until the water reaches our knees. Riden hisses through his teeth when the salt water reaches his first gunshot wound.

"Take a deep breath," I say, even as the water starts filling me. I feel myself changing, inside and out.

And with no more hesitation, I pull him under with me and begin to swim.

My heart races. Pure joy surges through me to feel so full, to be surrounded by the sea. To a human, it would be freezing cold. But not to me. It is soothing and revitalizing and refreshing. I can feel strength and health pouring into me as I start swimming at an impossibly fast pace.

And I can feel my body change.

My hair lengthens, takes on a life of its own as it swirls and whips through the water. My skin whitens, changing from the tan color the sun gave me to the color of white pearls. My nails lengthen and sharpen ever so slightly. I can breathe even while under the water. I can move effortlessly through it. I can see as well as if I were on land, night or day. I feel connected to the sea life around me. The snails on the rocks deep below me. The fish swimming far to the right. The plants swaying in the light current below. Even the tiny creatures that can't be seen with my eyes. I can still feel them.

I want nothing more than to swim and simply enjoy the feel of the water flowing by me as I propel myself forward.

But a weight prohibits my swim.

I almost forgot. There's a man with me. His eyes are open, even through the salty water. He's watching me with clear astonishment.

As he should. I am power and beauty. I am song and water. I rule the sea and all creatures within it.

The man points upward. Then he gestures to his throat. A trail of blood mixes in the water, flowing behind us. A nearby acura eel smells it, but then it senses me and flees in the other direction.

The man shakes me, gripping my arm. I return my attention to him. Ah, he is drowning. He needs air if he is to survive.

I will relish watching him squirm and drown. It'll be an enjoyable spectacle as I continue to swim and become one with the soothing waters. Perhaps I'll dance with his lifeless body afterward.

He begins kicking his feet, trying to reach the surface on his own, but his injuries are too great for him to manage it, and my grip is too strong for him to ever get away.

Finally, he stops struggling. Instead he puts his hands on either side of my face, straining to look into my eyes. He presses his lips to mine once before he is still.

At that simple motion, something awakens inside me. *Riden.* This is the man who got himself shot by helping me escape from Vordan, and now I'm letting him drown.

Instantly, I swim for the surface. He's not breathing, even above the water. I need to get him to land. I sense around me for interruptions in the water, looking for something large that resists the flow of the natural currents around me. There is a ship not too far off. Riden's ship. They must be searching for him.

Faster than anything else in the water, I swim for the ship. Like a bird in the air, I pass through effortlessly, mounting league after league.

I'm swimming toward my other captors yet again, but I cannot hand myself over to them without a plan of escape. Panic sets in. There's no time. Every second that passes is a second that brings Riden closer to death. I need to get to the ship now.

I don't halt my movements toward the ship, but I submerge my head and start singing. From below the water my voice is clear. Clear and sharp as a bell. It travels fast, reaching the ears of those on the *Night Farer*. The power of my song is limitless when I am in the ocean. The sea keeps nourishing me, feeding me so I never tire.

Reaching out toward the ship, I prepare the men for what is to come. They need to be ready for us. We cannot waste a second. I still can control only three men at a time, so I first reach out to Kearan, telling him to move the ship in our direction. Then I find Enwen and Draxen. I bring them to the ship's edge and hold Riden up, so it will be him that Draxen sees first.

"Lower a rope!" Draxen commands immediately.

As his men hasten to obey, I let out one more verse. This time I reach even farther out.

I'm forced to swim to the right, dodging the large knotted

rope that splashes me with water as it reaches its end. My body changes as soon as I'm hoisted out of the water, so quickly that no one can take notice. None can see my siren form unless they peer through the water, and I think it's safe to say that they were too far away to notice. But that is hardly a concern for me at the moment.

Draxen's men haul us up quickly. There must be at least five of them tugging on the rope. I have to grip the edge of the railing once I get to the top—it's difficult while holding on to Riden's weight as well. Otherwise they would have hauled me all the way over, and I probably would have broken a finger or my wrist as it jammed into the railing.

Draxen grabs Riden and lays him down on the ship's deck. I'm about to step forward to help when I'm seized by what feels like twenty men.

"Go grab Holdin!" he orders. Someone runs belowdecks.

"The ship's doctor can't help him," I snap.

I'm momentarily distracted by the filthy fingers at my body. They probe and push, straying to places they shouldn't. Places hardly necessary for restraining me. My muscles hurt from the strain. My pride hurts from the whole scene.

"What did you do to him?" Draxen demands.

That's it. I don't care if the whole crew witnesses this. They're about to die anyway. I slam my abilities into Draxen, ordering him to make his men let me go.

His crew hears me singing; they're perplexed enough by

that. But once Draxen orders them to let me go, they're dumbfounded.

He has to repeat himself, more loudly this time, before they listen. They must decide I'm not behind the change if they still obeyed Draxen's order. Good.

I rush to Riden, sit on the cold deck, and place a hand on either side of his head. I lower my head as though going in for a kiss. I need to force air back into his lungs. Plugging his nose with the fingers of my right hand, I blow into his mouth, willing the air to reach down into his lungs.

I wait a moment and then try again. Five times I do this, and nothing changes.

"No," I say, barely a whisper. I lie on top of his body, placing my head against his chest, a silent plea for it to start moving up and down, for his lungs to work, for his body to keep the life within.

This can't be happening. Not after he rescued me. Not after he let himself get shot to help me. He can't die now.

But there is water in his lungs. I can sense it beneath my cheek. And if I could just get it out . . .

I place my hands against his chest to make it look as though I'm using them to force the water from his lungs, but I know at this point they're useless.

I sing, so softly that only Riden can hear, were he awake. I tell his mind to stay alert. I beg the organs to remain steady. I cannot heal his wounds. I cannot speed up or change anything.

I can only reach his mind. I tell him not to give up. Not yet. He's not allowed to die.

When I've expelled some of the song from me, I pull at the water beneath me, the water in Riden's lungs. I cannot touch it, but I can sense it. And I *demand* that it come to me.

It does not move.

But I dig my fingers into Riden's chest, and pull—both physically and mentally. I will him back to life with every essence of myself.

And finally, the water sways upward. It drifts out of the lungs, through his flesh, sweats out of his skin, and comes into me.

"Now breathe!" I say and sing at the same time. I blow air into his mouth once more. Demand that his lungs start working. Riden's heart still beats, so if I can convince his lungs to pump on their own, he will be all right. He *has* to be all right.

Riden gasps, heaving in the loudest breath I have ever heard. It reminds me of a newborn babe taking its first breath. It is the sound of life.

I lean away from him and take a moment to breathe myself.

In seconds, they are upon me. Draxen must have regained his senses. A blade is shoved under my throat. Another presses against my stomach, digging in enough to scratch the skin. I can't even muster up the strength to care. Riden is alive. That's all that matters. His eyes are closed and his wounds still bleed. But he will survive.

"What would you like done with her, Captain?" one of the offending pirates asks.

"Take her back to the brig. I want five men down there watching her at all times. She's not to be given food or water. And don't talk to her."

Like a caged bird, I'm locked up. Again.

I'm really starting to hate this.

Chapter 20

THERE ISN'T A WORD for how cold I feel in the brig. Now that I can afford to think about myself, I register the effect of wet clothes and the brisk morning air. Small gaps in the wood allow faint breezes to escape into the ship. They rake against my skin, sending me racking with shivers.

My extra changes of clothes are no longer in here. I've no idea what Riden's done with them. Maybe the other pirates took them once my cell was unlocked. Fabric can be sold at a pretty price, and pirates are always looking to make a profit.

I sit on the floor, my arms wrapped around my legs. My toes have gone numb. I remove my boots and rub at them fiercely with my hands.

The men outside my cell do nothing. They hardly spare me a glance. Draxen was obviously responsible for this lot being chosen to watch me. They won't respond to any of my comments.

"Is it Draxen's intention for me to die or can I get a blanket?

"Oi, Ugly, I'm talking to you."

One man looks. His face reddens, and then he goes back to staring at the walls.

"How's it that Draxen managed to find a whole group of deaf men as my guards?

"Get me a blasted blanket, or I'll have your heads!

"Don't suppose one of you would like to toss me your shirt?" At this point I would take any foul-smelling garment, as long as it's dry.

Eventually I try to force myself to dry. I run in circles, wave my arms about—anything to get my blood pumping. But each thing I do sends more air onto my raw skin. I wish I were back in the water.

I remove as much clothing as I dare in this company.

How is there still water on my skin? How can there be so much of it? The truly terrible part is I could whisk it away, but I don't know what the consequences would be. Would I lose myself and become the siren? Or could I manage to keep my head like I did those few times with Riden's help? I don't know, but at this point, I can't risk it. Not with what's about to come.

I don't know how much time passes before I give up being

quite so careful. I sing a low tune to the man who looked up at my taunt. He seems to be the weak one of the bunch. *Get me a blanket!* I hurl the words at him in the form of a harsh song. Only he can hear the intent of the song. To the others, I'm making meaningless noise.

Abruptly, he gets up and leaves.

"Where yeh going?" another one asks him. He doesn't receive a response.

The enchanted man returns shortly. He hands me a blanket through the bars. "Just to get you to shut up," I have him say, to throw off any suspicions the others might have.

"About bloody time," I say. I rip the cloth from his hands and use it to wipe the water from my skin. Then I wrap myself in it. So much better. I can actually think clearly.

All I need now is to wait out the rest of the day. Possibly the night, too. I don't know how long it will take.

Yesterday and this morning have thoroughly exhausted me. I drift in and out of sleep. First I dream of Riden. He's healthy and well. He tells me again he's a better shot than I am. We take turns shooting at dummies. In the end, he wins. But this makes me realize this is a dream. In reality, he couldn't possibly beat me.

Then I dream of my father. He's demanding the map. Screaming at me from where I rest behind bars, refusing to let me out until I produce it. I search through my clothes, where I know I've put the map, but it's mysteriously not there. He tells me I'll never see the outside of the cell. The bars start moving closer, crushing my skin.

I gasp out loud. The men on the other side of the bars snort before going back to their dice and drinking.

A few moments later, I slink into blissful sleep once again, thinking about the last song I uttered before being pulled back aboard this ship.

It won't be long now.

∝

I wake to the sound of gunshots. A huge smile stretches across my face.

It's time.

"All hands on deck!" Draxen shouts from above. My guards all hurry up the stairs, leaving me alone below.

After flipping over the table in my cell, I check the leg for my lockpicks. They're still here. All that time and Riden couldn't figure out how I got out of my cell.

The fight above is loud. There's screaming and grunting. Swinging limbs and clanging metal. Cursing and collapsing.

Eventually, I hear rapid stomping; it's distinct from the rest of the ongoing battle. Probably because it's closer. If I had to guess, I'd say someone rolled down the stairs. Shame, that. Probably will hurt like mad the next day if the poor bastard isn't already dead.

"Captain, you down here?"

"Over here!" I shout back.

Niridia's face comes into view, followed by two more members of my crew. I could jump for how glad I am to see them.

"Got your beckonings. Wallov came to me the moment he heard you singing," she says. She looks me up and down. "You can't be in a good mood. You look terrible."

I cringe. "Don't remind me."

Niridia grins. She's one of the most beautiful women I've ever seen, but that's not why she's my first mate. We met five years ago, both the daughters of pirates. Niridia's my senior by one year, but she follows orders and fights nearly as well as I do. With hair the color of the sun and bright blue eyes, she's a complete contradiction, as anyone who's seen her fight can attest.

"How's the situation up top?" I ask.

"Shipshape, Captain," Niridia says. "Tylon's men have nearly half of them on their backs already."

"Tylon's here?" Venom creeps into my voice.

"Sorry. He caught me leaving. I didn't tell him where I was going, but he followed."

"Bloody hell, that man needs to learn to mind his own business."

"You know how he is."

Yes, but I'm still going to have a long talk with him when this is all done. Tylon captains one of the ships in my father's fleet. And lately he's gotten it into his head that the two of us need to be . . . involved. A notion my father no doubt persuaded him of. I, however, want nothing to do with the arrogant piss pot.

"Wouldn't be too harsh on him, Captain. His men helped a few of the girls up top when they were in a tight spot."

"I'm sure. And how many times did the girls have to assist his idiotic crew?"

"Plenty."

"I thought so."

"Shall we go join the fight, then?" Mandsy asks eagerly from where she stands between Niridia and Sorinda.

"Sword?" I ask.

"Here, Captain." This from Sorinda. The raven-haired girl produces my sword out of seemingly nowhere. Sorinda hides more weapons on her than a spy does secrets.

Ah, my cutlass. One of the first gifts my father ever gave me. I had Sorinda hold on to it for me while I went on my mission. I can see she took good care of it. There's no one I'd trust more with a weapon than Sorinda.

Seeing them again warms me. Now I want nothing more than to be back on my ship, but first things first.

"Let's help the boys and girls upstairs, shall we?"

"Aye," they all respond together.

We trod above deck and engage in the fight. It's utter chaos. I have only a moment to register friend from foe as I try to remember the faces of all the men from the *Night Farer*. This would be far easier if Tylon's men weren't mixed in with Draxen's. Instead of simply killing all the men on the ship, I now have to be wary of the pirates who serve under my father in Tylon's crew. To be fair, a couple of the men are mine. But I know every member of my ship so well, it'd be impossible for me to mistake them for anyone else.

There are people still trying to board the ship, eager to join the battle. Draxen and his men don't stand a chance, but they're putting up a fight. Most of them are, anyway. I see Kearan sitting on the deck, drinking, not a care in the world. Not much of a fighter, that one.

I spot Draxen. He's fighting two of Tylon's men at once. For a moment, I wish one of them would kill him. Riden can't blame me for that, and I do so want to see him dead. But I know that no matter by whose hand he falls, Riden will still hurt from the loss. I hate that I keep proving Vordan right. I care about Riden's pain. I don't know why, but I do.

Before my eyes, Draxen slays one of Tylon's men. The other steps back a couple of feet. Then he advances with a new fury. Bad move, that. The poor man's not thinking clearly. He will only join his friend.

Draxen kills him, too. The pirate falls to the deck as Tylon boards the ship. Seeing a man kill one of your own men is a terrible sight. It helps you pick your targets during a battle. And Tylon races for Draxen immediately.

This needs to stop. Now.

Tylon is an excellent fighter. He's been pirating a good six years of his life, ever since he was a lad of twelve. Now he's one of my father's most trusted men and a good match for any pirate captain. I couldn't say who would win in a fight.

This makes me unaccountably nervous. I can't risk Tylon winning, but how would it look if I intervened?

Oh, for stars' sake!

I race forward, jumping between the two men who are still a good ten feet from each other.

"Alosa," I hear Tylon say from behind me.

I ignore him for now. "Draxen, you need to stop this. Tell your men to surrender, or more will die."

Draxen looks at me, his eyes filled with blood lust. Surrendering is the last thing he will consider, even at the cost of the lives of all his men. He advances toward me, determined to end me once and for all.

I'll just have to knock him out again. But how will it look to everyone else if I don't kill him?

Suddenly, Draxen's eyes are no longer on me, and I hear swords drop to the deck.

What the—

I turn around, though I already suspect what I'll find.

The pirate king has arrived.

I look around the ship, spot Niridia, and catch her eye. The message conveyed in the look I give her is obvious. *Did you do this?* She shakes her head once. *No.*

My next action is to kick Tylon in the shin.

"Ow," he says.

"You brought him here?"

"Of course. You obviously called for help. Why wouldn't I bring him here?"

"Because we don't need his help." I make a sound akin to a growl. Then I advance to the ship's edge. "Hello, Father."

"Do you have it?" he asks. He does not look pleased. My father is a bear of a man. Dark brown hair and beard. Wide-set shoulders. Over six feet tall. You don't have to meet him beforehand to know who he is. My father commands attention in the same way the winds command the waves.

"Of course," I respond.

I reach a hand into the single pocket on my breeches and pull out the small orb. Draxen was so concerned for his brother's life, he did not think to check me for the map again. He might not have even realized it was no longer in his possession.

In a very businesslike manner, I place the map into my father's waiting hands. He looks over the glass, confirming I've given him what he wants.

"Now explain yourself. Why did you call Niridia?"

Everything is silent, halted. All the men and women hold

Draxen's crew at gun- or sword-point. My father doesn't care about their discomfort. He'll take as much time as he wants to question me. It's as if everything stops for him. It has always been this way.

"I needed a way off the ship. I had the map and needed a way to transport it."

He looks at me, slightly disbelieving. "Why didn't you bring this ship to me?" Before I can answer, he holds up a hand to silence me. "Niridia?"

"Aye, sir!" Niridia shouts from where she has two men held at gunpoint.

"Tell me, where did you find my daughter when you boarded the ship?"

"She was—"

"In the brig," I interject. Niridia would lie for me. She'd die for me, too. And in this case, they would be the same thing. My father may do many things to me, but I know he would never kill me. He would not show the same courtesy to anyone who lied to him.

"It was a minor setback," I say. "I was kidnapped off this ship. Vordan Serad came for me."

"Vordan?" My father's face darkens. He has a deep contempt for his competitors. "How did he know you were here?"

"He had a spy on the ship."

"What did he want with you?"

"He was curious about my . . . skills. He locked me up and

284

forced me to do things for him." I try to keep the conversation as unrevealing as possible since we have listening ears.

"What did he learn?"

"A lot, I'm afraid. But he already knew most of it. Said he had a spy high up in your ranks."

My father's eyes pass over his men quickly. "Be that the case, I will deal with it later. Was your escape difficult?"

I hold myself straight. "I handled it fine."

"And Vordan?"

"Dead."

"Did you search his body for his map?"

"Aye. It wasn't there, and the circumstances of my escape didn't allow me time to do a search of the area."

"Really?" my father asks doubtfully. He has trouble seeing how others are unable to complete even the most difficult of tasks. "And why was that?"

Because I had to get Riden away to safety. "His whole crew was nearby. They were being alerted to my escape. I did not have time on my side."

"Time?"

I'm really starting to hate his prying questions. They always unnerve me, but I try to keep my temper in check. My father is a good man. He has to keep a tough face in front of the crew, even during his dealings with me.

"It was difficult enough taking down Vordan's massive bulk and escaping. I needed to get out of there."

Now Kalligan looks at me strangely; I cannot guess the reason for it. "Describe Vordan to me."

"He was tall," I say. "Over six feet. Well-muscled. Bald on top with a brown beard. Had five gold hoops in his left ear—"

"That wasn't Vordan."

"What do you mean?"

"Vordan is an unremarkable man. Average looks and build. Brown hair. Casual clothes. He likes to blend in, in a crowd. Although, he does have a rather obvious habit. Likes to flip a coin over his fingers."

My mind feels as though it physically expands as the information seeps into my ears. My jaw drops.

"Clever bastard!" I exclaim.

"What?" my father asks.

"He was there. *He was here*. He was the spy on the ship. He wanted to observe me for himself, but he didn't want me to know who he was, so he let one of his men pretend to be him. He ensured that all the attention was kept away from himself." That's why he was the one who had the key to my cell. And he would have been the one carrying the final map piece.

Father looks up suddenly. He grabs me by the arm and hauls me to the side just as Draxen lands right where we'd been standing, his sword pointed at the pirate king. He must have climbed the netting when all the attention was on my father and me.

Damn idiot! If I'm bothering to save his sorry arse, Draxen could at least make it easy for me!

My father's men move forward, prepared to protect their king.

"No," he tells them, holding up his hands to halt them. "I'll handle the boy." He draws his sword and prepares to duel.

"Father," I say hurriedly.

"What?" He keeps his eyes on Draxen, but I can see the look of annoyance on his face.

"Death by your hand is too good for him and his crew. Let me take them captive." I smile in a way I hope is convincing now that Father's glanced my way. "I'd like to return the courtesy they have shown me while I was aboard their ship." It shouldn't matter to me if Draxen dies, or anyone else in his crew, but it does.

I wish I could sweeten the deal with a little song. But my powers of persuasion don't work on my father, unfortunately. Actually, none of my abilities work on him. He's the only man I've ever met who is immune to all my abilities (though I now know my powers of seduction don't work on men like Vordan—or whoever that man was pretending to be Vordan). It probably has to do with the fact that he's my father. His blood runs through my veins.

Kalligan finally looks at me with approval, and it warms me to see that look on his face. "Very well. Take who you will. Kill the rest. Can't have any of them going free. Dump their bodies in the sea and bring me back this ship."

"Aye, sir."

"And when you're done and cleaned up, come find me. I'm expecting a full report." The pirate king leaves the ship, taking his men with him. Tylon and his men follow.

My crew have already removed all the weapons from Draxen's men. They are now moved before me in a line and forced to their knees. Several of my girls have to wrestle Draxen's sword from him. Even though he's surrounded, he still won't go down without a fight. But he's forced to the ground in line with everyone else.

I survey them slowly, letting the fear sink in. I have experienced a great many things while on this ship that I'd rather forget. These men will not suffer the same misfortunes. They'll only face death or imprisonment. So a little fear is healthy for them right now.

"This feels oddly familiar," I say to the pirates who are now at my mercy. I knew this day would come; I just hadn't expected it to feel so good. "Who wants to live? Should I be merciful? Or should I kill you all like you tried to do with my crew when you captured me?" I address that last part to Draxen specifically.

"Do what you will, woman," Draxen says, spitting on the deck.

I hadn't expected him to face death so nobly. "Your men should be disappointed that you don't even try to bargain for their lives."

"If it's all the same," one pirate pipes up, "I'd prefer to live." This from Kearan.

I smile. "Very well. Wallov, Deros, take this pirate to the brig." Wallov and Deros are the only two men in my crew. They are all muscle, both of them, and they're handy dealing with prisoners. Particularly large ones like Kearan. But their muscles are not the only things that make them useful. I need at least one man on my ship at all times. Men are the only ones who can hear my song. Or at least be affected by it. When I'm parted from my crew, it's good to always have a way to contact them quickly when they're within reach of my song.

"Take this one, too," I order, pointing to Enwen. "And the captain. Also, you should find an injured man, suffering from two gunshot wounds in the rooms off the main deck. Take him to the ship as well. Mandsy?"

"Aye, Captain?"

"See to him, will you?"

"Of course."

I order several more to be brought over, a few of the really young ones. It's harder to allow such youth to be taken from the world so easily. I'll let them go at the next port, and Kalligan will be none the wiser.

But the others, those who were cruel to me, those who are truly despicable lowlifes, like Ulgin—those I want to see rotting at the bottom of the sea.

"Kill the rest," I say.

Sorinda is the first to take out her sword. She starts stepping behind the men and slitting their throats one after the other.

Killing is practically an art for her. The way she moves is magical.

Everyone hurries to follow orders. The prisoners are taken over to the ship. I arrange for a few of my crew to stay aboard the *Night Farer* to steer her toward the meeting place. The bodies are dumped overboard, and everyone returns to their positions.

It is only when everything is sorted out that I can return to my own ship. When I finally step onto the deck of the *Ava-lee*, the taste of freedom hits me. I was never really a prisoner while on the *Night Farer*, of course, but there's something truly sweet about being home again.

Chapter 21

I TRAIL MY HANDS along the wooden railing as I walk. It was damaged once during a battle against a ship that tried to desert my father's fleet. A cannon from my ship tore through the opposing vessel's mizzenmast, and the whole thing managed to come down onto my ship, tearing through the railing and denting the deck. The crew and I quickly sailed for the island of Butana, where we stole wooden planks from the island's fine lumberyards. Nearly lost a member of the crew, too. Men with saws and axes chased us away, but even carrying heavy wooden planks, we still all made it out alive. We rebuilt the railing ourselves and replaced the damaged planks in the deck.

Each piece of this ship has a story. Each piece was fought

hard for and earned. It makes the whole so much more reward-ing, because it took so much effort to put her together.

I love my ship almost as much as I love my crew.

I see the door to my quarters, and I feel a strong pull in that direction, but I ignore it. There will be time to get comfortable later.

"Hiya, Cap'n," a tiny voice says from above. Roslyn sways down from a rope until her bare feet hit the ground. The wee lass is more stable swinging through the air than she is on flat ground.

I ruffle the girl's hair as I take in the faces of all my crew, promising myself that there will be time to catch up with every-one later. But there are a few things that must be settled first.

"Niridia," I say. No matter where I am on the ship, my first mate always manages to hear me. I swear I could whisper to her from down below and she'd hear me from the crow's nest. It's a fantastic ability of her own.

"Aye, Captain?" she asks, materializing in front of me.

"How many dead in the skirmish?"

"Don't beat yourself up over it. When there is fighting to be done, good men and women will be lost. And there's not one on this ship who isn't willing to die for you."

"How many?" I repeat.

"Two."

"Who?"

"Zimah and Mim."

292

I close my eyes and picture their faces in my mind. Zimah was one of the three who volunteered to come with me on the journey to get myself kidnapped by Draxen. She was a great tracker and a fine conversationalist. She had all kinds of stories to share about the places she'd been. I loved listening to her. Mim had a good pair of hands on her. Always willing to do what I asked, glad no matter what it was. A mighty fine pirate. I shall miss them both dearly. I hate to think it was because I called for help that the two of them died. I realize every man and woman knows what they sign up for when they join the crew, but still. I hate the constant losses that come with pirating.

"We will light candles for them tonight," I say.

"Already sent the order to Roslyn."

"Good." As captain, I have to push aside losses and focus on what's best for the crew. I hate that part, too. "We'll need a new navigator. Someone who can track and knows the lands and waters well."

Niridia nods.

A crazy thought comes to me. "I know just the man."

"Man?" Niridia asks. "Didn't you swear after Ralin that you'd never take on another man for the crew so long as we already had one?"

"Oh, don't remind me about Ralin. Couldn't keep his hands off the crew, that one. Despicable creature."

"He was a bit more bearable once you cut them off."

"Yes, shame he decided to leave our employ after that. Can't imagine what that was about."

Niridia smiles. "Some men don't have the stomach for being pirates."

"This one, if he's willing, should be well cut out for the job. He's more interested in his drink than in the girls. And he's so slow, he wouldn't be able to catch any of the women."

"Sounds like a fine specimen. How could we turn down such an able-bodied man?"

I laugh. "I missed you, Niridia."

"Missed you, too, Captain."

"I need to go belowdecks, but I should be back shortly. Get us going, will you? I want to get to the checkpoint as quickly as possible."

"Of course."

It doesn't seem right that the first place I should go once boarding my own ship, the *Ava-lee*, is the brig. I've spent so much time in cages, cells, and other forms of entrapment over the last month. It's hardly the sight I want to be met with now.

But there is lots to do, and why waste time?

Besides, Draxen's in my brig, and I want to gloat.

I tread belowdecks. The sound of my feet pounding on the wooden steps is much sweeter than when Riden was dragging me belowdecks on the *Night Farer*. Freedom is a sound unlike any other. And my ship is so much prettier. I doubt I could find its likeness anywhere.

The cells are all full. I like to keep the prisoners as separated as possible. Less chance of escaping that way. As it is, some have to share, two men to a cell. Not Draxen, though. He's the one to be especially wary of. He's all the way down on the end by himself.

I probably kept more of Draxen's crew than I should have. There will be plenty of opportunities for getting rid of them. Ideally, before Trianne runs out of food to make in the kitchen. Men are more expensive to feed.

Wallov and Deros stand to attention once I enter the brig. Draxen looks pointedly away from me.

"Why so sullen, Draxen?" I ask. "You got the best cell."

He ignores me. I smile as I look to my men.

"Good to see you, Captain," Wallov says. "Roslyn's been asking after you for quite some time."

"How is she coming with her letters?"

"Quite well. Likes to read everything in sight."

"Glad to hear it. It's good to see you both again. Sadly, I must cut the chatting short. We will have plenty of time to celebrate finding the map and to catch up later tonight. Right now, would you kindly bring me out that one?" I ask, pointing at a cell in the middle.

"The large one, Captain?"

"Aye."

"Sure thing."

They both enter the cell, Deros standing near the door

while Wallov goes in all the way. There are two pirates in this cell. The younger one stands up and tries to give Wallov some trouble, but Wallov shoves him backward, sending him to the ground and leaving a free trail to Kearan.

Kearan's slumped on the floor, but he stands quickly. "No need for force, mate. I've got no reason not to come willingly."

Wallov lets him walk back on his own, but he keeps an eye on Kearan. He's got strong arms and sharp eyes, that Wallov.

Deros locks the cell back up while Wallov brings Kearan to me. I'm standing back over by the entryway to the brig. No need for all the pirates to hear what I'm about to offer him. Might give them all the wrong idea. For Kearan is one of only two men I intend to recruit.

"Kearan?"

"Yes?" he asks, not bothering to tack on any sort of civil title. Even in such a dire situation, he has his come-what-may attitude.

"One of my good women died in the skirmish. A spot's opened up on my crew. I could use a navigator like yourself. Are you interested?"

"It's been only a month since you tried to kill me. Now you want to hire me?" He doesn't look confused or scared or even grateful. Just bored.

"I know. I'm questioning it myself."

"What'll happen if I say no?"

"You'll stay down here until I either kill you or ... well,

killing you is probably the only option." I don't want to tell him I'd let him go. He can't think he has too many options. Besides, once he spends some time on my ship, he won't regret the decision.

"With such gracious options like those, how can I choose?"

I cross my arms. "I think I'm being more than fair. You're lazy, and you wouldn't need to contribute all that often."

"In the meantime, will I stay down here?"

"No, you'll be on probation, free to roam the ship with a guard trailing you. Once I feel I can trust you, I'll remove that."

Kearan scratches at the stubble on his face, thinking it over.

I add, "We have a rather large rum storage."

"I'll do it."

"I thought you might say that. Now, report up top. Go introduce yourself to the helmsman."

"Aye." He starts to leave.

"Kearan." I stop him.

"Yes?"

"You will address me as 'Captain' from now on."

He looks down at the floor for a moment, as though this might change his mind. Finally, he says, "Aye, Captain."

"Good."

He leaves, and I grab Wallov's attention again. "Now I need that one. The man with the pearls."

Enwen is the only one in the cell. He comes strolling out as soon as it opens.

"Miss Alosa," he says. "I see the bracelet brought you luck after all."

"What?"

He points to my foot. I forgot completely that he'd tied his "siren charm" there. "Got you your freedom, didn't it? And I know my pearls still work because I'm here safe and sound on your ship. Are yeh a believer yet?"

"I'm afraid I don't believe in luck. Just skill."

"Sometimes I think they're the same thing."

I'm not sure what he means by that, but I don't really care at the moment. "It so happens I could use a good thief. Would you be willing to join my crew?"

He smiles. "Course. Don't care much where I sail, so long as there is plenty of coin to be found."

"Don't worry. I promise that where we're going, there will be more money than you can even fathom."

Enwen licks his lips. "In that case, I promise to be the best thief you've ever seen."

"Good. Report up top, then."

"Aye-aye."

As he disappears above deck, I realize I should have mentioned that he leave the thieving for when he's off the ship. Best not forget next time I see him.

I survey the remaining prisoners before speaking up. "The rest of you will remain here until I decide what to do with you. You needn't fear for your lives unless you try to escape." I look at Draxen during the last bit. "Then you have great need to worry."

Draxen stands. "What of my brother?"

"My best healer is seeing to his wounds."

"If anything happens to him, I'll kill you."

"Draxen, empty threats are useless. Your brother is in my care, and whatever I decide to do with him will be done. There is nothing you can do to change it. Understand?"

I may have made it sound a bit worse than it is, but I don't care. After so much time spent near Draxen, he should be glad I'm letting him keep his life.

I start for the surface, following after the two new members of my crew.

Though the pain of our loss is great, I think Kearan and Enwen will be nice additions. I have plenty of good fighters on the ship, but skilled thieves and navigators are hard to come by.

I breach the top and am greeted by the bright sun. It is a fine day with few clouds in the sky. The wind blows my hair over my shoulders. It's perfect for sailing.

I stop short when I find Kearan frozen in place, facing the stern.

"Kearan?" I ask, poking him in the back. He doesn't move.

I swivel around so I can look at his face. He's staring at something ahead. Attempting to follow his gaze, I can only guess he's looking at the aftercastle.

"Kearan?" I try again.

He opens his mouth, closes it again to swallow, and tries again. "Who is that?"

Oh, he's looking at a person. I take another look. "Niridia? That's my first mate at the helm."

He shakes his head. "Not her. The dark beauty in the shadows."

I look again. I hadn't even noticed Sorinda hiding in the shadow cast by the end sail. "That's Sorinda."

He doesn't look away. As far as I can tell, he hasn't blinked. "And what is her job on the ship?"

I smile. "She's my assassin."

"I want her to be the one to supervise me."

"What?"

"You said I was on probation and I would be supervised for a time. I want it to be her."

I have never heard Kearan talk so clearly. His words are usually accompanied by the slur that comes with constant drunkenness.

"Did you hear the part where I said she's my assassin? Don't mess with her. She'll kill you before you have time to blink."

"Then it shouldn't be a problem. She can make sure I don't step out of line."

Not twenty minutes ago, I assured Niridia that Kearan was more interested in his drink than in the girls. It appears I spoke too soon.

But to be honest, I'm dying to see how this turns out.

"Sorinda!" I shout.

She doesn't move her stance, but I see her eyes shift toward me.

"Come down here." I wave her over.

Like a cat, she slinks out of the shadows. Rather than taking the companionway, she leaps over the railing and lands without making a sound.

She is, as Kearan described, a dark beauty. Long black hair. Thin with elegantly pointed features. Though she's constantly trying to hide, when she comes into the light, there are few who stand out more. Niridia is an obvious beauty with features that almost look painted. Sorinda is like something forged out of nature. One of the beauties that only comes out at night.

She doesn't answer once she reaches us. She simply waits for me to speak.

Kearan stares at her openly. Sorinda pretends not to notice.

"This is Kearan. He's joined our crew. Going to be our new navigator. Right now he's on probation. Will you keep an eye on him for me?"

"I always have an eye on everyone."

I smile. "I know, but this one is officially your responsibility."

She sizes up Kearan. Her expression never changes much. It's always impossible to tell what she's feeling. But now her lips curve downward slightly. Kearan may be large and ugly, but there's no denying he's good at what he does—so long as he is properly motivated to do it.

"Very well," she says at last.

"Good. Now if you'll excuse me, I have one more prisoner to see."

Though Draxen's ship is bigger than mine, I've opted for more rooms up top rather than larger captain's quarters for myself. Since I actually care about my crew, I've had a room fashioned for treating injuries.

This is the one I start for.

On my way, I spot Enwen at the port side railing, surveying the crew. He's less of a concern to me than Kearan. I'll have someone keep an eye on him, but that can be sorted out later.

Mandsy leans over the cushioned table in the room, where Riden lies on his back, asleep. His breeches have been sheared at the thighs to allow easy access to the pistol wounds. The room smells of ointments and blood.

"How is he?" I ask.

"Things are looking really good, Captain. The ball has already been removed from his thigh. The shot at his calf went clean through. I bandaged him up as best I could, including the lighter cuts and stabs on his arms."

Something inside me relaxes, and breathing comes more easily. "Good. Has he been conscious at all?"

"Yes. He woke up once and looked at me funny."

"Did he say anything?"

"He said, 'You don't have red hair.' Then he fell back asleep."

She smiles knowingly. "He was awfully disappointed I wasn't you, Captain."

"Nonsense. There are plenty of redheaded women."

"If you say so."

"Alosa?" The voice is faint and unsteady.

"Riden." I step up to the head of the table so I'm in his line of vision.

"I'll just leave you two for a moment," Mandsy says.

"Yes, thank you, Mands."

She closes the door behind her.

His face is pale, but his chest still rises and falls, filling with air then releasing it. I never truly appreciated that motion until now. His arms and legs are covered in bandages. There's barely more skin than white strips of cloth.

"How do you feel?" I ask.

"Like I got shot. Twice."

"If you weren't so injured already, I'd beat you for what you did back there."

"Freeing us?"

I shake my head. "No, you idiot. Getting yourself shot! Twice!"

"Pain goes away eventually," he says. "Death is permanent."

"You're awfully lucid for a man who was shot."

He smiles before his face turns to seriousness. "I'm sorry for what those men did to you. I can't possibly know how awful it was for you, but I imagine it was horrific."

I look at him incredulously.

"What?"

"Do you see me?" I ask.

"Yes. What—"

"I'm standing. I have no injuries. No *gunshot wounds*, and you think *I* had a horrific time? I'm fine." Although I'm furious that Theris—the real Vordan—is still alive.

"How is my brother?" Riden asks.

"He's in my brig."

"Alive?"

"Yes, alive! You think I want a corpse stinking up the place?"

"Thank you, Alosa."

I wave him off like it's nothing. "I trust you find your own accommodations satisfying?" I ask when the silence becomes too long.

"I'm on a table."

"Yes, but it's the only thing in the room aside from Mandsy's case of healing supplies. Not a mess in sight. There's nothing for you to obsess over."

He laughs. When he's done, he asks, "What happens now?"

"Honestly, I don't know. My father and I have some planning to do. The men from your crew who are still alive, I'll drop off at some port. I can't let Draxen go free. He clearly won't let his defeat go, so he'll remain my prisoner for now. But no harm will come to him or you if I can help it."

He locks eyes with me. His expression is so grateful, so relieved—you'd think I'd made him king of his own island.

"You saved my life, Riden. I'm simply returning the favor."

"Is that really all it is?"

"Yes."

He takes a deep breath. "When we were on that island, I learned so much about you. I accused you before of enchanting me, of toying with my mind. I know now what it really feels like to be under your control. I realized you were being honest with me before, and that what I think—what I feel—has nothing to do with your abilities, but everything to do with you."

"Riden," I say, stopping him.

"Yes?"

"You've lost a lot of blood, and I'm pretty sure you were dead for a time. Maybe you should take some time to reclaim your strength—and your head—before you say or do anything mad."

"Like get shot twice?" he asks, relieving the tension in the room.

I laugh. "Yes, like that."

"Fine, but since I know so much about what you're capable of, would it hurt if I asked you a question?"

"You may ask." Doesn't mean I'll answer.

"What's so special about your birth? How did you come to possess the powers of sirens without fully becoming one? You said you'd tell me in exchange for the map. Though I didn't offer it to you freely, you have it now, and I'd still like to know."

Riden does know so much about me. He witnessed firsthand all the horrible things I could do to him if I wanted. Yet he still talks to me as though we're . . . friends, almost. I don't mind if he knows more. It's remarkable that he's accepting me as it is. Not that I should care whether he does or doesn't.

"My father followed his section of the map almost nineteen years ago. He wanted to see how far he could get with what he had. He and two ships from his fleet came across an island that had never been charted by any cartographer in Maneria, save the one who made the map to the Isla de Canta long ago." I know this story by heart. When I was little, I asked my father to tell it to me repeatedly. Now that I'm older, I realize it's a bit inappropriate for a young girl. But my father has always treated me as though I'm older than I really am.

"What was the island?" Riden asks.

"We do not know its name. Only that it is located on the way to the Isla de Canta. But its name is not important. What's important is what they found when they reached it."

"What did they find?"

"A lagoon. A lagoon where beautiful women bathed in the water. Thinking that they'd go and have some fun, several men jumped overboard, including my father. But instead of the women fleeing, screaming to get away, it was the men who shrieked until their heads disappeared below the water's surface."

"But your father survived. How?"

I smile, remembering when he told me the story of how he and Draxen took control of the *Night Farer*. "Don't interrupt. I'm getting there."

"Sorry."

"The siren is a strong creature. Stronger than any single man. When she finds her prey, she grips him by the shoulders and forces him down to the ocean's bottom, where she has her way with him."

Riden swallows. "How romantic."

I cock my head. "Would you say it is any more terrible than the intentions of the men who started for them in the first place?"

Riden is silent at that.

I continue. "A man will struggle and fight to save his life, but the siren will always win. And those sirens who conceive while underwater will give birth to siren children. Always girls, of course. Because sirens are always female.

"My father was grabbed by the most beautiful of them all. Their queen, even, he claims. She, like the others, pulled him down to the ocean's floor."

"And?"

"My father struggled at first. He fought with all his might, but it was useless. He knew he was going to die. And so, instead of struggling until the lack of air became too much for him, he decided he would become a partner in what was happening."

"You mean—"

"Instead of fighting, he returned her embraces and kisses. And for whatever reason, this saved his life. Because she brought him back to the surface. All the way back up onto land. For a child who is conceived by a siren on land will be more human than not."

"Stars," Riden says, all other words leaving him.

"My father, and those who stayed aboard the ships, left the island, having gone as far as they possibly could without the other two-thirds of the map, and sailed home. They were permitted to leave due to my father's encounter with the siren queen. She allowed them to keep their lives instead of sending all her subjects to finish them off.

"My father has returned to that island many times since then. But he's never seen another siren."

Riden doesn't say anything more. He's too lost in thought, trying to take it all in. Eventually, his eyes close, and I assume he's asleep. I stare at his closed eyelids. His deep, even breaths. His full lips. He's a strange man. Strange for having saved me. Strange for fighting so hard to save his awful brother. Strange for not fighting for what he wants—whatever that may be.

I suppose I will have plenty of time to better figure him out in the future.

There's still one-third of a map that needs finding.

ACKNOWLEDGMENTS

This novel wouldn't have made it to publication without the help of many people. First I want to thank my agent, Rachel Brooks, who took a chance on me, found a home for *Daughter of the Pirate King*, and continues to work to ensure its success. You're a superhero and fairy godmother all rolled into one, Rachel. Thanks for being awesome.

Huge thanks to the team at Feiwel and Friends, especially Holly West, my amazing editor. Your insights into plot and character are invaluable. You've really helped me get into Alosa's head and make this novel shine. I also appreciate the efforts of Starr Baer and Kaitlin Severini, who worked as production editor and copy editor, respectively.

Anyone else behind the scenes who I didn't work with directly but who still helped with *DotPK*—I was once one of those people and know you exist—thank you.

Alek Rose, as my college roommate, you suffered through my alarm going off an hour early so I could write and edit. You let me yak at you about new book ideas and never stopped cheering me on. Thank you, Eerpud.

Sarah Talley, Megan Gadd, and Taralyn Johnson, you are the best friends and critique partners a writer could ask for. Never change.

I'm so grateful to my beta readers: Gwen Cole, Kyra Nelson, Shanna Sexton, Jennifer Jamieson, Elizabeth Anne Taggart, Juliet Safier, Tyler Wolf, Samantha Lee, Erica Bell, Kyra Pierce, Grace Talley, and Candace Hooper.

I need to give a quick shout-out to the Swanky Seventeens, especially my agent sister Gwen Cole, for keeping me sane and sharing this crazy ride with me.

Thanks need to go to Elana Johnson, who was invaluable during the querying process for *DotPK*; to Brandon Sanderson, whose creative writing class taught me so much about successful magic systems; to Rick Walton, who taught me more than I ever could have hoped to learn about publishing; and to Kathleen Strasser, without whose help, I may have never started writing in the first place.

I also need to thank my aunt Krista and uncle Tim. I did the majority of the work on this book while I was finishing my last term of college and living with you. Thank you for opening your home to me. Thank you, Audrey, for helping me brainstorm character names. Thank you, Emmy, for letting me steal your room and read to you. Nathan and Jared, thanks for making sure I was never bored.

And, of course, I am forever grateful to my family, who supported me every step of the way. Thank you, Mom, Dad, Jacob, Becki, Alisa, and Johnny for your encouragement and long-suffering as you listened to me talk about the long road to publication.